THE GOLDEN AGE

IN

TRANSYLVANIA

BY

MAURUS JOKAI

Author of "Black Diamonds," "Peter the Priest," Etc., Etc.

TRANSLATED BY S. L. AND A. V. WAITE

Fredonia Books
Amsterdam, The Netherlands

The Golden Age in Transylvania

by
Maurus Jókai

ISBN: 1-4101-0704-3

Copyright © 2004 by Fredonia Books

Reprinted from the 1898 edition

Fredonia Books
Amsterdam, The Netherlands
http://www.fredoniabooks.com

THE GOLDEN AGE IN TRANSYLVANIA

CHAPTER I

A HUNTING PARTY IN THE YEAR 1666

BEFORE we cross the Kiralyhago, let us cast a parting glance at Hungary. I will unroll before your eyes a scene, partly the result of an adverse fate, partly of a dark mystery, representing joy and also deep sorrow. An incident of a moment becomes the turning-point of a whole century.

My soul is saddened by the images thus conjured up; the figures out of the past blind my sight. Would that my hand were mighty enough to write down what my soul sees in that magic mirror. May your impressions, your recollections, complete the scene wherever the writer fails through weariness.

*　　*　　*　　*　　*　　*

We find ourselves in the valley of the Drave, in one of those boundless tracts where even the wild beasts lose themselves. Here are primeval forests, the roots of which rest in the water of a great swamp encircled not by water lilies and reed-grass, but by giant trees whose branches,

7

dropping below the surface, form new roots in the quickening water. Here the swan builds its nest; this is the haunt of the heron and all those wild creatures one of which only now and then marches out into more frequented regions. On the higher ground, where in late summer the waters ebb, spring such flowers as might have been seen just after the deluge, so luxuriant and so strange is their mighty growth out of the slimy mud. The branches of ivy, stout as grape vines, reach from tree to tree winding about the trunks and decking the dark maples as if some wood-nymph had garlanded her own consecrated grove.

When the sun has set, life grows active in this watery kingdom; swarms of water-birds rise, and with their monotonous, gruesome cries sound the note of the bittern, the whistle of the turtle, and the four notes of the swan, now heard only in the land of fable, for there alone mankind is not; that kingdom still belongs to God.

Occasionally bold hunters venture to penetrate this pathless maze, making their way among the trees in small boats, often overturned by the long roots under the water many fathoms deep, although the dark grass, the yellow marsh flowers and the small dark-red lizard seem to be within reach of one's hand. Sometimes a thicket bars the way of the boat, trees never touched by human hand are rotting here heaped mountain-high thousands of years before. Those trunks that have fallen into the water have been petrified, and the grasses and vines have grown over them in such a tangle that they form a strong crust which sways and bends but does not break beneath the tread. This crust appears to stretch far and wide, but in reality one step too far brings death, so that this strange and remote region is but rarely visited.

On the south flows the Drave, whose rapid current frequently sweeps away the tallest trees, to the peril of the boatmen. To the north the forest stretches as far as Csakathurm, and where the swamp ends, oaks and beeches tower higher and mightier than any in all Hungary. Throughout this wilderness are wild beasts of every kind; especially the wild boar that wallows in the swampy ground; and here too the stag grows to his greatest strength and beauty. In the days that we write of, the buffaloes roamed through this wilderness, making nightly raids on the neighboring millet fields, but at the first attempt to catch them they plunged into the heart of the swamp and were safe from pursuit.

On the edge of the forest in those days stood a castle of so many styles of architecture that one must conclude it had been the favorite hunting-resort of some Hungarian or Croatian noble. The greater part of the building seemed to be a century older than the rest, in fact the oldest

part was merely a hut of oak logs rudely put together, its roof overgrown with moss and its
walls with ivy and periwinkle; over the door
were the antlers of a patriarchal stag; the later
lords must have entertained a pious regard for
its builder or they would have torn down this
hut. On the side toward the woods was a long,
barn-like building of one room, intended for the
large hunting parties of later times; here masters
and servants, horses and hounds, staid in friendly
companionship when the bad weather brought
them together. Around an old oak with wide-
spreading branches was a strange looking hermit-
age, the oak forming its single column of support; the entire hut had been built of the skulls
of boars taken in a single hunt. Finally, on a hill
somewhat higher than the rest, where the trees had
been cleared away stood the most modern building; it consisted of a small, tasteful hunting-castle,
with columns in front, tiled roof, marble ter-
races, oriel windows and other features of mediæval architecture. The bastions near by, begun
but left unfinished, the deep moats and the walls
stretching beyond all proportions, seemed to indicate that the man who had begun the building
had intended a stronghold, perhaps against the
Turks. Behind the building were still to be seen
two long culverins and a stout iron mortar with
a Turkish inscription that threw some light on
their origin; but the times and the spirit of the

times had changed, and later comers had built a Tusculan villa upon foundations intended for a fortress.

On one of the brightest days of the year in which our story begins, a large hunting party was stirring at the castle. Hardly had the sun sent his first rays through the dense trees when the boys of the stable and kennel led out the horses and the hounds straining at the leash and bounding to the shoulders of their keepers in their excited anticipation. Long wagons, drawn by six to ten oxen, had already gone to the meet to bring back the game. The villagers summoned to the chase, variously armed with axes, forks, or occasional guns, were divided into groups by the hunters. Some peasants, in parties of twos and threes, carried on their shoulders boats hollowed from the trunks of trees, to drive back the game if it escaped to the swamp. Men and beasts alike showed signs of haste and impatience; only a few of the older men took the time to sit over the fire and cook their bacon. At last the hunting-horn sounded from the castle yard, the company sprang with shouts of joy upon their snorting horses; the restless, yelping pack dragged their keepers this way and that; the hunters armed themselves,—in short, everything was ready and waited only for the lords and ladies. In a few moments a group of riders came down the hill attended by the squires; in

front rode a tall, muscular man, the lord of the
castle; the rest seemed involuntarily to have
fallen behind him. His broad shoulders and
well-rounded chest were of Herculean strength;
his face was burned by the sun and showed no
trace of age; his close-trimmed beard and heavy
moustache gave his countenance a martial aspect,
and the Roman nose and coal black, bushy eyebrows added to his features an imperious look,
though the melancholy curve of the lips and the
delicate oval of the blue eyes lent a certain poetic
expression to his knightly countenance. A round
cap with an eagle's feather covered his short
hair; he wore a plain, shaggy coat unfastened,
beneath which showed a white dolman of deerskin ornamented with silver; at his side hung a
broad sword in ivory sheath, and from his studded girdle of red shone the pearl handle of a
Turkish dagger. Next him rode a young knight
and a youthful Amazon; the knight could count
scarcely twenty years and the lady looked still
younger. Two people better suited to each other
could not be found. The young man had pale,
gentle features and rich chestnut hair curling on
his shoulders; a small moustache barely covered
his upper lip, his blue eyes wore a constant smile
of carelessness, if not frivolity, and had not the
strong sinews of his arm shown under his close-
fitting sleeves one would have taken him for only
a fanciful boy; on his head he wore a marten

cap with a heron's feather and his garments were of silk; from his shoulder hung a magnificent tiger skin, its claws serving for buckles joined by a sapphire clasp. He rode a coal-black Turkish horse with housings embroidered in gold, some woman's delicate handiwork.

The Amazon, to whom the youth seemed to be whispering many a sweet word, formed a complete contrast to him; she had an earnest, fearless, lively countenance; her eyes were brighter than garnets; she loved to curl her lip and draw down her fine, thick eyebrows, giving to her face an expression of pride, then when she glanced up again and parted her lips with a spirited smile, you might see a heroine indeed. Her dark braids hung over her shoulders half their length and then were looped back under her cap of ermine with its waving plume. She wore a silk riding habit fitting closely to her slender figure and falling in heavy folds over the flanks of her Arab horse. Figure and face called for homage rather than love; no smile played over these features, her great, dark, fathomless eyes rested many a time upon the youth as he bent toward her, shedding a rare charm, a fulness of love, a nobler, higher longing which means more than love, more than ambition, which is perhaps the self-consciousness of great souls who have a hint of their eternal fame.

Behind this beautiful pair rode two men whose

dress indicated their high rank ; one about thirty years old, the other a pale, elderly man with dress simple to affectation. It is worth while to mark this man's face, for we shall often meet him ; cold dry features, thin blonde hair and beard mixed with grey, a pointed cleft chin, scornful pale lips, quick watery blue eyes with red rims, jutting eyebrows, a high bald shining forehead which with every change of feeling was wrinkled in all directions. This face we may not forget. The rest—the Herculean rider, the smiling youth, the stately girl,—will hurry past us like fleeting pictures which come only to go ; but this last will accompany us throughout the entire course of events, ever appearing only to cast down or to build up, to determine the fate of great men and lands. The bald head moved nearer to the knight at his side who was testing his lance as if for a throw, and said to him in an undertone, evidently continuing a conversation:

" So, then, you Transylvanians will not have anything to do with this affair ? "

" Let me have a rest from politics to-day," answered the other, starting impatiently. " You have got so that you cannot live a single day without intrigues, but I beg of you, spare me to-day. To-day I wish to hunt, and you know how passionately I love the chase."

With these words he spurred his horse forward, and joined the stately knight.

Thus rebuffed, the older man bit his lips in vexation, then turned with a smile to the youthful knight riding before him.

"A glorious morning, gracious lord; would that our horizon were as bright in every direction."

"Would that it were," answered the youth, without really knowing what it was to which he was replying, while the beautiful Amazon leaned over and said to him:

"I don't know why it is but I cannot place any confidence in that man. He is forever putting questions and never answers any himself."

Just then the stately rider came up with the group of hunters, acknowledged their loud greetings and stopped in their midst.

"David," he called to an old grey-bearded hunter who came forward, cap in hand, "put your cap on. Have the drivers of the game all taken their places?"

"Every man is in his place, gracious lord. I have already sent boats to the swamp in case the beasts are frightened back there."

"You think of everything. Now start with the men and hounds and follow the road that we usually take; we alone are enough for the road I have in mind, we will go straight through the forest."

At once a murmur of astonishment and incredulity arose among the hunters.

"Beg pardon, gracious lord," said the old man, with his cap again in his hand, "I know the way, and no God-fearing man should make trial of it; the impenetrable undergrowth, the deep water and slimy ground threaten with a thousand perils; and besides, straight through the forest goes the wide devil's gorge that no human being with horse has yet crossed."

"We shall get over, my good fellow. We have already been through more difficult places. No bad luck befalls the man who follows me; you know yourself that fate favors me."

The hunter obediently made ready to march forward with the rest. At this moment the bald head rode to the noble's side.

"Gracious lord," he said, quietly, not to say sarcastically, "I consider it a great calamity for a human being to imperil his life for a mere brute, especially when he has urgent need of that life, but your grace has made the decision and I know it will be carried out. Still, have the goodness to look about you for a moment and remember that we are not all men here; there is a delicate lady in our midst, and to expose her to death for the sake of our adventure is surely want of tenderness."

During this speech the knight did not look at the older man but gazed fixedly at the young Amazon, and the glow of pride on his cheeks was brighter as he saw how calmly the stately

lady measured with her eye her unbidden protector, and with what proud self-reliance she
took her lances from her page, chose one, and
sharpening the point on her pommel, assumed
the position of a true matadore.

"Look at her," cried the knight, "do you feel
any anxiety for this girl, my niece?"

These words of the knight echoed loudly;
there was no voice like his, deep as thunder and
carrying far.

The young Amazon allowed the knight who
had called her his niece to put his arm about her
and kiss her blushing cheek, for in those days the
Hungarian woman still blushed even if the kiss
came from a kinsman's lips.

"Is it to no purpose that she sprang from my
blood? shall she not match the best man in fear-
lessness?   Have no anxiety for her, she will face
greater dangers than these and bring her husband
to them too."

With these words the hero put spurs to his
horse; the startled creature reared and plunged
but the hard knees of his rider brought him
under control.

"Follow me," he cried, and the brilliant company vanished in the thicket of the forest.

*   *   *   *   *   *

Let us arrive there before them.   Let us hurry
to the place where the stags take their noonday

rest in the shady grove, where the turtles sun
themselves and the herons bathe. What dwellings are these in groups of fives and sixes between
the water and the wilderness—these huts built
up on piles with round roofs clay-covered and
bound with twigs? Who built this dam, and for
what purpose, so that the water at the entrance
of their dwellings should never fail? Here
dwell the dear, industrious beavers whom Nature
has taught the art of building. This is their col-
ony. These thick beams they have hewn with
their teeth. They have shaped all this,—they have
dug down into the earth to build a dam, and
year after year they keep this dam in repair.
See, at this very moment comes one gliding out
from the lowest story of his dwelling below the
water; with what a gentle eye he looks around
him; as yet he has never seen a human being.
But let us go back to the day of the hunt. In
the shadow of an old hollowed tree was resting
a family of deer—stag, doe and little fawns. The
stag had stepped into the sunlight where he
might see his own shadow; his stately form seemed
to please him; he licked his bright coat, scratched
his back with his branching antlers and walked
proudly, stepping high with a certain affectation;
the movements of his slender figure were marked
by the play of his muscles. The doe lay lazily
in the muddy sedge; at times raising her beautiful head, her great dark eyes full of feeling, she

gazed at her companion or at the sporting fawns;
if she noticed that they were too far away she
gave a certain restless moaning cry, at which the
lively creatures would hasten to her, tumbling
over each other, leaping and bounding about the
mother, never an instant quiet, their limbs quivering and every movement quick and graceful.
Suddenly the stag stood fixed. Scenting danger
he gave a cry and lifted his nose; his nostrils di-
lated as he snuffed the air, pawed the ground and
ran restlessly about, angrily shaking his antlers;
again he stood still and his wide-opened eyes
showed instinctive fear; he ran to his precious
doe and with unspeakable tenderness they put
their two heads together,—they too have a language in which they understand each other.
The two fawns fled to their mother, their slender legs trembling. Then the stag with long,
noiseless stride, made his way into the forest.
The doe remained licking her trembling fawns,
who returned the motherly caresses with their
little red tongues. At every noise she raised
her head and pricked up her ears; suddenly
she bounded into the air; she had heard something hardly perceptible to human ear; far,
far away there was a sound in the forest; hunters know this sound well—the chase had begun.
The doe cast restless glances about her, then
quietly lay down; she knew that her mate would
come back and that she must wait for him.

Nearer and nearer came the chase. Soon the stag came noisily back and turned with a peculiar sound to his mate, who at once sprang up and with her young fled straight across the line of chase. The stag stood still for a moment, digging up the ground with his antlers, either with rage or to efface the traces of his mate's lying there. Then he stretched his neck and barked loudly in imitation of the hounds, to lead them on a false scent; a trick often observed by hunters. He then bounded away, tossing his antlers, and followed the doe. Ever nearer came the chase; with the barking of dogs was heard also the cracking of the underbrush and the shouts of the hunters. The forest became alive: the startled hares and foxes ran among the trees in every direction to escape the cries of the men. Now and then a fox fled in haste to a hole, only to bound back again frightened by the fiery eyes of the badger. Among the timid hares a grey striped wolf stood forgetful of his thirst for blood; switching his tail he looked about him for some possible escape and ran howling on, driven by the nearing voices.

Yet no one was hunting these poor creatures —a greater quarry was the game,—a stag with mighty antlers.

The hunting net was drawn closer and closer, already the dogs were on the track and the horn gave a signal that they were near the stag.

"Hurrah, hurrah!" rang out from afar. The hunters coming from the opposite direction halted and blocked the way. The noise of the pursuers came rapidly nearer. Suddenly, a peculiar noise was heard; the two deer with their young broke through the bushes and disappeared; between them and the hunters was a wide ravine; the noble quarry leaped like lightning over the tree trunks lying in the way, and at last reached the ravine. Before and behind were the hunters, but the pursuit from behind was more terrible; there were the knight, the fearless Amazon and the eager hunter. The stag bounded across the broad ravine without the slightest effort, raising both feet at once and throwing back his head; the doe too made ready for the leap but her young shrank back from the edge; then the doe gave out, her knees sank, her head drooped, and she stayed with her young. A lance hurled by the Transylvanian hunter pierced her side. The wounded creature gave a distressed cry, like the wail of a human being only more terrible. Even her murderer in his pity did not venture to approach her until her struggles were over. The two fawns stood sorrowstricken by their mother and allowed themselves to be taken alive. Meanwhile the stag, already across the ravine, dashed wildly toward the hunters before him, who blocked his way, and tossed his heavy antlers in fury. The hunters knew the courage born of despair which comes to these animals otherwise so timid, and throwing themselves to the ground, gave him free pass. Only a few hounds ran after him, but the maddened creature tossed them on his antlers and leaving them to roll on the ground in their blood, plunged on to the swamp.

"After him," roared the knight with thundering voice, and galloped at full speed to the ravine over which the stag had fled.

"May the Lord help him," screamed those on the other side, in terror; but the next moment their terror was turned to shouts of joy, for the horse with his bold rider was over. Of the entire company only two ventured to follow, the stately Amazon and the delicate youth. The two horses made the leap in the same moment; the lady's habit swelled out like a pennant in the breeze and she glanced backward as if to ask if any man had so much courage. The rest of the company considered it advisable not to try the bold leap, except Nicholas, the Transylvanian, who made a dash although his horse had already hurt his hind foot in the woods and the huntsman might have been very sure that he was not equal to the leap.

Fortunately for the rider, just before the spring his saddle-girth gave way and he fell on the edge of the bank, while the horse just reached it with his forefeet, and tumbling, fell into the

depths of the ravine. The three riders were
alone in their pursuit of the fleeing stag which,
once out of the circle, led his followers on to the
bog. The knight went first. The Amazon and
her comrade followed by a sweeping détour
through the tree trunks; just as they were on
the edge of the bog, there suddenly appeared
snorting before them two wild boars;—they had
come into the lair of these beasts which had been
deaf to everything around them as they lay in
the reeds and mud, only noticing the newcomers
when the young man's horse trampled to death
two young ones rubbing themselves against the
old sow. The rest of the young scattered into
the sedge while the old ones, with threatening
growls, turned upon the intruders. The sow
plunged blindly at the youth, while the boar
stood still a moment, his bristles raised and ears
pointed. He leveled his tusks and, with deep
grunt and blood-shot eye, charged at the maiden.
The young man hurled his lance from a safe distance at the sow; the whizzing weapon struck
into the hard skull of the creature, the point
piercing to the brain. The sow ran like a monstrous unicorn, the lance still sticking in her
skull, but her eyes had lost the power of sight
and she passed the rider and fell without a sound
at a little distance. The maiden waited calmly
for the raging boar; seizing her lance with her
left hand she aimed its point downward and held

her bridle firmly. The noble horse stood quiet against his raging opponent, pricking up his ears, and with a turn of his neck kept his eye on the boar so that just as the tusk would have entered the side, the trained animal bounded away, and at the same moment the Amazon bent over and hurled her lance deep between the shoulder-blades of the boar. The creature, wounded to the death, sank down with a groan, but made one more onset at the maiden, when the youth sprang like lightning from his horse and dealt him a final blow with his sword. Just then from afar was heard the sound of the horn ; the other riders who, by making a long circuit, had now overtaken the leaders, greeted the heroes of the day, the knight, the Amazon and the youth, with loud huzzas. The strongly-built man was bespattered with mud and the others did not look much better. Only the riding habit of the lady was without spot and without rent. Even in such circumstances as these, ladies know how to take care of their clothes. When the knight saw the monster that his niece had laid low, looking larger than ever now that in was stretched out in death, he appeared like one just realizing the peril to which his darling had been exposed, and cried out in terror, "My dear Helen!" Then he took her hand with a smile and glanced at the bystanders with triumph.

"Did I not tell you that she was of my blood?" Every man hurried forward to compliment the brave heroine, who on this occasion seemed to experience that extraordinary pleasure peculiar to the lucky hunter.

"Nicholas, my son, do the boars grow as large as that in Transylvania?"

The Transylvanian, already somewhat out of sorts from his recent accident, could not let this pass without denying that there was anything in Hungary better worth having than Transylvania could produce, so he answered sulkily, "Yes, indeed, and even larger." No reply possible could have so angered the knight as this;—to say to an excited hunter that there is better game anywhere than that he has just praised; and still more, that had been laid low by his own darling.

"Good, my son, good," growled the knight, "it remains to be seen."

With undisguised signs of annoyance on his countenance he turned aside from the ill-natured Transylvanian and gave orders to have the game carried back to the hunting castle. On the way thither he spoke no word except to his dear one, whom he flattered and extolled to the very heavens.

*   *   *   *   *   *

It was already late in the afternoon when the hunters sat down to their meal. The simple but appetizing food had been arranged on a large grassplot in the middle of the forest; wine and joy thawed out their spirits and they talked of this and of that, of the war and of the chase, of beautiful women and of poesy, which at that time was in great favor among the upper circles. But in spite of the merry conversation the knight could not keep from asking, in a tone of reproach, "So, then, there really is better game in Transylvania?" until the repeated question became irksome to the young man, who had not intended his reply to be taken with such seriousness.

The bald head saw the situation and attempted to give another turn to the conversation by taking up his beaker and proposing this toast;— "May God put the Turks in good spirits."

The knight in his vexation overturned his glass and replied angrily, "That He shall not! I have not grown old fighting against them to turn round now and pray for them. He is a fool who changes only to find a new master."

"The Turk is a gracious master for us," said the young man, with an ambiguous smile.

"Didn't I say so? With you, even the Turks are finer and greater than with us. So it is; in Transylvania everything is better than it is in Hungary; the boars are larger and the Turks are smaller than with us."

While they were talking the old hunstman David approached his master and whispered in his ear. The features of the knight lighted as by magic, and springing from his seat he cried, " Give me a gun."

Seizing his silver-mounted rifle, with a happy expression he said to his guests :

" Just stay here, there is a colossal boar near by. You shall see him, my son," he said, touching Nicholas on the shoulder. " Twice already have I given him chase, but this time I will have him. He is the genuine descendant of the Calydonian boar."

With that the knight directed his steps in eager self-forgetfulness toward that part of the forest pointed out by the huntsman, whom he commanded to turn back, for he would have no one with him.

" I do not know why it is," whispered Helen to the youth at her side, " but I feel as if I had cause to fear some peril threatening my uncle." The youth rose without a word and took his rifle. " Do not follow him," called out the Transylvanian when he noticed this move, " you would only anger him. Never fear, he will do it alone. A man that has wiped out entire armies of Tartars will surely be able to manage an unreasoning beast." And in this way the young man was held back at the very moment of departing. The men went on drinking and the maiden continued with her thoughts, from time to time glancing anxiously toward the forest.

Suddenly there was a shot heard in the forest;
all set down their glasses, and looked expectantly
in that direction. A few moments later came
the cry of a boar in pain; not the sound of a boar
at the point of death, but the rattling sound of
an interrupted struggle.

"What's that?" each asked of another.

"Surely he would call if he were in peril."

With that came a second shot.

"What's that?" all shouted, and sprang to
their feet. "Up! Up!" cried the maiden,
trembling in every limb, and the entire company
hurried in the direction of the shot.

*   *   *   *   *   *

The knight had gone only a few steps into the
forest when he came upon the boar at the foot of
a great oak. It was a monstrous boar with long
black bristles on his back and forehead; his skin
like iron lay in thick folds on his neck and his
feet were long and sinewy. He had dug himself a litter in the brush, where he now lay.
Where he had laid his monstrous head he had
torn up by the roots shrubs as thick as one's arm.
When the monster heard the steps of a man he
raised his head, opened wide his jaws and looked
sidewise at his opponent. In order to get a
better aim the knight had dropped on one knee,
and shot through the sedges at the beast just at
the moment when he raised his head. Instead of

hitting the skull the ball entered the creature's neck, wounding but not killing him. The wounded animal sprang up, and in his charge at the knight struck his crooked tusks together so that the sparks flew. Such a furious attack might easily have been avoided by a spring to one side, but the knight was not the man to avoid his antagonist. He threw down his gun, tore his sword from its scabbard, stood face to face with the boar and dealt a blow at his head which might have cleft it through and through ; but the dangerous stroke fell on the tusk, and upon this, hard as stone, the sword was broken in two at the hilt. Stunned by the blow the boar, though he plunged at the knight with his tusks, inflicted only a light wound in his thigh, at which the man seized the animal by the ears with both hands and a furious struggle began. Without weapon he fought the beast which turned its head with grunt and groan, but the steel-like grasp of the man held his broad ears with irresistible might and when the creature raised himself on his hind legs to throw his opponent, the knight with giant strength gave him a push and threw him over backward. True, he fell too as he did so, but he was on top and raising himself up, pressed down the wild beast struggling in vain against his superior strength, and seated himself in triumph on his belly. The boar seemed to be entirely conquered. His glazing eye grew dim, blood streamed from jaws and nose, he had ceased to roar and made only a rattling sound; his legs contracted, his nose hung down; in a few moments he must certainly die. The knight should have called to his comrades, only a little way off, or kept quiet until the boar bled to death, but this took too much time. He remembered that he had in his girdle a Turkish knife and he thought to put a quick end to the struggle, so he pressed down the head of the boar with one knee, that he might be able to spring when he drew out his knife at his side, and with one hand seized his girdle. Just then, a shot was heard in the forest; the overmastered boar, feeling the pressure of hand and knee lightened, with his remaining strength threw the knight off and dealt one last blow with his tusk. This blow was fatal—it tore the man's throat.

The guests and relations hurrying to him, found the hero dying beside the dead boar. With cries of sorrow they strove to bind his terrible wound.

"It is nothing, my children, nothing," said the knight, even then dying, and he was gone.

"Poor knight!" said the bystanders.

"My poor fatherland," cried Helen, raising to heaven her eyes heavy with tears.

The day of rejoicing was changed to one of mourning; the hunt to a funeral feast. In sorrow the guests attended the corpse of their best friend back to Csakathurm. Only the bald head took another direction.

"That is just what I said," he muttered to himself, "one needs his life for something more. Well, what matters it? there are still people elsewhere; I'll go to the next country."

*   *   *   *   *   *

So died Nicholas Zrinyi, the younger, the greatest writer and the bravest fighter of his fatherland. So died the man, who had been the favorite of fortune, the darling of his country, its protection and its glory. In vain would you look now for the hunting-lodge or the castle;— all is gone—the name, the family of the hero, even his memory. The general and the statesman have fallen into oblivion; one part only of the man is left, one part only lives forever,—the writer.

CHAPTER II

THE HOUSE IN EBESFALVA

WE now move forward one country; —one
country forward, and four years backward. We
are in Transylvania in the year 1662. Before
us is a dwelling, plain but of the nobility,
at the lower end of Ebesfalva, almost the last
house in the place. The building was planned
more for convenience than for fancy; on both
sides are stables for horses and for sheep, built
partly of stone, partly of plaster and partly of
wood; sheds for wagons, poultry-yards, open
barns, high-gabled sheep pens covered with straw;
in the rear is a fruit garden where one catches
sight of the arched top of a beehive, and finally,
in the middle of the courtyard stands the whitewashed dwelling of one wing, with shady nut-
trees under which is a round table improvised
out of a mill-stone. A stone wall separates the
court of the dwelling from the threshing floor,
where are to be seen piles of hay and great heaps
of grain, from the top of which a peacock utters
his disagreeable cries. It is evening; the men
have returned from the fields; the oxen are
loosed from their heavy wagons loaded with corn;
the sheep come with tinkling bells from the

32

meadow; the grunting swine hurry through the
open gate each to his own trough; the cocks
quarrel together on the nut-trees where they went
to roost at sunset; in the distance is heard the
sound of the evening bell; and from still farther
away comes the sound of the village maidens going to the fountain. The men look after the
cattle, one brings a great bundle of fresh-mown
grass, and another carries in a large pail of fresh
milk, fragrant and foaming. From the kitchen
comes the gleam of a blazing fire, over which a
maiden with round red cheeks is holding a great
pan that gives out the fragrance of food, soon
to be placed on the heavy green earthenware.
The farm hands sit round the mill-stone table,
eating heartily, while the patient house-dogs
watch them with thoughtful attention. Then
the dishes are cleared away and the ears of corn
are taken from the wagon and put under cover.
The peasant maidens of the neighborhood gather
for the husking; the more timid are frightened
for their lives by the mischievous lads who hollow out ripe pumpkins, cut eyes and mouth and
set a burning light inside to use as a lantern.
The more clever of the lads, seated on upturned
baskets, weave long garlands of the corn husks;
and over their quiet work ring out jolly songs,
and fairy tales are told of golden-haired prin-
cesses and waifs. Here and there a game is
played, not without kisses proclaimed to all the

world with loud shrieks. The children make merry if they chance to find a red ear in the corn. And so they sit and sing and tell stories and laugh over trifles until the heaps of corn are all gone. Then come the long farewells; down the length of the street they sing on their way home, partly in joyousness of spirit and partly to keep up their courage. Each one goes to his house, locks the door and puts out the fire; the shepherd-dogs throughout the village answer one another, the moon rises and the night watchman begins to call off the hours in measured rhythm, while the other villagers sleep unmindful of the golden proverbs of his song.

Only in one window of the manor house is there still a light: there only they have not yet gone to rest. The watchers are an old maid-servant, grown grey in service, and a younger one. The old woman is reading laboriously something from the Psalter that she already knows by heart from beginning to end. The young maid has sat down to her spindle as if she had not done enough through the long day, and is drawing the long threads of the silken flax, which yesterday she combed and to-day carded.

"Go to bed, Clara," said the old woman kindly, "if I sit up, that is enough. To-morrow you will have to get up early just the same."

"Surely I could not go to sleep before the return of our noble lady," replied the other, con-

tinuing her work. "Even though the men are
all at home I am afraid while she is not here;
but when once the noble lady comes I feel as
safe as if castle walls surrounded us."

"You are right, my child, she is worth more
than many men, poor soul! For many years all
the cares that belong to a man have rested on
her shoulders. She has to look out for everything; and as if that were not enough she has
leased beside the estate of her sisters, Madame
Banfy and Madame Beleky. How many lawsuits she has had to carry on with this and that
neighbor or kinsman! but they meet their match
in her! She goes herself to the judge and the
courts and is so clever that an advocate might
learn of her. Once, when my lord Banfy came
to play the gallant with her, thinking our gracious lady one of those grass-widows, how quickly
she showed him the door; the good man hardly
knew which foot to put first and yet he is one of
the royal judges. To pay for that he quartered
on us the head collector with a mixed crowd of
troopers. You were here then, weren't you,
when our noble lady had them driven out of the
village? How they took to their heels when
they saw that our noble lady herself stood there
with her gun."

"If they hadn't," boasted the excited maiden,
"I would have struck them over the head with
my oven-cloth."

"You see, Clara, when a woman is compelled to take care of a house alone for so long a time, to defend herself and her family with her own strength, she comes to feel just like a man. That is why our lady has that determined look, as if she had not been a maiden of high birth."

"But tell me, Aunt Magdalene," said the girl, drawing her stool nearer, "are we really never to see our gracious master again?"

"God only knows," replied the old woman, with a sigh, "when the poor man will be set free. I have a sure presentiment which I have told, but nobody listens to me. When the late Prince George became dissatisfied with his own country and set out to conquer Poland with the best Hungarian nobility, our Master Michael went with him. How hard I tried to keep him back, and so did his noble lady; for they had been married then but a short time; and the good master himself had no wish to go, he had much rather sit in the house and read books or build mills and take care of his trees, but honor bade him go. However, I insisted that he should at least take my son Andy with him; surely God ordained it wisely that he should go with him, otherwise we never should have heard anything more of our gracious master. For when the prince saw the beastly crowd of Tartars drawn up against him in the field he hurried home, while all the nobility were taken prisoners by

the heathen Tartars and carried off to Tartary to
bitter bondage. My son Andy begged so hard
that they finally let him come home, especially
as he had a wound that made him unfit for work.
He brought back the news that our Master
Michael was pining away there in imprisonment
and that the Tartars, when they observed in
what esteem he was held by the other prisoners,
took him for a duke and demanded such a fright-
fully high ransom for him that all his estate
turned into money would not pay it. However,
our noble lady was very happy when she learned
that her husband was still living, and went
round trying to raise the money. But neither
relatives nor good friends would help her, not
even for security, for in war-times people do not
like to lend on real estate. So she sold all the
valuables she had brought with her from home;
beautiful silver plates, bracelets set with precious
stones, gold cups that were heirlooms, beautiful
garments embroidered with silk and threads of
gold, rings, buckles, clasps, real pearls, in short
everything that can be turned to gold. Yet as
all that was not half of what the Tartars demanded she leased the estates of her sisters, and
had the fallow ground ploughed and the woods
cleared away to make room for grain fields. She
turned night into day to find time for all the
work. Nothing connected with farming that
would bring money did she leave undone; she

had loam-pits made and stone-quarries opened;
she raised cattle that the Armenian cattle drivers
bought; she herself went to market, took her
wine even into Poland, her grain to Hermanstadt,
her honey, wax and dried fruits to Kronstadt;
she even went as far as Debreczin to get a good
price for her wool; and how prudently she lived
all that time! she never took anything from her
serving people that belonged to them, but she
herself saved every bit.   In harvest time, when
she would be in the field all day long she would
often go a week at a time without having any
dinner cooked; her entire meal then would be a
small piece of bread, so small that a child would
not have been satisfied with it, and a glass of
cold water.   But you can take my word for it,
Clara, that no one ever saw her out of temper,
and no bitter tear ever fell on the dry bread
which was all she allowed herself in loyalty to
her husband."

"What do you mean by that?"

"Why, I mean that the money that she got
together in this way, by hard work and saving,
has been carried by Andy into Tartary at this
season every year to make up the ransom.   During this time the poor lady stinted herself in
every way."   The old servant wiped the tears
from her eyes.

"And what is the ransom required?"

I don't know exactly, my child.   Andy has

always brought back a paper on which the Tartar has written the amount received and what still remains to be paid, and the noble lady keeps it very carefully. Of course I do not like to ask any questions."

The maiden became silent and seemed thoughtful; the spindle went twice as fast in her hands and her heart beat more rapidly.

"My son Andy has gone on such a journey now, and I am expecting him back every hour; from him we shall know something certain."

At that very moment the outside gate creaked; a small wagon was driven noisily into the courtyard and the joyous barking of the dogs showed that it was no stranger who had come.

"They've come," cried the two serving women, and had just time to rise from their seats when Anna Bornemissa, wife of Michael Apafi, entered,—a well-built woman, almost as tall as a man; through the plain grey linen gown showed the slender but rounded outlines of a strong figure; she might have been thirty-six years old. Her face was one of those that give no trace of time until far on in years. She was sunburned, but with the bloom of youth and her healthy color this only heightened her peculiar beauty. Her glance was quick and masterful but its charm lay in the soul which it reflected. In her features there was nothing hard, rough or masculine; her brow was arched, smooth, free from wrinkles and full of nobility; her eyebrows were delicately marked, her eyes exquisitely shaped, with long lashes that only half shaded them; they were not the fierce black, but rather nut-brown eyes, showing fire and light, yet now so cold. The nose and the oval of her face were delicately formed, her lips when her mouth was closed were gentle and delicate. The rest of her features seemed to be making an effort not to share her smile, and the mouth when open was proud and authoritative.

"What, still awake!" she said to her maids. Her voice had a pleasant ring although the lower tones were subdued by sorrow.

"We wished to sit up for your ladyship so that you would not have to wait outside for us," answered the old woman, bustling about her mistress and taking the heavy cloak from her shoulders.

"Is not Andy back yet?" asked Madame Apafi, in a voice almost stifled.

"Not yet, but I am expecting him every moment." The lady sighed deeply. How much suppressed sorrow, how many vanishing hopes, what depths of resignation lay in that sigh! Before the strong soul of this woman passed the many sufferings of her joyless life, her struggles with fate, mankind and her own heart; her love had been grafted upon pain that could bring forth wishes only—no pleasures. Another year

of her life had passed, rich only in struggles.
With the industry of a bee, she had succeeded in
getting together a few offerings for the single
purpose of her life, and who knew how many
more such years there must be before she could
attain it: thus far, she had only work, patience
and a joyless love. Madame Apafi forced her
countenance back into its wonted coldness, bade
her servants good-night and was just going to
her room, when Clara kissed the hand of her
mistress, causing her to look at the maid with
astonishment. She felt a hot tear on her hand,
which had come in spite of the maiden.

"What is the matter with you?" asked the
lady, taken aback.

"Nothing is the matter with me," sobbed the
maiden, "but you—most gracious lady—I am so
sorry for you. I have for a long time been
thinking of something, but have never dared tell
it. We often talk of it—how our master has
been taken prisoner, and how hard it is to get
his ransom;—I mean my friends in the village;—
all of us have necklaces with much useless gold
and silver coin on them, and so we girls have
agreed to put this money together that we have
no use for and give it to you, gracious lady, to
send off as ransom for our master." Madame
Apafi pressed the hand of her maidservant and
a tear came to her eye.

"I thank you, my girl," she said, touched. "I

prize this offering of yours far more than I should if my sister Banfy had placed ten thousand gold necklaces at my disposal.   But God will help us." Just then a horse's hoofs were heard in the court-yard and the dogs began a tremendous barking.

"Who's that? Robbers, perhaps,—the red-coats," stammered the old woman, and neither of the serving women dared go to the door; but Madame Apafi took the light from the table, and boldly going to the door opened it so that the light shone far out into the courtyard.

"Who is that?" she called, in a strong firm voice.

"Us—I mean me," answered somebody, con-fusedly; and all three at once recognized Andy by the voice.

"Oh, it's you, is it? Come, be quick," called Madame Apafi, joyously, and pulled the evi-dently confused servant into the house. He stood twirling his cap, not knowing how to be-gin.

"Did you see him—speak with him?—is he well?" asked Madame Apafi, quickly.

"Yes, well," answered the boy, glad to find a starting point.   "He sends you greetings and kisses, my noble lady."

"Why do you look around that way?—whom are the dogs barking at outside?"

"Perhaps at the black horse; they are so glad to see him again."

"Did you give the money to Murza?"

Instead of answering Andy began rummaging in the pocket of his fur coat, and as the opening of the pocket was very high and the bottom seemed very deep, he turned all colors while he was searching for the paper, and trembled as he handed it over to his mistress.

"Is there much left yet? What did Murza say?" asked Madame Apafi, in a tone almost trembling.

"There is not much more,—you could almost say there was very little more," answered Andy, with downcast eyes, in his embarrassment fumbling with his hat.

"How much? how much more?" They all cried at once. Andy turned red. "There isn't any more!" he blurted out, and burst into a loud laugh followed by tears;—at once the lady caught the meaning of his words.

"Man," she cried passionately, seizing him by the shoulders, "you have brought my husband with you!" Andy pointed behind him and nodded in silence. He wept and laughed all at once but not a word could he speak.

With a cry such as one utters only in deepest joy, the lady ran to the half open door and there stood listening, Michael Apafi, long waited and oft lamented.

"Michael, my own dear husband!" cried his wife, trembling with feeling; and, beside herself, she fell on her husband's neck, whispering to him words too low to be heard, expressions of tenderness, joy and love. Apafi pressed his wife to his heart; no sound was to be heard save low sobbing.

"You are mine, mine at last," stammered his wife, after a long pause, recovering from the violence of her feelings.

"I am yours. And I swear to you that no country, no world can tear me from you again."

"Oh, my God, what happiness!" cried Anna, raising to heaven her face covered with tears of joy. "What joy you have brought back to me," again leaning on her husband and burying her face on his breast.

"If the whole world were mine I should not be rich enough to repay you for your loyalty to me. If I could call a kingdom my own I would give it to you, and that would be only a beggarly reward."

The husband and wife, exultant in their joy and love, remained undisturbed in their happiness. Until late in the night the light burned in their room,—how much, how much they had to say!

CHAPTER III

A PRINCE BY COMPULSION

A YEAR had passed since Apafi's return. In the manor house at Ebesfalva all was excitement. Before one pair of horses could rest another started out on the road. The servants were sent in every direction. There seemed to be great confusion in the house, yet nobody appeared troubled. To those who asked confidentially it was whispered that the wife of Michael Apafi might give birth to a child at any hour. The master did not for one instant leave the chamber of his suffering wife.

Suddenly a wild noise rang out in the court-yard; about twenty-four horsemen had arrived, led by a Turkish Aga. To the terror of the serving people the Turkish troops carried lances and knives.

"Is your master at home?" the Aga said, haughtily, to Andy, who in his terror had remained riveted to the spot. "If he is," he went on without waiting for an answer, "tell him to come out, I wish to speak to him."

Still Andy could not speak, at which the Turk with emphasis added, "If he will not come out I will go after him."

With these words he sprang from his horse and crossed the space before the entrance. Andy ventured to stammer a brief—" But, gracious lord,"— when the Turk cut him off with—" I should like it better, my boy, if you would stop your talk and go into the house."

Just then Apafi, attracted by the rattling of the lances, came out of his wife's room. He was terror-stricken when he faced his unexpected guest.

"Are you Michael Apafi?" asked the Turk, angrily.

"At your service, gracious lord," replied Apafi, quietly.

"Good. His majesty, the celebrated Ali Pasha, sends you word to enter this carriage without delay and come to my lord in camp at Klein-Selyk, and that without any attendants."

"That's a pretty story," muttered Apafi to himself. "I beg your pardon, worthy Aga," he added aloud, " just at present it is quite impossible for me to carry out this wish, as my wife is in travail, and any moment may decide her life or death. I cannot leave her now."

"Call a doctor if your wife is sick; and re-member that you will not restore her to health by bringing down the anger of the Pasha on you."

" Grant me only one day and then it does not matter if it costs me my life."

"I tell you, it won't cost you your life if

you only obey, but if you don't you may soon cause yourself trouble; so be reasonable."

Anna from her room heard the conversation outside, and full of anxiety called her husband to her. "What's the matter?" asked the sufferer, anxiously.

"Nothing, nothing, sweetheart, I have just had a summons but I am not going."

But Madame Apafi had seen the spear-points of the Turks through the window curtains and said in despair, "Michael, they want to carry you off!" and she pressed her husband convulsively to her breast; "they shall kill me rather than drag you off into slavery so that I lose you again."

"Keep quiet, my dear child. I am sure I do not know what they want of me. I certainly have not done the good people any harm. At the most they will demand a tax, which I will get together at once."

"I have a presentiment of something dreadful; my heartstrings tighten, harm has come to you," stammered the sick woman, and she broke out into violent sobbing and threw herself on her husband. "Michael, I shall never see you again!"

The Aga was getting tired of waiting and began to knock at the door and call out, "Apafi, here Apafi, come out; I cannot enter your wife's room—that would not be proper—but if you don't come out I will burn the house down over your head."

"I will go," said Apafi, striving to quiet his wife with kisses. "My refusal will only make matters worse; but as soon as they let me go I will be here at once."

"I shall never see you again," she gasped, trembling; she was almost in a swoon. Apafi, taking advantage of this momentary unconsciousness, left his wife and went out to the Aga, his eyes heavy with tears.

"Now, my lord, we can go," he said.

"Surely you are not going like a peasant, without a sword," said the Turk. "Gird on your sword, and tell your wife that she has nothing to fear."

Apafi went back into the room, and as he took down his heavy silver-mounted sword from the wall above the bed, he said to his wife, consolingly, "See, sweetheart, there cannot be anything disagreeable to expect, or I should not have been told to buckle on my sword. Trust in God."

"I do, I do trust in Him," said his wife, still kissing her husband's hand passionately and pressing him to her heart; then she began to weep bitterly,—"Apafi, if I die, do not forget me."

"Oh!" cried Apafi. He tore himself with bitter feelings from the embrace of his wife, and wished all the Turks born and unborn at the bottom of the sea. Then he jumped into the

wagon, looking neither to heaven nor earth,
but struggling all the way with a single thought
—that it had not been allowed him to leave
his wife when she had happened to fall asleep.

Hardly were they an hour away from Ebesfalva when the Turks caught sight of a rider at
full speed, who was evidently trying to overtake
them. They called Apafi's attention to it. At
first he would not listen to them, but when told
that the rider came from the direction of Ebesfalva he ordered the wagon to stop and waited
for the messenger. It was Andy who, waving
his handkerchief, came galloping toward them.

"What has happened, Andy?" called out his
master with beating heart, while his servant was
still at a distance.

"Good news, master," shouted Andy, "our
most gracious lady has a son and she herself is
out of all danger—God be praised!"

"Blessed be the name of the Lord," cried
Apafi, with lightened heart, and sent the messenger back. As soon as this chief cause of his
anxiety had vanished all his other troubles disappeared. He thought of his son and in the glow
of this thought began to believe that his Turkish
attendants were as good, respectable, civilized
people as he had ever seen. Late at night they
reached the tent of Ali Pasha. The sentinels
were sleeping like badgers; as far as they were
concerned one might have carried off the whole

camp. Apafi had to wait before the tent of the Pasha until he had dressed himself, when drawing aside the curtains, the Pasha bade him enter. There sat Ali with crossed legs on a rug at the back of the tent, and behind him two finely-clad Moors. On the rug that formed a partition in the tent, was outlined the figure of some one standing behind.

"Are you that Michael Apafi," asked the Pasha after the customary greetings, "who for several years was a prisoner of the Tartar Murza?"

"The very same, most gracious Pasha, the one to whom, in his mercy, he granted exemption from the full ransom."

"That will be made right. Murza granted exemption from the full ransom because His Excellency the Sultan commanded him to do so, and His Majesty will do even more for you."

"I hear these words with astonishment and gratitude, for I do not know how I can have deserved this grace."

"His Excellency has learned that you conducted yourself wisely, honorably, and like a man, in that sad imprisonment, and that you knew so well how to win the hearts of the other prisoners that although there is no respect of rank among prisoners they all had the highest respect for you. In consideration of this, and furthermore taking into account that the present prince, John Kemény, as he has plainly shown, intends to set himself free from the Sublime Porte, His Excellency has determined without further delay to raise you to the throne of Transylvania and to support you there."

"Me,—gracious lord! It is your pleasure to jest," stammered Apafi. It seemed as if everything was beginning to go round before him.

"Yes, you! You have no cause to wonder at this, for when my lord pleases pashas and princes are made, at a glance from him, slaves, beggars or corpses; and at another glance, common soldiers, nobles, or slaves step into their superiors' places. You were so fortunate as to come in for a share of his good-will. Make this to your advantage and do not misuse it."

"But, gracious lord, what an idea that I can become a prince!"

"That is my affair, I will make you one."

"But Transylvania has another prince, John Kemény."

"That is also my affair. I will settle with him soon."

Apafi shrugged his shoulders; he felt that he had never been entangled in a worse affair.— "That was a true presentiment of my wife's, that to-day a great danger threatened me," he thought.

The Pasha resumed the conversation. "Now then, without further delay, write an order for a convention of the States so that the ceremony of inauguration may take place as quickly as possible."

"I—who will come at my call? My lord, I am one of the least important of the nobles of my country: they will only laugh at me and say that I have gone crazy."

"And then they will become aware that they themselves have gone crazy."

"Then surely I could not send out such a summons, for, with the exception of the country of the Szeklers, Kemény has all in his power."

"Then we will send to the Szeklers, they will certainly come."

"And even among the Szeklers the more influential are unknown to me, for I am not one of them. There I know such people as John Daczo, Stephen Run and Stephen Nalaczy."

"Well, then, call these men, Run, Daczo, and Nalaczy, if you think they are honest folk."

Apafi began to scratch his head. "But suppose they came, where should we hold the convention? we have no suitable place. In Klausenburg my brother-in-law, Dionysius Banfy, is my sworn foe, and he is captain of the train bands. In Hermanstadt John Kemény himself lives."

"Certainly we have Klein-Selyk, we can assemble here." In spite of his distress, Apafi had to laugh. "There is not a house here where thirty men could find room at the same time," he answered, quickly.

"Yes there is, there is the church," replied the Pasha, "there you can hold your meeting. If that building is good enough to pay one's respects to God in, surely it is good enough to pay one's respects to men in."

Apafi did not know what further objection to urge. "Can you write?" asked the Pasha.

"To be sure I can," answered Apafi, sighing deeply.

"Because I can't. Well then, sit down and send your summons to the states."

A slave brought a table, parchment, and red ink. Apafi sat down like a lamb for the sacrifice, and by way of beginning made a letter on the parchment so large that the Turk sprang up in fright and asked him what that meant.

"That is an S," answered Apafi.

"Leave some space for the rest of the letters."

"That is the initial letter, the rest will be smaller of course."

"Read aloud to me what you are writing."

Apafi wrote with trembling hand, and read, "Whereas"— The Pasha tore the parchment away from him in anger and roared out, "'Whereas,—since'—what is the use of such roundabout expressions? Write as is the custom, 'We, Michael Apafi, Prince of Transylvania, command you, miserable slave, that as soon as you receive this writing, without fail you appear before us at once in Klein-Selyk.' Then stop."

It required some effort on the part of Apafi to make the Pasha understand that it was not the custom to use such terms with the Hungarian nobility. At last he gained permission to write as seemed best to him, only the contents were to be decisive and authoritative.

The circular letter was finished at last. The Pasha ordered a man to mount his horse at once, and gave him instructions to deliver this at full speed.

Apafi shook his pen and sighed to himself;— "I would like to see the man who can tell me what will be the result of all this."

"Now, until the convention assembles, stay with me here in camp."

"May I not go back to my wife and child at home?" asked Apafi, with throbbing heart.

"The devil! That you may run away from us? That is the way all these Hungarians treat the rank of prince. The men we do not wish lie down on us and beg for the honor, and those we do wish take to flight." And with that the Pasha showed Apafi to his tent and left him, at the same time giving the order to the sentinel stationed at the entrance as a mark of honor, to be sure not to let him escape.

"He got into a pretty scrape that time!" sighed Apafi, in deep resignation. The only hope that remained for him now was that the men summoned would not appear for the convention.

*   *   *   *   *   *

A few days later, in the early morning while Apafi was still in bed, there entered his tent suddenly Stephen Run, John Daczo and Stephen Nalaczy, with all the rest of the noble Szeklers to whom the letter had been sent.

"For God's sake!" cried out Apafi, "what are you here for?"

"Why, your majesty summoned us here," replied Nalaczy.

"That's true, but you might have had the sense not to come. What can we do now?"

"Enthrone your majesty with all due ceremony and if necessary, defend you in true Szekler fashion," said Stephen Run.

"You are too few for that, my friends."

"Have the goodness just to look out in front of the tent," began Nalaczy, and drawing aside the curtain, he showed him a crowd of Szeklers with swords and lances, who had remained without. "We are here *cum gentibus* to prove to your grace that if we acknowledge you as our Prince, this is not done in mere jest."

Apafi shrugged his shoulders and began to draw on his boots. But he was so thoughtful and melancholy with it all, that an hour passed before he was dressed, for he took up each article of dress the wrong way, and put on his coat before he thought of his waistcoat. Several hundred of the nobility had assembled in Selyk at his call, more than he expected or even wished.

When Ali Pasha came out of his tent, in the presence of all assembled he took Apafi by the hand and threw about him a new green velvet cloak, set on his head a cap bordered with ermine, and gave the States assembled to understand that they were to receive this man from this time as their true Prince. The Szeklers roared out a huzza, raised Apafi on their shoulders and set him on a platform covered with velvet that Ali Pasha had ordered built for him.

"Now let the lords betake themselves to the church—and do you give your oath to your Prince according to your custom and swear fealty to each other. The bells have already been rung at my order. Have mass said in due form."

"Pardon me, but I am of the Reformed Church," protested Apafi.

"That suits me all the better. The affair can be conducted with less formality. There is his Reverence Franz, the Magyar, he shall preach the sermon."

Apafi let them do as they would, only nervously stroking his moustache and shrugging his

shoulders when he was questioned. Nalaczy and
the rest of the Szeklers considered it proper to
meet him in the church with all the reverence
due to princes. The Reverend Franz extemporized a powerful sermon, in which he assured
them in thundering language that the God of
Israel who had called David from his sheep to
the kingly throne and exalted him above all his
enemies, would now too maintain his chosen one
in his good pleasure, though his foes were as
numerous as the blades of grass in the field, or
the sands of the seashore.

This little church could never have dreamed
that it would one day be the scene of a convention and a princely election. And Apafi could
certainly never have dreamed that all this would
have been fulfilled for him. He had neither ear
nor eye for the consecration nor for the sermon,
for his mind was constantly busied with the
thought of what might become of his wife and
child and where would they find refuge if he
should fall into the hands of Kemény and they
should be driven from house and home. Then it
occurred to him that somewhere in the land of
the Szeklers he had a brother, Stephen Apafi,
with whom he had always had the friendliest relations, and who would certainly take care of
them if he saw them in misery. These thoughts
made him forget everything about himself so
completely that when at the conclusion of the

assembly all present rose and began the Te Deum, he too arose, quite ignoring the fact that these services were in his honor. But some one behind laid his hands on his shoulders and pressed him down into his place, telling him in a low, familiar voice that he was to remain seated. Apafi looked around and fell back on his seat in astonishment, for the man behind him was no other than his brother Stephen.

"You here, too!" said Apafi to him, deeply affected.

"I was a little belated," said Stephen, "but I arrived in time and will stay as long as you command."

"Will you also run into danger?"

"My brother, our fate lies in God's hand, but we too have something in hand which will have a little to say," and with that he laid his hand on his sword hilt. "Kemény has forfeited the love of his country,—I need not tell you why. You have good cause to triumph and the ways and means will not fail you."

"But if it should prove otherwise? what is then to become of my wife—have you not seen her?"

"I have just come from there. That is why I was late."

"You have talked with her? What did she say about my affairs? Is she very much worried?"

"Not in the least. On the contrary, she is very much pleased, and thinks Transylvania could not have found a better prince; that you deserve this honor much more than any of the great lords, who have no thought except for tyranny or carousal, and she regrets very much that her child is still so young she cannot come to strengthen and encourage you."

"I should have been much better pleased had she been chosen prince," said Apafi, half in vexation and half in jest.

"Look out," said Stephen, "the young woman is so accustomed to managing affairs at home that if you do not keep the crown firmly on your own head we shall yet live to see her wearing it on hers. This, of course, I speak only in jest."

There is many a truth spoken in jest.

CHAPTER IV

THE HUNGARIAN PRINCES IN BANQUET

HIS Excellency, Prince John Kemény, was
meantime tarrying mid sport and pleasure in
Hermanstadt. This good lord had a perfect passion for eating, and would not have given up his
dinner if the last spoke in the last wheel of the
state carriage had been broken. Among his
counsellors his cook stood first. The entire town-
hall was at his disposal and had been taken possession of by his attendants. In the courtyard
spur-clanking cuirassiers amused themselves with
Transylvanian-Saxon serving-women. A few
German musketeers stationed on guard, had
leaned their weapons against the gate-post and
entered into friendly relations with the boys who
were carrying the food away from the table, at
the same time singing with merriment Hungarian
songs quickly picked up, and dancing as they sang.
On the other hand, the Hungarian guards were
sitting in their yellow cloaks with green fasten-
ings, leaning silently against the wall. They
gave no heed to the tankards of wine set in their
hands, except to pour them down at a single
draught and return the mighty cup to the
friendly butler. The latter could hardly hold

himself up—smiled at all, the happy and the unhappy, and marched off backward to the cook,
who, carrying everything on high, now brought
in on a silver dish a great tart decked with flowers and sugar, representing the Tower of Babel;
and again a huge porcelain bowl, from which
came the spicy fragrance of a hot punch; and
again a great wooden platter, on which rested a
whole roast peacock in all his plumage. With
difficulty could he make his way across the courtyard with his amazing burdens, for the crowds
had gathered there for the adjustment of their
affairs, and were waiting until the prince should
leave the table. Meantime they got wine, roasts
and pastry; everything except what they came
for—justice.

In the banquet-hall were the lords and ladies,
all somewhat mellow with drink. The meal had
lasted some time and was still far from finished.
French cookery seemed to have reserved its most
wonderful products for this princely feast. The
three natural kingdoms had been taxed to tickle
the palates of men. Everything considered appetizing and extraordinary, from the days of
Lucullus down to the time of the French gour-
mand, had been brought together there. All
kinds of native and foreign wines were taken
from great silver coolers and poured into richly
cut and colored Venetian glasses. The rarest
game, cooked in all sorts of ways, was set out on

silver dishes; then followed transparent, rosy, quivering jellies, preserved fruits from the Indies, ragouts of cocks' combs, delicacies made of snails, lobsters and rare sea fish, dishes that the guests could only by the wildest fancy imagine appetizing, after they were already sated with what was good; artichokes, oysters, turtles, the enjoyment of which I should, for my part, count a punishment, great pasties and rose-stained swans' eggs in large baskets, which the guests, by way of diversion could cook for themselves over a small spirit lamp placed before each one. Finally came countless other wonderful dishes, the names of which would be hardly recognizable by ordinary mortals and in abundance sufficient for six times as many guests. There were all kinds of spicy drinks to suit the taste of each one. Behind each guest was stationed a page, who as soon as the guest turned his head, immediately removed his full plate and gave him a clean one.

Behind the Prince stood the son of Ladislaus Csaki, who was proud that his son might fill the glass of the Prince, and the Prince needed to have it filled frequently. The Transylvanian feasters were wont to close their banquets by drinking each other down for a wager. John Kemény now called on the brave spirits for the wonted contest. Most of the guests declined the challenge. The sober ones expressed their thanks

for the honor and excused themselves; only three
took up the challenge. The first was Wenzinger,
leader of the German troops, the second was
Paul Beldi, general of the Szeklers and supreme
judge of the court at Haromszek, a fine-looking
man; his noble brow indicated rest, his gentle
eyes were brightened a little by the wine, his
silent lips opened in a smile; otherwise no effect
of the drinking was to be seen. Opposite him
was the third contestant, Dionysius Banfy, captain of the train bands at Klausenburg and
general of the troops, a medium sized, broad
shouldered, haughty man, with a touch of unbecoming affectation in his aristocratic countenance.

John Kemény was seated at the upper end of
the table and at either side sat the wives of
Banfy and Beldi. One of them, Banfy's wife, was
a young woman barely twenty years old, who since
her sixteenth year had been under the dominion
of her husband. She hardly dared to raise her
eyes, or if she did it was only to turn them to her
husband. On the other side sat Beldi's wife, between her husband and the Prince; hers was still
a dazzling beauty like that of a white rose, and
now lighted up by the cheer of the feast, the
healthy color seemed fairly to burn. There was
an eloquent charm in her eyebrows, and when she
let fall her lashes over her burning eyes her look
was fascinating. Bethlen's wife at the opposite

end of the table talked openly of the coquettish woman who had a marriageable daughter and yet dared appear with open bodice; but this gave all the more pleasure to the Prince, not less to the impetuous Banfy, and even to the gentle husband, who worshipped his wife.

The wager had electrified all the men, so that the music which sounded from the gallery throughout the feast now began to chime in with songs, when Gabriel Haller entered and hurrying to the Prince, whispered a few words to him with a serious look. Kemény stared at him, then emptied the glass in his hand and laughed loudly.

"Tell the news to the company that they too may know," he called out to Haller.

He hesitated.

"Out with it; you could hardly say anything more entertaining. Set your music to it, up there. It is a great joke."

The men all urged Haller to share his joke with them. "It is quite unimportant," said the man, with a shrug, "Ali Pasha has raised Michael Apafi to be Prince."

"Ha, ha, ha!"—The laughter went round the table. The Prince turned with absurd affectation first to one and then to another of the company. "Does any one of you know this man? Has anybody ever heard of him before?"

Banfy's wife clung with blanched face to her

husband's arm, while he, leaning his elbows on the table said, not without annoyance; "I am a distant connection of the poor wretch. In fact, he married a relative of my wife. He was a long time in slavery to the Tartars, and the Turks, who are now angry with us, have undoubtedly set him free on condition that he should allow himself to be made prince. He must have lost his wits entirely."

Again the men laughed loudly.

"We will crown him at once," said Kemény, sarcastically, throwing back his head.

"That has been done already," said Haller.

"Where? By whom?" questioned the good-natured Prince, with contracted brow.

"In Klein-Selyk, by the State Convention."

Kemény indicated by a motion of the hand and uplifted eyebrow that he did not fully understand this reply.

"Who was present? Surely all the men of importance in the country are here with us."

"There were present Stephen Apafi, Nalaczy, Daczo and others, a couple of hundred Szekler nobility."

"Well, we will count them up as soon as we are through with other affairs," said the Prince, contemptuously. "Give Gabriel Haller a chair."

"They are not waiting for us, but are already coming against us; they are in Schassburg now."

"I suppose they will drive us out,—Michael

Apafi with his two hundred Szeklers," said Kemény, laughing.

Wenzinger now arose and said in soldierly fashion; "Does your Highness wish me to have the army called together? we have eight thousand armed men. If it pleases your Highness, we will scatter these people so completely that there will be no two men left standing together."

"Keep quiet," replied Kemény, who looked down with contempt upon the whole business. "Sit down and drink. Let them come nearer, why should we take the trouble to go to them? we can certainly take them, bag and baggage.— I am sorry, Dionysius Banfy, that this man is a connection of yours, but out of consideration for you I will see to it that he is not broken on the wheel; I'll have him—stuffed."

This hit of Kemény's was received with roars of laughter.

"Bring a glass for Gabriel Haller, we will go on with our wager. Play the rest of that interrupted music."

Again the music rang out. The gypsy band played a Czardas. The men clinked their glasses and sang to the music. The servants outside joined in. The emptied glasses flew against the wall; there was not one among them who could not have dashed his glass in a thousand pieces except Gabriel Haller, who had come last and

was still sober, ashamed to smash the costly
Venetian glass.

"Break it against the table so the pieces will
fly," thundered the Prince at him, and Haller, in
obedience to his Prince, struck the glass lightly
against the table and snapped the stem, and then
bowed with respectful humility before his master.

Madame Banfy sighed as she thought of her
kinsfolk. Her husband, to prevent any one's
thinking that he was in the least concerned in
the affair, jumped from his seat and amid the
sounds of the Czardas invited the beautiful
Madame Beldi to dance. The little lady was
ready. Banfy grasped the beauty about her
waist, held her firmly and whirled her around. The
excited woman flew with the lightness of a fairy
on the arm of her partner. With that, the rest
of the men jumped from their places, seized other
women for a dance, and soon the entire company
was swept away in fantastic revelry, every one
clapping, dancing and shouting. Banfy was hot-
blooded and light-headed; he loved beautiful
women, and now in addition there was the glow
of the wine. When his beautiful partner once
more hung on his arm, her glowing cheeks came
so near him that he suddenly so far forgot himself as to press the bewitching woman passionately to his heart and imprint a hot kiss on her
cheek. Madame Beldi cried out and pushed the

bold man from her. Banfy, also startled at what he had done, cast a glance about him but everybody was so taken up with his own pleasure that, to all appearances, neither kiss nor cry had been noticed. However, Madame Beldi angrily left her partner, and when Banfy stammered out an apology, indicated to him that he should stay at a distance.

This kiss was to cost Banfy dear one of these days. Nobody had noticed it except the man whom it most concerned,—the husband. Beldi's eye had seen it. Let not anybody think that a husband who loves is not jealous. Even if he acts as if he had not seen, had not heard, he sees and hears and notices everything. He had indeed seen Banfy kiss his wife, although he acted as if he did not notice the confusion of his wife who, all excited, sought her husband. He took her hand and led her from the hall. Once outside he bade her make ready for a journey. "Where are we going?" asked his wife, quivering with excitement.

"Home to Bodola."

Of all the guests Dionysius Banfy alone noticed that two had vanished from the hall.

CHAPTER V

In a part of the country of upper Weissenburg, as soon as you have left the Pass of Boza or made a détour of the ravine in the footpath around the mountain heights, you catch sight of the valley of the Tatrang. On all sides are low mountains covered with light fog, and in the background the sky-piercing heights of the foothills of Capri, bright in the early autumnal snow. In the fog-wrapped valley are four or five hamlets with whitewashed houses, from which the smoke arises amid the green fruit trees. The little stream of Tatrang winds clear as crystal between the quiet villages, forming here and there waterfalls with snowy mist. The clouds hang so low over the valley as to shut out with their golden veil first one object and then another from the observer on the mountain-height. There is Hosszufalu with its long street; and the church of Trajzonfalu reflects the sunbeams from its painted metal roof. Tatrang is right on the bank of the stream, at this point crossed by a long wooden bridge; far in the distance appear dark and misty the walls of Kronstadt and the outline of the citadel, at that time still unharmed

Farther down in the valley are the scattered dwellings of the little village of Bodola, its church high on a hill; opposite the village stands a small castle with broad towers and black bastions with battlements; the western bastion is built on a steep rock. But it is only from afar that the castle looks gloomy; as you draw nearer you see that what appeared a dark green growth on the bastion is a garden of flowers. The great Gothic windows are decorated with sculpture and painted glass. Up the steep cliff is a well-kept, winding path, with mossy stone benches at every turn; at its summit is a parapet and the pointed turrets of the castle are painted red and topped with fantastic weather-vanes.

The road to Kronstadt through the Boza Pass leads to this little castle in a few hours, and at the very time when John Kemény had abandoned himself utterly to pleasure in Hermanstadt, a long line of horsemen was moving out of the castle; there might have been two thousand Turkish riders, recognizable from afar by their red turbans and their snow-white caftans; with them were a few hundred Wallachian howitzers in charge of men in brown woolen cloaks and black turbans. The way was so narrow here that the horsemen could ride only two by two, and those in the rear had hardly emerged from the mountain pass when the first riders were already in Tatrang. Their leader was a medium sized, sunburned man, with eyes like an eagle's; there was a long scar across his forehead; the sharp upward turn of his moustache indicated an unusually hot temper, an impression confirmed by the short, crisp speech, the proud turn of the head, and the abrupt movements. Beyond the village he called a halt to await the rear; at the very end rumbled two baggage-wagons and a melon-shaped calêche, the entire baggage of the Turk. A child followed, whose serious expression and gleaming short sword seemed hardly appropriate to the full round face; he might have been twelve years old. Within the carriage, the curtains of which had been thrown wide open to give free play to the evening breeze, sat a young woman of possibly two and thirty, whose dress was partly Turkish, partly Christian; for she wore the loose silk trousers and short blue caftan of Turkish women, but had taken off her turban. Her face, contrary to Turkish custom, was unveiled, and she looked calmly out of the window at the country and the passing peasants.

Beyond the village the Turkish leader marshaled his troops, evidently accustomed to some discipline. At the head of the left wing was the young boy; the right was led by a strong man.

"My brave men," said the Pasha to his troops, "you will encamp here. Let every man keep his place beside his horse and not lay down his

arms. Ferhad Aga with twelve men will go to
the village and say to the justiciary most respect-
fully that he is to send four hundred-weight of
bread, as much meat, and twice as much hay and
oats, for which he will receive four asper the
pound,—no more and no less."

The Pasha then turned to the Wallachians.
" You dogs, do not think that we have come here
to plunder. Do not stir from your places. If I
find that a single goose has been stolen from the
village, I will have your captains hung and you
decimated."

Then he chose four horsemen from the company. " You will follow me. The others are to
rest. We will continue our march to-night. In
my absence, Feriz Bey is in command."

The small boy saluted. " As soon as Feriz Bey
receives word from me to leave you, you will
be in command of Ferhad Aga until my return."

With that the Pasha struck spurs to his horse
and galloped off to Bodola with his escort of four
men. Then the boy called Feriz Bey by the
Pasha, rode forward with soldierly bearing and
in the clearest, firmest tones gave order to dismount. His Arab steed, with foaming bit reared
and plunged, but the little commandant went on
with his orders as if he did not notice the mad
leaps of his horse. Meantime, the Pasha continued his ride toward the castle of Bodola. The
lord of the castle, Paul Beldi, had just returned

the day before with his wife from the court of
Kemény, which he had left without parting
words, and was standing before the dwelling
when the Turkish riders came into the courtyard.   In those days the relations of Transylvania and Turkey were such that a visit of this
kind might take place without previous announcement.   As soon as the Pasha caught sight
of Beldi he jumped from his horse, hurried up
the steps to him and presented himself briefly.

"I am Kutschuk Pasha.   Since my road lay
through this country I have come to speak with
you, if you have time."

"Your servant," replied Beldi, giving his guest
precedence as he showed him to the castle salon.
It was a square room, with the walls painted in
Oriental landscapes; in the spaces between the
windows were great mirrors in metal frames;
the marble floor was covered over with large,
bright rugs; on the walls above the windows
were portraits and trophies of old weapons of
strange shapes and settings; in the centre of the
room was a large table of green marble, with
claw feet, and here and there easy chairs uphols-
tered in leather, with heavy carvings.   Opposite
the entrance a door led to the terrace from which
was a wide view of the snow-covered mountains.
The evening light streaming through the painted
glass cast a bright reflection over the faces of the
men as they entered.

" In what way can I serve you ? " asked Beldi.

"You are well aware," replied Kutschuk, "that at present there is a great division in the country over the princely succession in Transylvania."

" That does not concern me and I do not intend to take sides with either party," answered Beldi, guardedly.

" I did not come here to ask you for help or advice in this affair. The question is to be settled by the sword. What has brought me to you is purely a family affair and concerns me and me only."

Beldi, in amazement, bade his guest be seated and said to him, " Speak."

" You may have heard that there was once here in Transylvania a Mademoiselle Kallay, who fell in love with a young Turk and became his wife ; naturally, without the knowledge or consent of her parents."

" I do know about it. They used to say that the young Turk knew as well how to conquer a woman's heart as a foe on the battlefield."

" Perhaps so. Conquests in war have meantime effaced the traces of love from his cheeks. As you see, my face is crossed this way and that with scars. For the man who married that woman stands before you."

Beldi looked at the Pasha with astonishment.

" I have loved this woman without ceasing and

with adoration," continued the Pasha; "this may
sound strange to you, coming from the lips of a
Turk, but it is true. I have no other wife. She
has borne me a son of whom I am proud. Now
my affairs are in so critical a condition that I
must either work wonders with the help of God,
or fall in battle. You know that the religion of
Mohammed sets a high value on death in battle,
so that this causes me little anxiety; but I am
thinking of my wife, who if she should lose me
and my son would be placed in a most doubtful
position. In Turkey, she would be exposed to
persecution because she had remained a Christian; in Transylvania, because she had married a
Mohammedan; there through my relatives and
here through her own. For that reason I turn to
you with a request. I have heard you spoken of
as a man of honor and of your wife as a worthy
woman. Receive my wife into your family. I
have sufficient property for her so that she will
be no burden to you in that respect; she needs
only your protection. If you promise to grant
me this request you can count on my friendship
and gratitude forever, the command of my sword
and my property and, in case I survive, of my
life."

Beldi grasped the Pasha by the hand. "Bring
your wife," he said, in cordial tones, "my wife
and I will receive her as a sister."

"Not as a sister, I beg of you," said Kutschuk,

laughingly, " with us that is equivalent to enmity. So then, I may bring her ? "

" We shall be happy to have her with us," replied Beldi, and gave order to his servants to return to Tatrang with the Pasha's followers and bring his carriage from there by torch light Kutschuk sent word that Feriz Bey was to come too. Meantime, Beldi presented Kutschuk Pasha to his wife, and it gave him no little pleasure to find that she remembered the Pasha's wife as a friend in her youth, whom she would meet again with natural interest and joy.

In the course of a few hours the carriage arrived and rolled heavily over the stone-paved courtyard. Madame Beldi hurried down the steps to meet the Pasha's wife, and as the latter stepped from the carriage received her with a cry of joy. " Katharine, do you know me still ? " She too recognized her playmate of old and the two friends rushed into each other's arms, kissed each other and said sweetly, " How handsome you have grown ! " " What a stately woman you have become ! "

" See, this is my son," said Katharine, pointing to Feriz Bey who, dismounted from his horse, was now hurrying forward to help his mother from the carriage.

" What a fine boy ! " exclaimed Madame Beldi, charmed ; she threw her arms around the handsome, rosy-cheeked child and kissed him again

and again;—if she had only known that this
child was no longer a child, but a general!

"I too have children," said Madame Beldi,
with the sweet rivalry of maternal feeling.
"You shall see them. Does your son speak Hungarian?"

"Hungarian!" asked Katharine, almost hurt.
"Does the child of a Hungarian mother speak
Hungarian! How can you ask such a ques-
tion?"

"So much the better," said Madame Beldi,
"the children will become acquainted the more
easily and they will belong to one family hence-
forth. Our husbands have arranged that with
each other and it certainly will please us."

The affectionate mother threw her arms around
her friend again, took Feriz Bey by the hand,
and brought them both into the midst of the
family circle, where they chatted uninterruptedly
and asked and answered thousands of questions.

In the little boudoir was a cheerful open fire;
large, beflowered silk curtains shaded the windows; on an ivory table ticked a handsome clock
set with jewels. In the back part of the room
an easy sofa covered with cornflower blue velvet
invited one to rest. On a centre-table covered
with a handsome Persian rug was a massive silver
candelabrum in the form of a siren who held up
a wax candle in each hand. In front of the fireplace stood Madame Beldi's children; the older,

Sophie, a maiden of thirteen years, tall, delicately built, with shy glance, appeared to be arranging the fire. She still wore her hair in childish fashion in two long, heavy braids reaching almost to her heels. This girl afterward became the wife of Paul Wesselenyi.

The second child, a little girl of four, knelt before her older sister and scattered light sticks on the fire. Her name was Aranka, the Hungarian for gold-child; her hair was in golden curls falling over her little shoulders; her features were animated and her eyes as well as her hands in constant motion, interfering with her sister in one way or another; she laughed innocently when the older girl at last became angry.

The two children rose when they heard steps and voices at the door. As soon as the older girl caught sight of the strangers she tried to smooth out her dress, while Aranka rushed noisily to her mother, and catching her by the dress looked up at her with a smile on her little round face. Katharine embraced the older girl who timidly offered her forehead to be kissed.

"And your cousin, little Feriz, you must kiss him, too," said Madame Beldi, and brought the two reluctant children together, who hardly dared touch each other's lips. Sophie turned red to her very ears, ran out of the room and could not be persuaded to come back that evening.

"Oh, you bashful Mimosa," said Madame

Beldi, with a laugh. "Aranka is braver than you are, I am sure. You are not afraid to kiss Cousin Feriz, are you, darling?"

The child looked up at Feriz and drew back, clinging to her mother's gown, with her large, dark blue eyes fixed on Feriz. Feriz Bey on his side knelt down, embraced the child and imprinted a hearty kiss on her round, red cheeks. Now that this first step had been taken the acquaintance was made for Aranka. She bade her Turkish cousin sit down beside the fireplace, and leaning against him she began to question him about everything she saw on him, from the sword hilt to the feathers on his turban; nothing escaped her.

"Let us leave the children to play," said Madame Beldi, and led her friend out on the balcony from which was a view of the valley of Tatrang flooded with moonlight. While the men talked seriously and the children gave themselves up to play, the two ladies began one of those confidential conversations so dear to young women, especially when they have so much to tell each other, to ask and to inquire, as these two had. Madame Beldi sat down beside Katharine, took her affectionately by the hand and asked half in jest;—"So your husband has no other wife?"

Katharine laughed, but there was a little vexation with it, as she said;—"I suppose you think a Hungarian marries a Turk only to be his slave. My husband loves me dearly."

"I don't doubt it, Katharine, but that certainly is the custom with you."

"With *us!*   I am no Turk."

"What then?"

"A Protestant like yourself. It was a Protestant who married me—the Reverend Martin Biro, who lives in Constantinople in banishment, and to whom my husband in his gratitude gave a house where the Transylvanians and Hungarians living in Constantinople can meet for worship."

"What, does not your husband persecute the Christians?"

"No, indeed. The Turks believe that every religion is good and leads to heaven, only they think their own religion is the best; for in their opinion theirs leads the way to the heaven of heavens. Besides, my husband has a kind heart and is much more enlightened than most Turks."

"Then why couldn't you bring him over to the Christian faith?"

"Why not? perhaps because whenever the story-tellers relate the romance of a Turk who fell in love with a Christian girl, they end the tale with her bringing him to baptism and exchanging the caftan for a coat. In this case they have a romance in which the wife follows her husband and sacrifices everything for him."

"You are quite right, Katharine, but you see it takes me some little time to become accustomed to the thought that a Christian, a Hungarian woman, can have a Turk for a husband."

"But consider, my good friend, God might not have counted it such a good service on my part if I had brought my husband over to our religion, as he does that I left him in the religion in which he was born. A Christian renegade, the most that he could have done would have been to take his place in the Church. But now, as one of the most influential Pashas, he can transform the fate of any Christian in Turkey to one so favorable that the Christian subjects of other lands crowd thither as to the Holy Land. How often, when he has received his portion of the war-plunder, has he handed me a long list on which were marked the names of my imprisoned countrymen whom he had set free for a large sum. He has expended immense treasure for this purpose, and, my darling, the reading of such a list gives me more pleasure than would the most beautiful Eastern pearls he could have bought for the same treasure ; and such a deed raises him higher in my eyes than if he could say all the psalms by heart. Beside, he is not at all the man whom you would expect to change his opinions in the least for God or man ; then, too, if he were ready to give up his religion I could no longer trust his love, for he would cease to be the same man I knew and loved—a man who, when he had once said a thing, stood firmly by it and never yielded to any fear or persuasion."

Madame Beldi embraced her friend and kissed her glowing cheeks. "You are right, my good Katharine. Our prejudices prevent us from entertaining more than the general opinion. It is true, love too has its religion. But what of your country? Have you never thought of your country?"

"Know my love for my country from the fact that I am now sacrificing to that the life of my husband and of my child, whom I see now probably for the last time."

The expression of Madame Beldi's face showed that she did not fully comprehend the meaning of her friend's words and Katharine had begun to explain this to her when the servant announced that the gentlemen had already been for some time in the dining-hall and were waiting only for the ladies. Madame Beldi led the way. The children were so far on in their friendship that Aranka let herself be carried into the dinning-room by Feriz Bey, while she played with his jeweled feathers.

When Katharine saw a large decanter of wine before her husband she seized it quickly and changed it for a glass carafe of pure spring-water. Madame Beldi noticed it and glanced inquiringly at her embarrassed friend.

"He never drinks wine," said Katharine, by way of excuse. "It hurts him for he is somewhat passionate by nature." Kutschuk raised Katharine's hand to his lips with a smile. "Why do you spare the truth,—that I never drink wine because the Koran forbids it,—because I am a Turk."

Beldi shook his head at his wife and to give the conversation another turn pointed to the children sitting side by side.

"Your son, Kutschuk Pasha, seems to feel quite at home already. You will see what a Hungarian we shall make of him before your return."

At that Kutschuk looked up quickly and proudly at Feriz and both looked at Beldi. In an instant the child's countenance changed completely, and he was wonderfully like his father; the same firm glance, the same proud toss of the head, the same haughty brow.

"Your speech leads me to infer, Beldi," said Kutschuk, "that you think I have brought my son only to leave him here with you."

"You surely will not take such a child into battle!"

"Such a child! He commands four hundred spahi horse, has already taken part in three engagements, had two horses shot down under him, and in the coming war is to lead the left wing of my corps."

The Beldis now looked in astonishment at the

child who, conscious that all eyes were directed toward him, strove to assume a proud look.

"But you will at least stand beside your son in the contest?" said Madame Beldi, anxiously.

"By no means. I shall lead the centre and he will look after his division. At his age I was already wearing the Order of Nischan and I hope he will not return without having won it, too."

"But suppose he should come to a hand-to-hand fight and be in danger?" asked Madame Beldi, with growing anxiety.

"Then he will be fighting as befits him," replied Kutschuk, stroking his moustache, that seemed to rise of its own accord.

"But he is far too young to enter a contest with men," said Madame Beldi, with an expression of pity.

"Feriz," Kutschuk called to his son, "take a sword from the wall there and show our friends that you know how to swing it like a man."

The boy sprang up and chose from the weapons hanging on the wall, not a sword but a heavy club, seized it at the very end of the handle and swung it with outstretched arm so easily in every direction that it would have been a credit to any man. His proof of strength was rewarded by a general cry of astonishment.

"Kutschuk, give me the boy!" said Beldi.

"With all my heart. Will you give me your daughter?"

" Which one ?   You may have your choice."

" The one next him.   When she is grown up
she will be just a match for him and we shall
both have a son and a daughter."

Beldi laughed good-naturedly, the two women
smiled at each other and Kutschuk Pasha looked
with satisfaction at his son, while the latter drew
the heron's feather out of his turban, tore off the
jeweled clasp which had been most pleasing to
the little Aranka, and gave it to the child with
generous gallantry.   The little maid reached for
the costly present timidly, without the slightest
suspicion of either its material or moral worth ;
but when once the trinket was in her hand she
would not have let it go for anything in the world.
The parents suddenly became silent.   True, their
expression was a smiling one, but their eyes were
serious.

CHAPTER VI

THE BATTLE OF NAGY–SZÖLLÖS

MEANWHILE Michael Apafi assured by Ali Pasha that help would come to him in a short time, advanced on Schassburg and there awaited the change of fortune. John Kemény came against him with a great army of German and Hungarian troops in imposing numbers, and he himself was a bold general in time of action. Michael Apafi could make but slight opposition. He had a few hundred stiff-necked Szeklers incapable of discipline, together with the blue janissaries who had stayed behind as bodyguard for him; in all not the tenth of Kemény's force in point of strength. By the advice of Stephen Aapfi the Prince determined to stay in Schassburg on the defensive until he could be joined by the auxiliaries from his Turkish patron. This decision was pleasing to the Saxon burghers, for behind the walls of their own town they knew how to defend themselves, but in open field they were never quite comfortable. With the Szeklers it was just the opposite. It was Nalaczy's mission to keep them in a warlike frame of mind. One evening he brought them to such a state of excitement at the inn that with the dawn they went noisily to the windows of the Prince and swore roundly that the gate must be opened to them for they were determined to attack Kemény and fight it out to the death. The Prince and his advisers came down in terror and strove in every way to make them understand that Kemény's troops were more numerous than they; that the half of his army was made up of muske-teers while on their side none but the Saxons knew how to use firearms; that if they should make a sally by one gate the enemy would rush in by the other and all would be confusion. But the man who thinks he can clear a Szekler's mind of an idea once gained is much mistaken.

"We are either going to be led against the enemy or we are going home," they shouted. "We positively will not consent to stay here ten years like the Trojans, for we are needed at home. Portion out to every man the number of the enemy that falls to his share, these he shall strike down and then take his discharge. We do not wish to stay here and be besieged and starved out, and then thrown to the dogs and rats."

"If you do not wish to stay, my friends, you may go," was the final decision of Apafi, "but it would be madness for me to be drawn into an engagement."

The Szeklers said never a word but took up their knapsacks, shouldered their spears and

moved out of Schassburg as if they never had
been there.   From this time on the Szeklers
were Apafi's enemies and remained so until his
death.

The next day Kemény's forces were beneath
the city walls, where Apafi had barely armed
men enough to guard the gates.   Wenzinger was
the man who best understood the art of war.
This general, true to the principles of the military
art in which he had been trained, first inspected
the ground, then carefully occupied any point
which could be of any importance, taking care
to cover the besieging forces in every direction ;
in short, in accordance with a systematic method
he prolonged his preparations so that when at
last he was ready to begin, at that very moment
came the news that the Turkish auxiliaries were
approaching on the double-quick.   Thereupon,
still in accordance with his system, he assembled
the scattered troops and made ready to meet the
approaching Turks.   But John Kemény was in
the way.   He feared that if the Turkish force
proved large his forces would have to take flight,
and in that case with Schassburg in the rear they
would come between two fires.   He preferred to
wait the attack of his enemy and withdrew
from the town altogether, taking up his position
in Nagy-Szöllös in a spot that will for some time
still to come be known as an important battlefield; from that point he watched calmly the

advance of Kutschuk Pasha's horsemen into Schassburg.

Apafi, in his anxiety over a state of affairs into which he had fallen through no fault of his own, had not eaten anything for three days, when word was brought him that the auxiliaries had come. It was already late in the evening when Kutschuk Pasha, after a forced march over rough mountain paths, entered the city. Apafi rode forward to greet the Turk, whom he looked upon as his guardian angel. Great was his astonishment when, after carefully surveying the line, he learned that they were barely equal to the fifth part of the opposing force.

"What does your Grace intend with this small force?" he asked the Pasha.

"God knows, who from above orders the fates of men," answered the Turk with characteristic fatalism; and did not take the Prince into his plans any further.

That night the Turks encamped in the public square in front of the Prince's dwelling. At last Apafi could sleep again after so many restless nights. It was such a satisfaction to him to hear the snorting of the horses under his window and the clanking of the sentinels' swords, that he fell asleep with a light heart amid these quieting sounds; then too there was the thought that with these troops he could hold out for some time, when—something might happen. Long before dawn he was wakened by the rattling on a board which called the Turkish horsemen to breakfast. "They breakfast early," thought the Prince, turned over and fell asleep again. As he dozed it seemed to him that he heard dervishes singing; their song is of a kind to make a man sleep even if he felt wide awake; but soon his Excellency was roused again by the sound of trumpets. "What are they doing in the middle of the night?" he cried out with annoyance; he got up, looked from the window, and saw that the Turkish riders had already mounted, though it was still dark; and with another sound of the trumpet the entire company rode out. The noise of the hoofs on the pavement and the words of command scunded out in the night.

"What a restless fellow this Pasha is!" thought Apafi, "he does not give his army any rest even at night, and that too after so many hardships," and with these thoughts he went to bed again, fell into still sweeter sleep, and woke late in the morning. The sun was high in the heavens when Apafi rang for John Cserei, at that time his factotum. His first question was,

"What is the Pasha doing?"

"He withdrew from the town during the night and sent back a messenger who has been waiting since dawn."

"Let him enter," said Apafi, and began to dress in haste.

With Kutschuk's messenger entered Stephen Apafi, Nalaczy and Daczo. They too had been waiting two hours for the Prince to awaken, and besides this they were eager for the Pasha's message.

"What news? Speak quickly," called Apafi to the messenger.

The latter stood with arms crossed, bowed to the ground, and began,

"Excellent Prince, my lord, Kutschuk Pasha, sends you the following message through me, 'Stay quietly in Schassburg and keep good hope; with the troops under your command guard the walls and gates.' Meantime my lord Kutschuk Pasha will advance against John Kemény and enter into an engagement with him wherever he finds him. It will be a struggle unto death, even if he should perish with his entire host."

This announcement so confounded the Prince that he could find no word of reply. Kutschuk Pasha in point of numbers was equal to the fifth of Kemény's force; besides, his troops were worn out with forced marches. The man who could hope for victory at such a time must believe in miracles.

"Let us prepare for the worst," said Stephen Apafi, "and put our trust in God."

That was the most sensible speech to be made under the circumstances. Michael Apafi let affairs take their course, any man who chose might

guard the walls. The guards left their soldiers
to look out for themselves and the soldiers did
not trouble themselves much about the walls.
The fate of the land lay in God's hand, literally
speaking, for the hand of man was withdrawn.
The Prince did no more than to order old Cserei
to keep watch in the church tower and let them
know when he saw the troops moving.

* * * * * *

Meanwhile John Kemény had halted in Nagy-
Szöllös, which was a few hours distant from
Schassburg. He made his headquarters in the
little parsonage, and the little room is still shown
where he rested for the last time, and the round
hill in the garden on which stood a summerhouse
where the Prince had begun his last meal but had
not finished it.

The Hungarian forces consulted for a long time
with Wenzinger and the Prince about the course
of action. Some advised taking the town by
storm and others maintained that they should be-
siege it and starve the people to submission.
Wenzinger shook his head.

" Permit me, my lord," said the experienced
German, " to express my opinion. I am an old
soldier, have been through all kinds of campaigns,
know the value of superior forces in war and also
of good positions, and know how to balance the
two. I have learned by experience that often a

hundred men under favorable circumstances are more difficult to displace than a thousand. I also know what a difference the spirit of an army makes. I know too the importance of taking into account the different kinds of weapons, and the importance of nationality. We have ten thousand men and there are barely three thousand drawn up against us. But we must take into consideration that the greater part of our Hungarian force consists of horsemen, and that it is impossible to storm a city with horsemen—still less possible to compel a Hungarian on a horse to dismount and fight on foot; furthermore I would remark that the Hungarian is a brave fighter when drawn up against foreigners, but whenever I have seen him against his own people, —and I have frequently had the opportunity, he has been so lazy and indifferent that it seemed as if he could hardly wait to turn his back on the battlefield. We have a force of men that are very good on the defensive, and if we had them behind the walls of that town we could hold out against a force of ten times that number; but except behind fortifications they are of no use. They are strong enough to defend a bastion but too weak to storm one. Then we have no cannon for storming so we must send to Temesvar for cannon, and before they can arrive over those roads—and it is a great question too whether the commander will send us any—Ali Pasha may return with fresh forces, while we shall have spent the time here to no purpose. So I maintain that we had better wait here no longer. We are in no condition to take the enemy within the walls by force or siege. We cannot suppose him so mad as to be drawn into an open engagement. The wisest thing for us under these circumstances is to go without delay to Hungary, there get troops and cannon, and then make it our object to force the enemy into a field engagement."

Kemény, who was not accustomed to listen for any length of time to words of reason, could hardly wait for Wenzinger to come to a pause; as if the plan of action was of the most trifling importance to him, he interrupted with frivolous impatience,

"Let's put it off until afternoon. General, after dinner everything looks different."

"No, indeed, not after dinner," said the German; "there is no time to be lost. We are in the midst of war where every hour is precious and not in the Diet where an affair can be dragged out for years."

At this hit the Hungarians laughed loudly, seized Wenzinger by the arm, and dragged him with jests to the table, saying,

"You know we have plenty of time after dinner."

"Many such soldiers whom no one can command would quite meet my views," said Wen-zinger, half in jest and half in vexation, and then he spoke no more during the meal, but drank the harder.

During the dinner John Uzdi, captain of the scouts, entered the extemporized banquet-hall with terror in his face. In his extreme haste speech almost failed him.

"Majesty—I saw great clouds of dust in the direction of Schassburg, and coming this way."

The Prince turned his head with humorous nonchalance toward the messenger; "If it is any pleasure to you to inspect those clouds of dust, why keep on looking at them."

Wenzinger sprang up from his place.

"I too must see them," he said, and ordered his horse brought forward at once. "Evidently the enemy has come out to draw us nearer."

The rest did not allow themselves to be dis-turbed but went on with their pleasures. After a few minutes Wenzinger came hurrying back; on his features could be read that secret joy which a soldier always feels when his plan nears success.

"Victory," he cried, as he entered, "the enemy is moving off, bag and baggage; provided only he is not doing it for appearances, and is not avoiding a battle, all's won."

At this news some of the men rose and began to buckle on their swords, but the Prince did not leave his place.

"Are they still far away?" he asked the general, calmly.

"Half an hour distant," answered the other with glowing countenance.

"Then let them come nearer, and meantime sit down beside me."

"The Devil I will!" said the general, angrily, "I have hardly time to assign the army their positions."

"What is the use of assigning them positions? Let them march in a solid column so that the enemy will be frightened to death at the mere sight of them."

"Quite right. However, I do not wish to frighten them away but to surround them. One half of the army I will draw up against them, and the other I will arrange as follows: one division shall steal through the grain fields and cut off the enemy's retreat in the direction of this city; another shall fall on his flank just above the millstream; and the third shall be stationed as rear guard. Your Majesty with his court shall join the rear guard."

"What," said Kemény, roused at last, "I in the rear guard! Hungarian Princes are in the habit of going first in battle."

"That was well enough in former times, but in a combined assault, so precious a life that must always be looked out for is only in the general's way, and has a disturbing effect on the movements of the troops.   But if it is your Majesty's express wish, then I give over the command to you and take my place in the rank and file.   Let your Majesty take the command.   Here only one can be general."

"Stay at your post and arrange matters as you will, only let me choose my position as I wish, and it shall not interfere with yours."

And Kemény staid at table with a few of the men.   Wenzinger had hardly time to make the necessary arrangements when word was brought the Prince that the army was in line of battle. Kemény rose calmly from his place, girded on his sword, but forbade them to put on his coat of mail.

"What for," he cried, "is the heart beneath any bolder?"

Then he had his finest horse led forward, which tossed his head so fiercely that two men could hardly hold his bridle.   The spirited black beast reared and plunged; his nostrils steamed, the white foam flecked his breast and his long waving tail reached almost to the ground. Kemény swung himself into his saddle, drew his sword and galloped to the head of the army. Everybody was astonished at the fine rider.   He adapted his movements to the horse as if they were one creature.   When the high-spirited horse reached the front he began to slacken his pace, struck his hoofs on the ground and seemed to salute the army with his head.

The men broke out into a loud huzza. At this moment the Prince's horse stumbled and fell forward, breaking the silver bit in his mouth; only the greatest skill and presence of mind saved the Prince from plunging over his horse's head. His attendants crowded about him.

"That's a bad sign, your Majesty," stammered Alexis Bethlen. "Let your Majesty mount another horse."

"No, it is not a bad sign," replied Kemény, "for I staid in my saddle."

"However it would be well if your Majesty would not ride this horse. He will keep stumbling now that he has been frightened."

"I intend to stay on this horse just to show that I do not give in to omens and am not afraid of them," replied Kemény, defiantly, and ordered the bridle with broken bit to be taken away and another brought. Just then Kutschuk's trumpeter sounded for the attack.

*   *   *   *   *   *

The Turkish horsemen were drawn up in the form of a crescent with the ends turned backward, and in the centre rode Kutschuk Pasha. The Turkish general on this occasion wore a costume of unusual splendor. His caftan was of heavy silk embroidered in flowers of gold; under this a dolman woven in threads of gold, and around his waist a costly Oriental shawl; his

sword was studded with precious stones; in his
turban was the entire wing of a gerfalcon, with
a diamond clasp. He rode a fiery Arab steed
with slender neck, long braided mane and flow-
ing black tail. The proud creature tossed his
head and shook the fringed housings; there was
a kind of gold net over his body with leather
knots at the ends from which hung large golden
crescents hitting against each other. As soon as
Kutschuk Pasha came in sight of the princely
troops of Kemény, he prostrated himself on the
ground and kissed the earth three times, raised
himself as many times to his knees, lifted his
hands and devout face to heaven and cried
"Allah, Allah!" Then he mounted his horse
again, ordered his son called to him, tore a falcon
feather from his turban, and said as he stuck it
in the boy's cap, "Now go to the left wing of
the enemy and try to fight bravely, for it is better that you should fall by the enemy's hand and
I should see you dead than that you should
flee and be obliged to fall a sacrifice to my
sword."

With these words he put his hand on the
weapon at his side. Feriz Bey bowed with an
expression of the deepest homage, kissed his
father's robe and galloped proudly to his appointed post. He seemed to know that all eyes
were now directed to those falcon feathers that
his father had placed in his turban. The Pasha

then rode along the front of his host and spoke
to his men :

"Brave comrades, now you see the enemy with
your own eyes. I will not say whether their
numbers are great or small, for you can see for
yourselves. They are many more than we, but
trust in Allah and fight bravely; it is more
honorable to fall here sword in hand, than to disgrace numbers by flight. We are in the middle
of Transylvania; whoever runs away will be
hunted down by pursuers before he can get to
the borders, but even if any one should escape
the Sultan will have him killed. We have no
choice but victory or death."

Then he turned to the Wallachians and addressed them in hard, angry tones :

"Well do I know, you dogs, that you are ready
to ride off at the first shot, but I have given
orders to the troops stationed on the outside to
shoot down any one of you who so much as
looks backward."

Then the Pasha took his place at the head of
the host and with unsheathed sword gave the
sign to the trumpeter. As he once more sur-
veyed the troops he noticed that the Moors in
their metal caps stationed behind him had
reached for their guns and made ready to aim.

"What do you mean!" growled the Pasha.
"Down with your muskets! The enemy has
more of them. Nothing but swords now! Let

every man ride boldly against the enemy and
when I give the sign, bend low on his horse and
gallop forward without trembling."

The army obeyed the command. The Moors
slung their weapons on their shoulders, drew
their broad swords and marched forward following the Pasha. Kemény's troops stood before
them like a wall of steel. In the first line the
musketeers and behind them the infantry. In
the centre was Wenzinger and on the right wing
John Kemény. The troops on the flanks marched
stealthily behind the mill and the grain fields
to attack the rear. When the Turks were almost within shot of Kemény's army Kutschuk
Pasha turned round and cast commanding glances
at his soldiers right and left, at which they in-
stantly dropped their heads on their horses'
necks, swung their swords forward, struck spurs
into their horses' flanks and rode madly into the
lines of the enemy.

"Allah! Allah! Allah!" rang out three
times from the lips of the assailing Turks. At
the third shout there came a tremendous report.
Kemény's musketeers had at that moment fired
in line at the assailing horsemen and their ranks
were for the instant enveloped in smoke. Gen-
erally speaking such firing does little harm in
war, causing more noise than destruction. In
this case only two Turks fell with their horses,
the rest galloped forward under the hot firing.

Wenzinger saw that his artillery had no time
to load again and gave command for the infantry to advance. If these troops could have
stood their ground against the attack of the
horsemen until the artillery could load again, or
until the flank troops could have fallen on the
Turks in the rear, Kemény would have won the
battle, but the ranks of the infantry were broken
through at the first onset, and after a desperate
engagement largely mown down. Thereupon
the defenseless musketeers fled in great numbers
and by their cries threw the rest of the army
into the utmost confusion. Wenzinger tried to
restore order at once by giving command for a
retreat along the whole line, and had this been
carried out the engagement might have taken
another turn. But the horseguards who were
under the command of the Prince, by Kemény's
orders stood where they were; the rest of the
troops changed their position and continued to
fight with those opposite them. The Pasha suddenly turned from the pursuit of the musketeers
in their mad flight and fell upon Kemény with
his entire force. The latter, attacked in front
and on the side at the same time, lost his wits,
and as there was neither time nor space for an
orderly retreat, plunged frantically along the
first way that opened. Naturally he did not notice in such a flight that he was riding down his
own infantry, then in retreat, since the horse-

guards who had charged in disorderly assault at
the rank still in line, and trampled down their
own troops, had prevented the use of the re-
serves ; so the whole army was brought into confusion and disorder.

The infantry threw down their weapons and
fled, pursued by the horsemen of both armies ;
any still remaining in line were trampled to
death by the horsemen. Neither the genius of
the leader nor the self-sacrifice of a few brave
men availed to restore order. The wild flight in
one part threw the rest into confusion. The battle was completely lost. In the general panic
that reigned the Prince too fled. As he had
been in the front ranks of the battle he was now
at the rear, and could with difficulty escape his
pursuers in such a tumult. The Turks pursued
closely and knocked down all within reach.
Close on the track of the Prince followed a
young Turk, and as his horse carried a much
lighter weight he soon overtook the Prince. By
the falcon's feather waving in his turban could
be recognized Feriz Bey, son of Kutschuk Pasha.
His features were ablaze with a youthful glow,
those of the Prince were dark with rage and
shame. During the flight he often looked back
and gnashed his teeth. " To flee from a child is
a disgrace," he cried out in his anger. Several
times he tried to stop but his maddened horse
swept him along. Meantime the youth had

come so near that he began to show his sword. At first the Prince did not consider the strokes of the boy worthy his attention, but as the latter coming nearer grew bolder and bolder, the Prince drew his sword and returned the blows.

"Don't come any nearer, you bastard," shouted Kemény, furiously, "or I'll deal you a blow that will knock your very breath out."

By this time Feriz with a bound of his horse reached the side of the Prince and aimed a Damascus blade at his neck, while Kemény leaning back, drew his sword for a fearful blow. The two swords were whizzing through the air, when Kemény's horse stumbled again and fell with a broken leg. This gave his blow another direction, and instead of hitting Feriz as he had intended, he struck the head of his own horse and cleft it in twain just as the young Turk's sword gleamed against Kemény's forehead. The Prince, falling from his horse looked darkly at his foe : the blood was streaming from his forehead. Once more he struck his spurs into his horse and the poor creature struggled to his hind feet, only to fall backward with his rider still clinging to him, and rider and horse were trampled under the feet of the pursuing enemy. During the wild conflict nobody paid any attention to the spot where the Prince had fallen.

Several days later in the Schassburg market-place his torn coat and broken weapon, found and offered for sale by some Turkish freebooters, were bought by Michael Apafi and laid away for safe-keeping in the treasury at Fogaras. Apafi ordered a careful search for the body of the fallen Prince, that he might bury it with due honors, but nobody could distinguish the Prince's corpse among the stripped and mutilated.

*   *   *   *   *   *

When the battle was won Kutschuk Pasha ordered the trumpet sounded to call back his men from the pursuit of the conquered foe. At the sound of the retreat the Turkish horsemen came bounding back man for man, in marked contrast to the usual custom of Turkish armies, who are as disorderly after victory as their vanquished foes. Kutschuk had accustomed them to stern discipline. The men returned blackened with smoke and covered with blood, but none more so than Feriz Bey; in his coat were the holes made by many balls and he rode his third horse since the beginning of the conflict; two had been shot under him. Kutschuk embraced his son without a word, kissed his brow, fastened his own Order of Nischan on his breast and exchanged swords with him, a mark of the highest honor among the Turks of those times.

Ferhad Aga, the leader of the right wing, was brought in dead. He had received all kinds of wounds and was completely covered with shots,

spear-thrusts, and sabre-cuts. Kutschuk sprang
from his horse, fell weeping upon the corpse, covered it with kisses and swore by Allah that he
would not have given this man's life for all
Transylvania. He did not go into town until
Ferhad had been buried. The dervishes surrounded the body at once, washed it, wrapped it
in fragrant linen, and the Pasha himself selected
a sunny spot under the trees. There the dead
man was laid with his face toward the East, a
spear with waving pennant was planted above
the grave, and a guard of men set for three days
to keep off the witchlike Djinns from the body
of the fallen one.

CHAPTER VII

THE PRINCESS

AFTER the battle of Nagy-Szöllös John Kemény's faithful followers fled to Hungary and transferred their allegiance from the fallen one to his son Simon Kemény. But his sinking fortunes had few friends, and while the faction of the younger Kemény grew daily less, Apafi's gained from day to day. By his triumph he won over the best and most distinguished of the town, the judges, nobility, commanders of the fortresses, in short everybody hurried to do him homage. The State in a body recognized him as Prince. Only a few places where Kemény had left German garrisons, still resisted, among these Klausenburg. Kutschuk Pasha brought Apafi with a strong force under the walls of this town. He had a tent pitched for him in sight of the old town in Hidele. At that time it was a place of thatched huts, and there the new Prince received deputations. By early dawn Apafi was fairly besieged by the hosts of visitors and place-seekers. At first the newly-chosen Prince, carried away by the novelty of his agreeable position, was able to fulfil the wishes of everybody and refused hardly a request. As soon as Nalaczy and Daczo learned that he had his boots on, they were with him and announced great crowds of people outside the tent eager for entrance. Apafi made haste to dress that no one need wait. He could hardly expect to satisfy everybody. Among the throng was Ladislaus Csaki; he came to offer the Prince as page the same son who had filled Kemény's glass a few weeks before. Apafi could hardly express his pleasure at this offer. Then came Gabriel Haller who bowed countless times and in the name of his two companions made an elaborate speech to Apafi. Apafi could scarcely conceal his childish pleasure in being called Excellency, a title used in Transylvania only for great princes. He invited Gabriel Haller at once to dine with him. At the back of the tent a raised seat had been placed, which the modest Prince positively would not accept until his brother Stephen had forcibly set him there. He received everybody standing and accompanied each one to the door when he went. Then they came singly to present themselves, make requests of the Prince, or swear allegiance.

At the Prince's side stood Nalaczy, Daroczy, Stephen Apafi and John Cserei, who repeatedly urged the Prince to sit down. The oaths of allegiance were received, the commanders of the citadels laid their keys in the Prince's hand and then followed visits.

First came Martin Pok, the jailer at Fogara,

with the humble request that he should be made captain of this stronghold instead of the foreign incumbent who had fled with Simon Kemény. Apafi promised to remember him. John Szasz came next, supreme judge in Hermanstadt, to make complaint that his fellow citizens had persecuted him and beg the Prince for help. Apafi took him under his protection. Then followed Moses Zagony who begged that the Prince would most graciously set him free from certain taxes imposed by Kemény and still in arrears. He too went away comforted by Apafi.

Last of all came before the Prince, a Szekler of the mountains, in short peasant coat and jacket of fur, who, he said, came sent from Olahfalu to bring Apafi the oath of allegiance in the name of his people, and to make his strange requests: first, that Olahfalve should be permitted to be only two miles distant from Klausenburg (the actual distance between the two places was more than twenty); secondly, that there should be a law enacted that if a man had not a horse he should go on foot.

The Prince received these strange requests with laughter. They seemed to put him in extremely good spirits and the young student, Clement, sought to take advantage of this. He was a crooked-nosed, high-cheeked youth, wrapped to the chin in a foxskin, who knelt before Apafi and handed him a roll of parchment that with the aid of his friends Apafi took and unrolled. Within, he found a green leaved tree showing the complete genealogy of his family. In this document he was connected with the Bethlens and Bathorys, taken back to King Aba and on the way connected with Huba, one of the seven leaders of the Magyars. But the good man did not rest even here; the lineage extended even to Csaba, youngest son of Attila. On the mother's side it went still further to the daughter of the Emperor Porphyrogeneta, and on the father's side to Nimrod the first king on earth. This flattery seemed to annoy Apafi somewhat, but he had not sufficient decision to order the flatterer out of the tent. He rolled up the genealogy, put it behind him and undertook to satisfy the impertinent poet with a few ducats. But that did not disturb the Prince's good-humor in the very least. It seemed as if he must express especial thanks to each man for approaching him, and show him the obligation that he felt; and after he had received and listened to the various suppliants, as if this were all too little, he turned to Nalaczy and Daczo with the question, "Is there nothing that I can do for you? What reward shall I make you for the fidelity with which you have stood by me from the first?"

Nalaczy and Daczo had for some time been puzzling their minds as to what request they might make that should not be too small.

"I leave the reward of my trifling services to the generosity of your Excellency," said Nalaczy, thinking that without doubt the Szeklers would now receive a new captain instead of Beldi.

"The little that I have done for your Excellency does not now deserve mention," said Daczo, but it occurred to him that the position of Captain of the train bands at Klausenburg, left vacant by Banfy's flight, would be an appropriate one.

Apafi was well-disposed toward them and perhaps might have made these excellent but useless people his privy counsellors, but to their great misfortune, at that very moment there was a tumult at the entrance to the tent. When the guard drew back the curtain Kutschuk Pasha entered. The Prince sprang from his seat and would have hurried to him, but his brother Stephen pulled his coat and whispered in his ear:—

"Maintain your dignity in the presence of the Turk; he is only a subordinate Pasha while you are Prince of Transylvania."

In spite of the warning Apafi was not satisfied until Kutschuk made him a sign to be seated, and although the Turk remained standing before the Prince, the impression on the bystanders was that Apafi appeared amiable and grateful and Kutschuk haughty and dignified.

"How can I thank you for your exertions in

my behalf?" Apafi asked the Pasha, with true feeling.

"Not to me, but to the Sultan have you cause to be grateful," the other replied, drily. "I was only following out his wishes when I placed you on the throne of Transylvania. Your enemies, with God's help, I have laid low, except for a few strongholds still in their possession; as soon as these are won my task is at an end. The rest is my affair. To-morrow I march to the siege of Klausenburg and shall not rest until the city is taken at any cost; when that stronghold has fallen the rest will go of their own accord."

"Then in your judgment it is not necessary that I should order the country troops to horse?" said Apafi.

"I do not need them," replied Kutschuk. "Let them stay at home and look after their own affairs. My troops will do it all."

Apafi was going to thank the Pasha for his generosity, when he suddenly became aware that the eyes of all were turned toward a side entrance of the tent, where somebody had entered without announcement. The Prince looked in that direction, and what he saw caused him to forget for the moment Transylvania, Kutschuk Pasha and Klausenburg. There before him stood his wife, the beautiful and stately Anna Bornemissa.

Her look was indeed princely. How well this

imperious countenance knew how to maintain a
friendly and yet proud gaze! No adornment
was noticeable in her costume, but was there any
need of precious stones where such speaking eyes
gleamed? Did this royal figure need velvet and
ermine to be recognized? Apafi saw her to-day
for the first time since his departure. She was
as beautiful as ever. Accustomed now to good
fortune and comfort, her features had gained a
transparent gleam; her eyes, long unfilled with
sorrow, were brighter than ever; the smile of her
lips that had known such joy only a short time,
was all the sweeter, and her figure formerly
slight had now gained in roundness. The gracious dignity of her figure and movements suited
her well.

When Apafi caught sight of his wife he forgot
all propriety and dignity, hurried toward her,
seized her hand, drew his trembling wife to him,
as was his wont when a plain nobleman, and
kissed her mouth and cheeks in a way plainly
audible to the assembled states. Anna nestled
into the embrace of her husband, offered her beautiful lips to his kisses, and at the same time her
great serious eyes, over her husband's shoulder,
seemed to be searching the faces of those assembled in the tent, resting a longer or shorter time
on each individual. The embrace seemed on
Apafi's part to have no end, until Anna with a
smile freed herself and said:

"You are lavishing all your effusions on me alone; there is some one else here who claims his share."

She motioned to her maid, Sarah, who with smiling countenance had followed her mistress into the tent, and now disclosed to Apafi's eyes a beautiful sleeping child that, covered with a silken wrap, the maid had lulled in her arms.

Beside himself with joy, Apafi took the child in his arms and kissed the round angel-face again and again. The child woke up, endured the kisses and embraces without a cry, and tugged at his father's beard, to the unspeakable joy of his parents.

The men standing about thought it fitting to congratulate the Prince on his paternal joy.

Apafi turned to them and said:—"Do you see how serious he is? he does not cry, because he is a man."

Anna beckoned Stephen Apaffi to her and whispered to him:—"I trust the gentlemen will not be annoyed if family joys and cares withdraw the Prince from public affairs for a few minutes."

"Your ladyship has taken the words out of my mouth," replied Stephen. "I was just on the point of speaking to them."

With that he turned to those present and begged them to leave the Prince to himself for the few moments claimed by family ties, and to withdraw to the adjoining tent. The gentlemen considered the request natural and left the tent, Kutschuk Pasha leading.

Anna took the child from her husband's hands, gave it over to Sarah and sent them away.

When they were alone Apafi approached his wife with new expressions of tenderness. She took her husband by the hand, looked him earnestly in the eye, and said:

" It is to the Prince that I have come."

This earnest look cooled Apafi a little, which did not escape Anna's notice, and she drew toward him again affectionately.

" It seemed to me probable that the Prince might need me more than the husband," and then she added with her irresistible smile, " I hope you will not misunderstand my intentions in this."

Apafi put his arm around his wife and drew her to him. The throne was quite wide enough for both.

" You are right. It is well you have come. There is always something lacking when I cannot see you. You certainly deserve to come nearest my heart; I am not in the least afraid to lay your mind in the balance with any man in the circle."

" Who are all these men ? " asked Anna.

" You shall know them by their names. The

tall, slender man is Ladislaus Csaki who has just offered me his son for a page."

"No time lost there. It is only a short time since the boy was serving Kemény."

Apafi's face darkened a little.

"The man with the heavy moustache is Gabriel Haller."

Anna clapped her hands with surprise.

"Is that he?"

"What fault have you to find with him?"

"That he has always served your enemies as a spy. He brought Kemény the first news of your coronation, and he was the one who announced the approach of Kutschuk Pasha."

Apafi's face grew darker still.

"And I have invited the man to dine," he muttered between his teeth.

"What do Nalaczy and Daczo wish, that they are here on so friendly a footing?"

"They are my faithful partisans who have been on my side from the beginning."

"Do not for that reason give them the first positions in the land. In a large sphere of activity, simple, ignorant men do more harm than sensible antagonists. Reward them, but only in proportion to their work."

"That I will," said the distressed Prince, and strove in every way possible to make the rôle of husband prominent throughout the rest of the scene, but Anna did not stop.

"What is John Szasz trying to get from you? I saw him too."

"The poor fellow is being persecuted," replied Apafi, curtly, for he began to weary of this fault-finding.

"There are bad reports in circulation about this man. It is said, and plainly, too, that he carried off a young girl from Saxony, and when he had wearied of her had her poisoned. The parents have begun a prosecution and he sees no safety except in winning your favor by flattery."

Apafi started up furious. "If that is true I will show Szasz the door; he shall not find protection with me."

"And for what purpose is the noble ragged Szekler here, I should like to know? His face seemed to me to indicate subtlety, for the Szekler is never so sly and dangerous as when he looks simple."

At this question the Prince was overcome with merriment. Fairly choking with laughter, he said, "He was the deputy of the people of Olahfalu."

At the mention of this name Anna too could hardly repress a smile.

"Poor people, all sorts of untrue stories are told of them; their minds work strangely."

"You understand everybody perfectly. Now explain the meaning of the demand which the Szekler has made of me. He begged for two things. In the first place that the distance between Olahfalve and Klausenburg from this time on should be considered only two miles."

"Oh, the sly simpleton," said Anna. "They already have the privilege of offering their lumber for sale at a distance of two miles and now their purpose is to open a market for themselves in Klausenburg as well."

"You are quite right," replied Apafi, convinced. "Now their second request seems somewhat suspicious to me, although it had nothing to do with their public affairs. They wished it to be established by law that anybody who had not a horse should go on foot."

"I understand," said Apafi's wife, after short reflection, "Olahfalu has recently been made a post-town, and on this ground the couriers, as they pass through, often demand horses. The good people are weary of the burden and for that reason wished a new law which should enforce going on foot for the couriers."

Apafi stamped angrily with his foot.

"The villain, to allow himself such a jest. You will see how I shall pay him for that. But it is time to admit the gentlemen again."

"One word more, Apafi," said Anna, with a winning glance, throwing her arms around her husband's neck. "I noticed Kutschuk Pasha among those waiting. I suppose he came to take leave."

Apafi drew back startled.

"On no account to take leave. Surely you understand that we are here to take Klausenburg by storm? This depends on Kutschuk Pasha."

"Michael," said his wife, entreatingly, and laid her hands on his shoulders;—"will you allow Klausenburg to be taken by the Turks? do you forget that the Ottomans have never of their own accord given back a Hungarian stronghold once taken by them? do you not remember that Klausenburg is the capital of your country and that those within its walls are your own people, of your country and of your faith? will you expose them to the rage of assailants? they who might otherwise be your friends are pagans and foreigners, whom you cannot allow to prevail against your own people. Did not your heart sink when you saw the walls of Klausenburg? could you look at these dwellings, these towers, without remembering that they are the homes of your people, the churches of your God into which the besiegers would throw their firebrands? Could you look at these walls without seeing on them mothers huddled together with their young children in their arms, crying out to you that within dwelt your own people, an innocent, true-hearted folk? and could you make your entry into the capital city of your own country over the fallen bodies of these women and children?"

Apafi stood up, his forehead bathed in perspiration. In his confused expression were traces of involuntary repentance.

"No indeed, Anna, no indeed! do not think me so heartless. I who could never withstand a woman's tears, could I be insensible to the sorrow of an entire people? but what can I do? I had intended to call out the troops of the country, to invest the city and to compel the garrison to yield; but what could I do with Kutschuk Pasha? he is determined to take the city by storm at once, and I can find no valid reason to bring against it."

"Be calm. All those in command of Turkish troops now in Transylvania have received firmans ordering them to join the army of the General-in-chief at Neuhaüsel as soon as possible. Kutschuk has doubtless received a firman of this character."

"I did not know that. Is that the reason he has been in such a hurry to storm the town?"

"You too will receive such an order from the Turkish Council of State. Under the pretext that this order has already come it will be an easy matter to prevail on the Pasha to abandon the siege of Klausenburg."

"I will try it, Anna. I will do it," replied Apaffi, pacing back and forth in the tent. "I owe it to my people. Better abandon those walls than force my way through with fire and sword."

"You must not do that either," answered his

clever wife. "There are ways and means of getting possession of the stronghold beside taking it by storm."

Apafi stood still and looked at his wife inquiringly. She drew him to her and whispered as follows: "Before you reached the walls of Klausenburg, I commissioned Raldi and several other of our faithful followers to try to win the garrison over to our side; this morning our spies brought me word that the infantry are so won over to us by promises and the force of circumstances that at the first sound of the drum from here they are ready to open the gates and give themselves up to you, bag and baggage. The cavalry alone cannot then offer further resistance."

Apafi in amazement said, "You certainly were created for a prince."

Anna took her husband gently by the arm, led him to the throne and made him take his seat.

"The sceptre is no toy, Apafi," she said, earnestly. "Never forget that posterity and eternity sit in judgment on princes. Every deed and every word of a ruler may mean safety or destruction to millions. Therefore consider everything that you say or do. Now I am going. Be firm."

Anna kissed her husband on the brow and as she did so her glance fell on the roll of parchment of the traveling student.

"What kind of campaign plan is this?" she asked, taking up the parchment.

Annoyed, Apafi tried to take it from her hand, but he was too late. Anna had unrolled it and as she looked at the tuft-hunting pedigree, cast a reproachful glance at the prince who stood before her with downcast eyes.

"Did you have that drawn up?" she asked him, quietly.

"No indeed!" answered Apafi, quickly. "An impertinent poet brought it to me."

"Throw it into the fire," said his wife, calmly.

"That is what I meant to do. I got rid of the author by means of a few ducats."

"He deserved a thrashing, and not gold," said Anna, angrily; then her features grew gentle again. She looked her husband straight in the eye and said in kindly tone;—"Be strong; be a Prince. Grant protection to the faithful, pardon to those who return in penitence, and scorn to the flatterer."

With these words she bowed low, kissed her husband's hand and was gone before he could reply.

Apafi then sent for those in waiting to return. It was very evident from the expression of their faces as they entered that they thought they might now ask and expect everything good from the Prince, for the happiness of the previous family scene would naturally leave him in a

state of mind in which he could not refuse anybody.

Stephen Apafi was the only one cool-headed
enough to observe the change in his brother's
features during this interval. Genuine princely
firmness, dignity and energy seemed now en-
throned upon this countenance.

"Faithful comrades," began Apafi in a strong
voice without waiting for any one to speak;—
"in respect to the requests with which you have
approached us, it is our wish to send you away
with a just and worthy answer. Your oaths of
allegiance we have received with due appreciation
and hope you will not cease to remain constant
in your loyalty. You, Ladislaus Csaki, we hereby
permit to return home to share the peace of the
family circle; as for your son we will have him
maintained in foreign lands at our expense until
he seems fitted for our service."

Ladislaus Csaki thanked him gloomily for the
favor granted of returning to the peace of his
own family circle, when he would so gladly have
remained with his family at court.

Gabriel Haller the Prince passed over as if he
did not see him, and turned to Nalaczy and
Daczo, who made every effort to appear humble.

"My faithful friend, Stephen Nalaczy, in consideration of your active zeal for us we appoint
you first chamberlain at our court; and you, John
Daczo, we appoint Lieutenant of Csikszerda."

Both men looked as would any one who had expected a great reward and received a very small portion. They could hardly express their thanks to their Prince for his favor, so great was their chagrin.

Meantime Martin Pok had pressed forward that he might not be left out, and completely hid the worthy Cserei, who was standing modestly behind the others.

"Why do you stand so in the background?" said Apafi, beckoning to him.

Thinking that the signal was for him, Martin Pok advanced still farther.

"We meant you, Cserei," continued the Prince. "Do you think we do not know how to search out our tried and faithful followers? Your fidelity and wisdom are known to us and for that reason we deem it advisable to appoint you Captain of the castle at Fogara."

Martin Pok was so amazed that he looked up at the ceiling to see if it was falling.

"Martin Pok on the other hand," continued the Prince, "we confirm in his former position. He will remain jailer of the same castle."

Martin Pok gasped. Cserei wished to remonstrate, but the Prince motioned to him to keep quiet.

The next in turn was John Szasz.

"The charge of a great crime has been brought against you, which we have neither desire nor

power to free you from.   You will be taken under guard to Hermanstadt and we advise you
to try to defend yourself there as well as you
can."

John Szasz looked in astonishment to right and
left.   He was utterly unable to comprehend what
had happened.

"You, Moses Zagoni, will give in your accounts
to the next treasury officers."

Zagoni considered it advisable to address words
of consolation to Szasz by way of concealing his
own discomfiture.

Now the Prince came to the messenger from
Olahfalve, and it was high time; for while the
Prince had been portioning out these different
favors the smile had gradually vanished from his
countenance and the comical old countryman was
now at his own expense to restore cheerfulness
to the company.

"What I promised you,"—said the Prince
turning toward him, and in doing so he could
scarcely conceal his amusement;—"remains
pledged to you.   Olahfalve shall be just two
miles from Klausenburg, if that is of any advantage to you; and also everybody who has not a
horse shall go on foot if you wish it; but I make
this condition; that you shall not bring any tim-
ber to Klausenburg to sell, and that you furnish
the post couriers the necessary teams."

The Szekler shook his head, scratched it and

raised his eyes to the Prince as if to ask with a look how Apafi had found out his dodges.

The Prince could not keep from laughing at the embarrassed expression of the Szekler and at that the others laughed unrestrainedly. But the Szekler who had thus far smiled confusedly, now grew serious at the general outburst, tossed his head back defiantly, looked furiously at the lords, drew up his coat and hurled these words at those standing around:

"Listen to me, you lords! I will stand it from the Prince that he makes fun of me, but I will ask you not to laugh at my expense."

The Prince motioned them to be silent, and to turn their attention called up the traveling student, Clement, who slouched in on his long, thin legs, looking as if he would fall on his knees at any moment.

"We have given orders to our treasurer," said the Prince, "to pay you from our own private purse for the work which you have done, three groschen."

"Your Excellency says"— stammered out the poet.

"You heard perfectly well. Three groschen, I said; that is the price of the writing material you have spent on the work. Hereafter employ your time more profitably."

Then the Prince signified that the audience was over. They left the tent with low bows.

Kutschuk Pasha alone remained. During the entire scene the Pasha had shaken his head in surprise, as if he would not have expected this from Apafi, and when he was left alone with him he noticed that it was no longer necessary to urge Apafi to maintain his princely bearing toward others. Apafi wore a friendly look, but in his friendliness one saw princely condescension.

"With regret we have learned," he began, turning to the Pasha, "that we must shortly lose you, whose bravery we so admired and whose friendship we so honored."

The Pasha hurriedly drew near in surprise.

"What does your Excellency mean?"

"In consequence of those firmans which order the Transylvania guards to assemble in the camp of the Grand Vizier, it will be our misfortune not to see you in our circle longer."

Kutschuk bit his lips angrily. "Whence could he get his information so soon?" thought he.

"We would gladly retain you, for your person is more precious to us than any other. We know that the commands of the Sublime Porte demand immediate obedience, and therefore that you may not for us draw down the displeasure of the Sublime Porte, we have so conducted the taking of Klausenburg that we shall march in without any assault; in that way you will be relieved of the burdensome task of maintaining

your troops here any longer. As for your services in establishing our position as Prince, we
will settle this in person with the Vizier, as we
too have been summoned to Neuhaüsel."

During this speech Kutschuk Pasha with folded
arms stared in wonder at the Prince's firm
glance, and when the Prince had concluded still
kept the same position without answering a
word.

Apafi went on calmly:

"However, to express even in a slight degree the gratitude which we owe you individu-
ally, accept from us this slight remembrance,
more as a token of our high esteem than as reward."

And the Prince took from his neck a gold
chain set with beautiful jewels, and hung it about
the neck of the Pasha. Kutschuk stood still riveted to the spot. He watched the Prince closely,
and wrinkled his forehead gloomily. Then suddenly he began to laugh and said:

"Well done, Apafi, very well done! I observe
you are in the habit of giving your intelligence
over to your wife for safe-keeping. Salem Ale-
ikum."

And the Pasha went off shaking his head.

Apafi with lightened feelings hurried to his
wife.

Gabriel Haller waited for some time at the
door, until an attendant informed him that the

Prince was dining with his family and then he
stole away.

A few days later Apafi made his entry into
Klausenburg with fife and drum.

CHAPTER VIII

AZRAELE

AGAIN we are in Hungary, among the mountains of Homolka, in that part of the country where no one has yet cared to dwell. In a circuit of ten miles there is not a single village to be seen. Over the entire mountain chain not a single roadway; even the footpaths break off suddenly in the rocks, either leading to a waterfall covered over with leaves, or to an abandoned charcoal hut where no grass could grow in the sooty vicinity.

While the sunbeams lie aslant over this region, drawing over it a gilded veil of mist, we can hardly distinguish a single object of the panorama. Gradually a broad ravine draws our attention. The mountain peaks which seemed to close in all sides are blue grey, and in the centre of this ravine rises a huge, solitary rock, looking just as if it had fallen from heaven. A hasty glance passes it by lightly, but a more careful observer discovers a small wooden bridge, supported on piles, which appears to connect this circle of mountain summits with one of the steep walls adjoining. Gradually we become aware that this trestle is not the work of nature; those stones forming walls which appear to continue the mountain heights are really the work of man's hand. It is a massive rock-bastion built as high as its support. And as the walls are built out in all directions as high as the steep edges of the cliff, it looks as if it had grown out of the rock, and as if the vines clinging to the walls were there simply to form a natural tangle.

In the year 1664 the eye that glanced over these walls might see within magic buildings. Corsar Bey, the terror of the country, inhabited this stronghold, and at his bidding hedges of roses sprang up on the bastions, and the castle stood in a grove of orange and pomegranate trees. On all sides could be seen those splendid buildings which Oriental pomp erects for the moment's pleasure: spacious domed buildings overlaid with sky-blue enamel where the sun mirrored itself; gay painted towers on the bastions with balconies decorated with Moorish carvings, and on these vases of flowers; slender white minarets covered over with vines; lattice-work kiosks with slender gilded columns, the whole as light as a card house; nothing but gilded wood, painted glass, enameled tiles, and gay-colored rugs. From the pointed roof-tops waved gay flags and high above all shone a golden crescent. Every kiosk, every dome, every min-aret was adorned with crescents and flags. It seemed a magic castle ready to vanish; but the walls surrounding this delicate structure were impregnable. On all sides were impassably steep rocks behind which the pursued, if he once reached them, could defend himself against a hundred times as many. The guards stood day and night with lighted fuse by the cannon, which Corsar Bey had had cast on the spot, as there was no way of conveying such defence there. Two of these fiery-throated monsters were turned toward the bridge, to blow it to atoms in case of attack.

From this vantage ground Corsar Bey roved the land, plundering and killing defenseless people; if he fell upon an army he ordered his Spahis and Bedouins to turn about and while he, taking advantage of the mountain paths, fled to his castle with the booty loaded on beasts of burden, the Timariots, stationed in reserve, made a barricade of trees and stoned to death those who dared follow into the valleys.

Sometimes he allowed his pursuers to follow him close to the castle, and while they shot at the walls of cliff with their small cannon dragged up with the utmost difficulty, and thought to starve him out, he would play the trick on them of bursting out from some subterranean passage to rob and burn in their rear. Every attempt to surprise him, to surround him, was in vain. The inhabitants of the surrounding villages began to withdraw to more remote places to escape this frightful neighborhood.

After the battle of St. Gotthard, (1664) in which the Turkish general lost twelve thousand men in an engagement with Hungarian and Austrian troops, a twenty years' peace was concluded between the Porte, the Transylvania principality and the Emperor, which left the Turk in possession of all the fortresses conquered or built in Hungary. The men of these fortresses now carried on the war on their own account; robbing and burning where they could. The Sultan could not hold each one accountable; all he could do was to empower the complainants to seize the disturbers of peace and do with them as they would.

In these times five or six counties, a few nobles, or the people of single villages would combine to carry on war against the foe within their borders. The country did not concern itself and furthermore could not have done so had it wished. The Roman Emperor was engrossed in the Spanish Succession, the Sultan in a war against Venice, the lesser antagonists struggled as they could.

*   *   *   *   *   *

Now, away from our sight, cold outer world— narrow panorama of mountain and horizon without charm. Arise before us, magic halls! We see a magnificent apartment, the splendor of which bears us to a more beautiful world, while thought flitting from object to object, grows weary of the beautiful and luxurious, sought out by fancy and employed to form a poetic, charming whole.

On a purple couch in the most splendid room of the castle lay Azraele, Corsar Bey's favorite. Beside her rested a live panther, stretched out like a gay footstool, and played with her hair like a young kitten.

*   *   *   *   *   *

The clatter of horses' hoofs was heard ringing out from the winding way that led through the valley and Corsarburg. The noise was heard through the woods long before the riders could be distinctly seen. Soon they reached the height where the road, climbing to the mountain ridge runs along its length. It was Corsar Bey with his robber band. First came the beasts of burden laden with spoils. From the full leathern sacks gleamed church treasures; then came the Bey himself with his gay horsemen recruited from all classes; spahis clothed in silk and carrying long spears. Bashkirs with bow and arrow, Bedouins in white cloaks with brass-hilted swords. The Bey was in his prime, his thin beard and moustache barely showed on his brown face, his high cheekbones and broad chin gave him a bold, cruel look. His dress was covered with jewels in barbaric profusion. His troop followed him in silence. Blood was clinging to all their garments:

some had not taken the trouble to wipe it off
their faces. The beasts trotted quietly toward
the castle urged on by fellahs, while the troop
followed them along the mountain ridge.

*   *   *   *   *   *

The shadows of night had fallen.

" I am afraid," said Azraele.

" Why are you afraid ? " said Corsar.

" I have had bad dreams," replied Azraele,
trembling. " I dreamed that the Giaours
stormed your castle by night and murdered you.
I tried to throw myself down from the battlements but could not, and I was caught. A Christian had me. Oh, it was frightful."

"Don't be afraid," said Corsar. " The Koran
says only the birds can fly and no one can get
into this castle who has not learned to fly. But
even if it were possible you need not be afraid of
falling into the hands of the infidels, for there
under the entrance is a fuse reaching to the powder houses ; if all is lost you have only to touch
that fuse with the night lamp, and the entire
place will be blown to atoms, with us and our
foes."

" What a comforting thought," said Azraele.

Suddenly she sprang up again with a scream.
" Do not you hear the noise of the Djinns ? " and
she trembled in every limb.

The Bey looked around him in terror. A storm
raged without ; the weather vanes creaked. From

the tops of the minarets the wind threw the tiles on the kiosks below. The lightning flashed and the thunder made the crags tremble.

"Do you hear these invisible creatures howling and rattling the closed windows with their mighty hands?"

"By the shades of Allah, I do," said the man, his eyes fixed with fear.

"Have mercy, have mercy! Away from this house, you bad spirits," cried Azraele. "May the sunbeams strike you and the darkness bury you. Go torment the Christians. May your wings break on the top of our crescents as you float over them. Ha, how their eyes shine! Spirit of Allah, cover us, that they may not see us with their eyes of fire."

The great, strong man trembled like a child. His superstitious fear had taken all strength out of his heart.

"Do you hear how they murmur? Say a prayer quickly aloud and stop your ears, so you shall not hear what they say."

At this moment the frightful storm broke in a window pane and the wind rushing in shook the curtains and made the lights flicker.

"Ah, do you see him?" cried Azraele. "Be still, don't look, don't open your eyes. Cover your face. Asafiel, the angel of Death is here. Don't you feel his cold breath? Hush, cover yourself up, perhaps he does not notice you."

Corsar clung to Azraele and covered his face with his hands.

"What do you want?" called Azraele, as if she were speaking with a visible spirit. "Whom have you come for, black shade, your eyes glowing with blue fire? There is nobody here but me. Corsar has not come. Come later, come an hour later. Away with you, black creature! May Allah crush you!"

Corsar did not dare open his eyes.

"Away with you, I say."

At this moment the lightning struck one of the bastions and shook the mountains to their foundations. When the sound of thunder ceased, a light fall of rain began on the roof; the roar of the storm grew more and more distant; was heard dully near by and howled mournfully in the distant woods.

"He has gone," whispered Azraele, in a barely audible tone. "IIe promised to be back in an hour. Corsar, you can live just one hour."

"One hour!" repeated Corsar, with dulled senses. "Oh, Azraele, where can you hide me?"

"That is quite impossible. Asafiel is relentless. One hour more and then he will carry you off."

"Bargain with him. If he must have dead men, I will have a hundred slaves beheaded. Promise him blood, treasure, prayers, burning villages, everything. Only beg him to spare my life."

"It is of no use. In my dreams I saw your sword broken in two. Your days are numbered. There is only one way of escape for you—one way of baffling this bloodthirsty angel. Some one of the dead must exchange names with you and Asafiel when he comes for you must drag him off in your stead."

"That is right. That is right," stammered the strong man in fear. "Find me such a dead man who will exchange names with me. You know the incantations. Go call up somebody from his grave; promise him everything, fellah or rajah, I will give him my name and take his. Go, hurry."

"You must go yourself. Throw your cloak around you. Leave your weapons here; spirits are afraid of sharp iron. We will go down into the churchyard under the castle walls, set fire to amber and borax over a tripod, plunge the magic staff into the most recent grave and so compel its inmate to appear before you. When the spirit has appeared you must take three steps toward him and call out three times bravely, 'Die for me!' Then the spirit will vanish and Asafiel will not call for you."

"But you will be near me," said the timid Corsar.

"I will be at your side. Now hurry. An hour is a short time."

Corsar threw on his cloak and repeated the beginning of a prayer the end of which he could not recall.

"Be careful not to wake the guards," said Azraele, cautiously, "if a human being should by chance hear us the power of the enchantment would be broken, for they might utter a prayer that would contradict ours. We will saddle our own horses and go down by the secret path. We must not say a word on the way and you must not look behind."

The Bey was ready. He put on his furlined cloak he was so cold. Azraele called to the panther lying on the rug,

"Oglan, you shall go too and keep watch. If we meet a wild beast you shall defend us."

As if he had understood the words of his mistress the panther rose on his hind feet and laid his paws on her arm, and the trembling man clung to her on the other side. A strange group! A pale woman wrapped in white, and by her side two princely creatures, a haughty man steeled for conflict, and a panther; both mastered by a glance from her, driven to joy or to despair.

*   *   *   *   *

The Moslem churchyard below the castle is planted with cypresses. Amid these dark trees of mourning are the graves rising ghostlike with their layers of white stones. At the sound of the approaching steps a grey wolf ran out from the graves, otherwise the place was absolutely desolate. The clouds were broken after the storm; and here and there might be seen the dark blue sky with stars like diamonds. The raindrops were falling from the trees. The rumbling of the thunder was still heard occasionally in the distance and the lightning played over the mountain tops brightening all with its white light.

The figures reached the churchyard by the underground passage and dismounted from their horses beside the graves. Azraele laid the reins of both horses in Oglan's mouth. The clever beast stood still on his hind feet and held the two snorting horses more firmly than any post could.

The man and woman reached a high grave with its stone just showing among the branches of a weeping willow. "It is hardly probable that a slave rests under this stone," whispered Azraele to the trembling knight; she placed her magic pan on the stone and lighted the amber and borax which blazed up and cast a white vapor over the grave. In the distance was heard a slight rustling and Corsar's horse whinnied restlessly.

"What's that?" asked knight.

"The Djinns," answered Azraele. "Don't look behind you."

Then she raised the magic wand and uttered an incantation over the grave interspersing it with unintelligible words.

"Restless spirit, appear at my command. Whether you are beneath the dark tree of Hell, or in the garden of the houris. Whether you sleep bound by chains of fire, or on beds of roses, hear my call. Flee through the air, cleave the darkness and appear before me in living form as you were. Appear!"

At the words she struck with her wand against the side of the stone, and there rose up from behind a figure wrapped in white.

"Now take three steps toward him," said Azraele to the dazed knight, "and speak to him."

Corsar Bey approached the figure before him with tottering steps, and said in a hoarse, quavering voice:

"My name is Corsar Bey; and you, accursed shade, who are you?"

"I am Balassa," said the spirit with a clear voice.

The white shroud fell off and revealed a mighty man with unsheathed sword in his hands.

"Corsar Bey, you are my prisoner," he said to the Turk, who stood petrified at the sudden turn.

The next moment the Bey put his hand to his side and not finding any sword there, ran with a cry of rage to his horse, threw himself into the saddle and used his spurs, but Oglan held the horse firmly with the bridle in his teeth, and when the horse tried to move, the panther dug his claws into him and held him back.

"To Hell with you, you cursed beast," yelled Corsar, foaming with rage, and gave the panther a kick.

But the panther only pulled the bridle this way and that, stood in the horse's way and frightened him with its leaps, compelling him to circle about.

"Speak to your beast, Azraele," screamed the Bey, turning around, and looking for his beloved saw her in the arms of the young Hungarian.

At this instant the churchyard became alive. The Hungarian soldiers who had been lying concealed tore the Bey from his horse. Even when thrown to the ground he tried to defend himself with stones.

"A curse upon you," said the vanquished outlaw.

The troops moved past him along the secret passage to his castle, and an hour later by the light of his burning castle he saw his favorite ride away mounted behind Balassa.

CHAPTER IX

THE PRINCE AND HIS MINISTER

A FEW years had passed since Apafi rose to his princely rank. We are in the period when, in consequence of the sudden death of Nicholas Zrinyi the party of Hungarian malcontents had lost their standing and most of them had gone to Transylvania, which country was rejoicing in Home rule, owing to the rivalry of the German and Turkish monarchs. True, the country paid the Sublime Porte a tribute, but in its diets it could make what plans it would; and if the Tartars did burn the villages of the country to the ground, in that very act they gave proof that they did not consider the country their own. All the fortresses were in the hands of the Prince, who could maintain as many soldiers as he had means to pay, and carry on war whenever he found himself in a position to do so. Furthermore, if it gave him any satisfaction, he could even dupe the Turks.

The Turk did not find anything to object to in the constitution of the country; in its privileges, its patriarchal aristocracy, its Latin language and Hungarian costume, nor in its many religions; all that did not concern him. He pitied from his soul the poor people who gave so bright an outlook to the affairs of the country. He did not exert himself in the least to procure them a more exact acquaintance with his own simple system; in this respect he was like the Turk in the story, who when he saw a Hungarian eating with his open knife in hand, sat down behind in confident expectation that the Hungarian would put out his eyes in carrying his knife to his mouth, and when he saw that this did not happen, went away in the pleasant belief that it certainly would happen a little later.

 * * * * * *

Great changes had taken place in Ebesfalva in this time; the princely residence was no longer the simple manor house. At some distance from that, on a height, the Prince had a castle built with a high square tower, and from each corner rose small pointed turrets; the entrance was guarded by two stone lions, and on the façade was this inscription in high relief:

" Fata viam invenient."

Beyond the carved columns along the front was a corridor connecting one wing of the castle with the other; the windows were all made with pointed arches and with antique decorations, and the inner court was reached through an arched passage under the building. In this courtyard instead of plows and wagons we now see rampart guns and long culverins. Instead of farm boys,

we see outside the gates guards in yellow cloaks
and red hose. To reach the Prince's office you
must pass through long passage-ways and echo-
ing apartments where pages announce your arrival from door to door, and when at last the reception-room is reached you stand not in the
presence of the Prince but of Michael Teleki, his
first counsellor. He is the same bald-headed
man whom we met on that memorable day that
saw the death of Nicholas Zrinyi.

In early days the good man had been only a
captain fallen into disfavor with George Rakoczi.
Since then his affairs had prospered and he was
now chief captain of Kövar and all powerful in
the name of the Prince. His mother was the
sister of the Princess. Through the protection
of his aunt he came into the protection of the
Prince. Once there Teleki needed no further
support; his comprehensive mind, his extended
acquaintance, his statesmanlike training made
him indispensable to the Prince, who preferred
to bury himself in his books and antiquities and
considered himself hindered by anything that
took him from his family or his studies.

His reception-room to-day was crowded with
men who wished to speak to his Excellency.
They were the Hungarian fugitives whom the
Prince seemed to hold in special horror. These
restless, gloomy people, always in quest of war,
did not suit the placid, meditative nature of the

Prince. Now he shut them all out, and admitted only, of all his courtiers, a learned pastor, John Passai who had a professorship in Nagy-Emged, and was dear to the Prince on account of his learning. Apafi's office looked more like that of a student than a ruler. The walls were covered with bookcases, in the corners were maps, and on the narrow spaces remaining were clocks, which the Prince wound up himself. The chairs and sofas were covered with books needed at once, so that often when the Prince received the visit of a friend he did not know where to seat him. Sometimes even the floor was covered with maps, dusty documents and open books; if Teleki entered at such a moment he would have to pick his way with as much care as a man looking for a dry path through the mud.

At this moment Apafi and the pastor stood before a table on which lay some old coins. Apafi looked carefully at a gold piece, turned it in his fingers and held it to the light. Passai stood in front of the Prince like a post, hat in hand, with knitted brows. Apafi twirled the coin and studied it on both sides.

"Those are not Roman letters," he growled, "neither are they Greek nor Arabic; and they certainly are not Hunnic. I have never seen such characters. Where were they found?" he asked, turning to Passai.

"In Varhely, when the Wallachians were clearing away the old temple."

" Why did they clear it away ? "

" It was an old ruin that they called a Roman temple."

" But it cannot have been a Roman temple, for it is not a Roman coin."

"I agree with you, but the Wallachians are in the habit of calling every ruin in Transylvania Roman."

" But why did they clear it away ? "

" The villagers thought they might burn the statues for lime."

" O godless people ! " cried Apafi, "to make lime out of rare works of art.   Did you not try to save at least part from destruction ? "

" I bought a cover of a sarcophagus adorned with sculpture, and a well preserved sphinx; but it was not convenient for the Wallachian who was moving them to lift them whole, so he broke the statues in five or six pieces that he might carry them in his cart more easily."

" He deserves to be impaled ! I will have a law passed that nobody hereafter shall dare lay hands on any antique."

" I am afraid your Excellency will be too late, for when the people learned that I was paying for their stones, the story went abroad that I was hunting for diamonds and carbuncles in the stones, and they broke them all up in such small pieces that now they might be used for writing sand."

"Have you spoken with the Lord of Deva about the mosaic?"

"He will not let it go at any price. He said that none of his ancestors had ever sold any of their possessions. If he would only allow it to be moved from the spot where it was found,— but he will not even consent to that. As it is the corn-stall stands over it and the oxen lie on the figures of Venus and Cupid."

"I have a great mind to confiscate the property and so get possession of the priceless treasures," said Apafi, with the zeal of a student, and again turned to examine the puzzling coin.

At this moment Teleki entered the Prince's apartment with an important air, took some writing from a silk envelope, opened it and placed it in Apafi's hand. The Prince appeared to read it with care and knit his brow as he did so. Suddenly he called out, "They certainly are Dacian letters!"

"What!" said Teleki, astounded, with wide open eyes. He could not comprehend how the Prince had found Dacian writing in the letter handed him.

"Yes, I am positive. I remember reading, perhaps in Dio Cassius, that the Romans had medals struck with a Dacian inscription and on the obverse the picture of a headless man. Here it is."

"But your Highness," said Teleki, with annoy-ance, "the writing that I handed you"—

Now for the first time Apafi noticed that there was a parchment in his hand waiting to be read, and sullenly gave it back to Teleki.

"I have told you already that I did not wish to see anybody to-day. In a month's time the Diet will be convened and then the Hungarians may talk about their affairs as much as they will."

"But, I beseech your Highness," replied Teleki, satirically, "this writing has nothing to do with the Hungarians, but with his grace the Tartar Khan."

"What does he want?" said Apafi, and glanced at the parchment, but when he saw its length he laid it aside. "I will make short work of him. Who brought the letter?"

"An Emir."

Apafi girded on his sword and went into the reception-room.

"Good-day, good-day," he said, hastily, to those assembled. In this way he made an end of their long greetings, and gave a searching glance through the throng.

"Where is the Emir?"

At this the Tartar deputy came forward. He stood boldly before the Prince with an air of consequence.

"Salem Alech."

"What is it?" said Apafi, curtly.

The Emir measured the Prince keenly with his piercing eyes, threw his head back and said:

"My lord, the gracious Kuba Khan sends word to you, Prince of the Giaours, that you are a false, faithless, godless man. You gave your word of honor that we should live as neighbors and how do you conduct yourself now? A year ago it happened that in passing through Saxony we visited cities the names of which a true-believer may not utter, and there took our usual plunder in due form. They were always profitable, but as some of them were not quite quick enough in the payment of the tribute, at the command of his Grace, Kuba Khan, they were burned to ashes as punishment, that they might improve. Then did they improve? Not at all. For when we visited there again this year we found only the bare walls that we had left before. The unbelieving dogs fled before us and left us only a search. So then, my lord the mighty Kuba Khan sends word to you to know what kind of a Prince you are that you allow these unbelieving dogs to leave their towns and make fools of us. Formerly when we came the hay had been put in barns, the grain threshed and the cattle fatted; now we find nothing but weeds, with hares and other unclean creatures that you unbelievers are accustomed to eat. And that we may not take our revenge, the towns are

not built up again. Now if you do not wish
to bring down upon your head the wrath of
the mighty Khan, see to it that you order those
fugitives back to their towns, and send word to
the rest of the Saxon towns that have surrounded
themselves with inaccessible walls, to open their
gates to us. Otherwise we will visit you in
Klausenburg with fire and sword and leave not
one stone above another."

During this speech Apafi had several times
grasped his sword. Then he reconsidered and
said calmly:

"Go back, give greetings to your lord, and tell
him that we will give him satisfaction at once."

Then he turned his back on the messenger and
would have left the room at once, but Teleki
placed himself in his way.

"That is not enough, your Highness. Once
for all there must be an end made of this dog-
headed Tartar's coming into the presence of the
Prince of Transylvania with such a speech."

"Then speak to him yourself."

Teleki advanced toward the Emir with an
earnest, dignified expression, looked him fixedly
in the eye, and said firmly:

"Your lord is indeed the ruler of Tartary, and
my lord the Prince of Transylvania, and his
Majesty, the Sultan is one lord of us all. Know
then that his Majesty the Sultan did not make
your lord Khan of Tartary to dwell at Vienna,

nor did he set Michael Apafi on the throne of Transylvania to support your lord. Go back to your land and do not come here any more to wonder that a town burned down by you one year is not built up the next. We will take care that the houses are rebuilt and also that the bastions are made high enough to keep you off. If you have any desire to pay us a visit in Klausenburg we will take care that you do not have your trouble for nothing, and shall know how to greet you from afar with our good cannon."

The Emir fumed with rage; his eyes were bloodshot, his hand felt for his dagger and he stammered out:

"If a slave should make such a speech in the presence of my lord he would have his head cut off at once."

Apafi now touched Teleki on the shoulder and said:

" Good, Teleki! you spoke like a man."

The Emir turned on his heel and hurried out of the room, shaking his fist.

This scene put Apafi into a good humor, especially toward Teleki. The minister read this in the Prince's face and took advantage of it at once. Taking one of the bystanders by the hand he brought him up to Apafi and introduced him in these words:

"My future son-in law, your Excellency."

An introduction under any other title would probably have been evaded by Apafi, but in this form it was impossible not to accept it. He found himself compelled to look at the young man. He was a fine-looking, slender youth and had no trace of a beard. With his feminine features the only sign of the man was his independent bearing. Apafi was pleased with him.

"What is the name of your son-in-law?" he asked Teleki.

The latter answered with a peculiar smile:

"Emerich Tököli, son of Stephen Tököli."

At mention of this name Apafi grew serious and said:

"Your father was a good friend of mine." But he did not offer him his hand.

"I know that," replied the young man, "and for that reason I sought your Highness."

"If only he had not been such a disturber of the peace. It is well that you have not followed his counsel. I remember well the contest between the defeated and half-crazed David Zolyomi. Both had married daughters of Bethlen, who had received as dowry in common the castle of Bajda-Hunyad; one had one-half, and one the other; after the two men had taken counsel together they gathered their servants in their respective castle-yards, began battle and shot at each other from the opposite windows; both had a great love for war. Your father was in battle just before his death. In the very hour of death he needed the thunder of cannon and the tumult of the siege. It is well that you are not like him. You look gentle."

"That is praise undeserved," said Tököli, proudly. "I too was in the stormed castle and defended it until my father fell."

Apafi heard this with displeasure. However he wished to show interest in the youth and so after a pause he asked:

"And how did you happen to save yourself?"

At that Emerich turned red and did not answer at once.

Teleki told the truth as if excusing the youthful fire of the young man.

"He is so young that in woman's clothes he easily escaped the notice of the besiegers."

This amusing explanation put Apafi in good humor again. He stroked the bright red cheeks of the boy and motioned to Teleki to introduce the rest of the men. They were all of them Hungarian fugitives. The Prince exerted himself to meet them kindly. Just then an official entered and announced,

"His Excellency, the ambassador of France wishes to be admitted."

Evident confusion came over Apafi. He drew Teleki to him and whispered in his ear,

"I will not, I cannot receive him. Go out

and speak with him and explain the matter to
him."

Apafi slipped quickly out of the reception-
room, rejoiced that this time he had rolled off the
burden on Teleki. However he stood and listened at the door thinking that there might be
some sudden outbreak after his back was turned.
And something did happen, though not of a
character to make one's hair stand on end. The
ambassador uttered a jovial laugh, and with that
all in the room burst out laughing as if at a word
of command.

"Something strange must have happened,"
thought Apafi, "to force these men to such of-
fensive laughter," and he opened the door part
way. But he could not fully open the door, for
the learned Passai, renowned for his gravity, had
fallen into such a fit of laughter that he leaned
against the door of the private office.

"Let me in, Passai," said the curious Prince;
and when the door was opened the cause of the
general laughter became clear. The worthy
minister stood in the middle of the room clad
in Hungarian costume. You cannot imagine
anything more comical! the good man, aside
from the fact that he was quite stout, was
smooth-shaven and wore always a friendly smile;
but this unusual costume gave him an appearance
so ridiculous that only a Hungarian can appreci-
ate it. Everybody knows that the Magyar cos-

tume for men shows the figure very plainly. Then too the worthy Frenchman moved about so helplessly in his tight hose and spurred boots that it seemed as if he might lose his footing any moment. He had forgotten to put on his scarf, which added to the comical effect of his costume, his long curled wig, making him look for all the world like a lion, and his round hat with a long heron's feather completed his droll appearance. Apafi saw no reason why he should not join in the laughter.

With the French ease in mingling jest and earnest the ambassador tripped up to him and said,

"Your Highness, you have so many times refused me admittance that the idea occurred to me that perhaps I did not come in appropriate costume, and as your Highness sees, results have proved the wisdom of the idea for now that I have approached you in Hungarian costume I have been so fortunate as to see you."

"Parbleu!" replied Apafi, with difficulty, suppressing his desire to laugh. "I am always glad to see you. The only condition I impose is that politics shall not enter into our conversations. But you have no sash, and without the sash the Hungarian costume is as incomplete as the French costume without culottes."

Saying this the Prince took a jeweled sash and himself fastened it about the figure of the ambassador.

"And what does this mean? who told you to stick your handkerchief in your trousers? only a haiduk does that, a nobleman puts his in his calpac. But what a fine handkerchief that is of yours!"

"Is it not a beauty?"

"It is, indeed, with its silk wreaths and gold and silver embroidery around the hem. Paris alone can furnish the like."

"But the truth is it was made in Transylvania."

"Incredible!"

"And what is more in Ebesfalva."

Apafi looked at the Reverend gentleman in astonishment.

"And I am not to know the skilful hands that busy themselves in this way!"

"Your Highness does know them. The name of the maker is in one corner of the handkerchief embroidered in beautiful Gothic letters."

Apafi looked at each corner of the handkerchief in turn; no two were embroidered alike; in one was a wreath of oak leaves, in one a trophy, in the third a Turkish, a Hungarian and a French sword fastened together with a ribbon, in the fourth under a Prince's crown was embroidered the name Apafi.

The Prince read the name aloud. The bystanders looked at him timidly expecting an outburst of anger. To the astonishment of all a smile played over the Prince's lips; he put the handkerchief in the Reverend gentleman's hat, put this on the ambassador's head, and said with very good humor:

"So you have succeeded in winning over my wife?"

The minister laughed at the ambiguous joke.

"But you will not win me," added Apafi, laughing.

The minister bowed low; then held his head erect and said significantly:

"Those mightier than I will accomplish it."

At this moment the door opened and a servant announced:

"Her Highness Anna Bornemissa, wife of Apafi, wishes to be admitted to the presence of the Prince."

Apafi looked at Teleki.

"This is your work."

Teleki answered calmly: "At your service, Highness."

"Did you bring the ambassador to the Princess?"

"Even so, Highness."

"Then it was you who advised him to appear in this masquerade that he might the more readily draw me out."

"That too was my work, your Highness."

"A very foolish plan on your part, Michael Teleki."

"That remains to be proved, your Highness," thought his minister, in proud consciousness of his clever superiority.

Madame Apafi entered the room. Her bearing was princely as was her dress. The gentlemen present vied with each other in greeting her. Apafi stepped quickly toward her, drew her arm within his and endeavored with marked consideration to take her to his private room.

"Let us stay here," said the Princess. "It is time enough to look at your Dutch clocks later; at present there are more serious affairs before us; the gentlemen from Hungary are waiting for a hearing."

"I know already what they wish, and have said that I will not hear anything more on the subject."

"Then you will listen to me. Yes, to me. I too am a Hungarian and make supplication to the Prince of Transylvania for help in the name of my Fatherland. That it may not be said that I influenced the Prince's will in secret, I have come here publicly before his throne and beseech him for protection for Hungary, whose sons are called strangers here in Transylvania where her daughter is the princess."

It was evident to all that Apafi would have much preferred to listen to men rather than to his wife, but he was caught this time. She stood before him as a suppliant, and there was no way of escape. Teleki ordered the pages outside not to give admittance to any one else. Apafi sat in an armchair in feverish excitement, and listened to the words of his wife. But before Anna could begin her speech the rattling of a coach was heard in the courtyard, and shortly after came the sound of decided footsteps through the corridor, and an imperious voice familiar to all inquired if the Prince was within.

When the page attempted to stand in his way a still more authoritative voice called, "Out of the way, boy." At the same time Dionysius Banfy pushed his way into the room. He was just as he had alighted from his carriage. His cheeks were redder than usual and his eyes blazed; he went directly to the Prince and said without preliminaries:

"Do not listen to these men, your Highness, do not listen to a word they say."

The Prince greeted Banfy with a smile and the words, "Welcome, kinsman."

"Pardon, your Highness, that in my haste I forgot to greet you; but when I heard that these Hungarians had gained audience here I was beside myself. What do you want?" he went on, turning to the Hungarian nobleman. "It is not enough for them that they have brought their own country to ruin by their restlessness; they would like to drag ours down too."

"You speak of us," said Teleki, with cold

scorn, "as if we belonged to some Tartar race
and had been driven here from God knows what
strange, savage country."

"On the contrary, I have spoken of you, my
lords, as people who from the very first have by
your restlessness involved Transylvania in a
course leading to destruction. The Hungarians
are, to a man, stupid."

"I beg you not to forget that I too"—said
Madame Apafi.

"It is with no pleasure that I see the will of
your Highness is authority here."

Madame Apafi turned to her brother-in-law in
injured pride:

"I shall not for that reason cease to remain
your well-wishing relative," and with these
words she left the room.

"You might have spoken to the Prince more
becomingly," said Teleki, sharply, to the great
lord.

"What have I said to the Prince, as yet?"
asked Banfy, shrugging his shoulders. "I cannot get anywhere near him with you in the way.
So far, I have only spoken against those, and
shall continue to speak against those who have absolutely no right to stand at the foot of the throne.
I mean you too, Michael Teleki. I know very
well why you have this Hungarian campaign so
much at heart. It is not enough for you to stand
first after the Prince in Transylvania, you would

like to be Palatine of Hungary as well. What a delusion you are cherishing! The French promise help to Hungary. Hungary promises Teleki the Palatinate. Teleki promises Apafi a crown; and all are lying, and all are going to deceive one another."

"My lord," replied Teleki, bitterly, "is it allowed to speak so to guests, to kinsmen who are unfortunate and in exile?"

"Nobody need instruct me in magnanimity," replied Banfy, proudly. "Guest and fugitive have always found refuge with me; and if these fugitives wish us to share our home, our fatherland with them, here is my hand; I receive them to a share. But in the same way in which I should have the sense to forbid my guests to set fire to the house over my head, so do I protest against setting fire to the country. And if they do not stop trying to disturb the peace once more prospering in our country I will use every means to have them driven out."

"These words need not surprise us," said Teleki in bitter satire, turning to the noblemen, "My gracious lord has been of late years pardoned by the Prince. Before that time he was in arms against us."

Apafi sat uneasily. "Have done with this quarreling. You are dismissed. As you see my counsellors are in opposition and without them I can do nothing."

"We will bring it before the Diet," said Teleki, solemnly.

The Prince withdrew, greatly annoyed, to his private room, and the lords went out the other door.

Banfy looked at him proudly as he went away and then straightened his fur cap.

"My good standing is at an end," he said mockingly as he went away.

Teleki looked after him coldly.   When all had gone Teleki whispered a few words to a page, who went away and soon came back with a curly-haired blonde youth.

It seems as if we had already seen this young man at some time, but for so short a time that we cannot at once recall him.   Over his warm dress hung a beggar's pouch, and in his hand was a knotted stick.

"So at last you allow me to come into the presence of the Prince," he said in a somewhat imperious tone to Teleki.

"Take your place here at the door," replied the minister.   "The Prince will soon pass on his way to dinner; you may then speak with him."

The young man with the beggar's pouch sat for a long time at the Prince's door, until Apafi finally appeared and the beggar placed himself at once in his way.

"Who are you?" asked the Prince astonished.

"I am the ransomed knight Emerich Balassa,

who was once named among Hungary's most influential men, and who now stands before your Highness with a beggar's staff."

"You were concerned in that conspiracy, I believe," said Apafi, who appeared unpleasantly affected by the scene.

"I was not, your Highness. If you will deign to listen to my story"—

"Tell it."

"As you well know there was once in Hungary a notorious Turkish robber-knight, by name Corsar Bey, who for a long time laid waste the upper country and whom the united powers of the counties could not succeed in bringing under control, in his rocky fortress. This man I caught by stratagem and in such a manner as to win over to my side his favorite. Under pretext of an apparition she enticed him alone outside the castle. I was duly informed, fell upon him with my men who had been concealed in the forest, and took him captive with his favorite, one of the most beautiful and unprincipled of women."

"I have already heard the story, Balassa. That was a worthy deed."

"Then hear the rest, your Highness. No sooner was the news of the capture spread abroad than the Palatine demanded of me most emphatically to give over my prisoners to him. The Turks had already offered me sixteen thousand ducats for the two, but I would not let them go at any price, and sent word to the Palatine that if he wished to call a Bey his own, he must crawl out from behind his wife's shadow and catch one for himself. I had caught mine for my own use."

Apafi laughed loudly. "You gave him the right answer."

"At that the Palatine became angry and by the Emperor's command sent troops against me who were to take my prisoners by force. His Excellency your brother-in-law, Dionysius Banfy, had at that time found refuge in my house and I introduced to him this woman who had completely befooled me. He was to flee with her to my castle, Ecsed. But when I saw that the Palatine interfered with every attempt of mine to deliver Corsar Bey over to the Turks for the offered ransom, and yet all he wanted of him was to cut his head off like any other freebooter's, I gave the Turk poison, which he took gratefully for the sake of escaping justice. Then when the Palatine's troops came they found only the dead body which the Turks took off my hands for a thousand ducats."

"Naturally the Palatine was angry with you for that," said Apafi.

"I had good cause to be angry with him, for I had lost fifteen thousand ducats by him; yet he succeeded in getting a writ of arrest against me from the minister. I scented it in time and got together my valuables, intending to flee to

Transylvania until the affair had been forgotten. Then I hurried to my castle Ecsed where, as I have said, Banfy had been sent before me with the Turkish woman. On the way I learned that Banfy had been pardoned by your Highness and restored to his former position. I rejoiced not a little that in him I should find a powerful protector here. Imagine my astonishment when I reached Ecsed to find the woman gone without a trace, and I learned from my castle warden that Banfy had taken her with him and left a letter for me. In the letter was written: 'My friend: Learn from this that a man should never trust another with his horse, his watch, nor his love.'"

"What!" cried Apafi. "Is that the truth?"

"Your Excellency can see his writing," replied Balassa, and drew from his pouch the letter referred to. "The woman must be hid somewhere in his forest of Banfy-Hunyad, I suppose."

"That is monstrous!" said Apafi, glowing with anger. "Can a man with such a beautiful, noble wife, my own wife's sister, so far forget his duty as husband! I'll not forgive him that."

"Pardon me, your Highness, I have nothing more to do with Banfy. My complaint is now urgently directed against Kapi."

"What have you against him? It is unheard-of to have so beautiful a wife and yet keep a Turkish slave woman!"

"This Kapi was the man who had the use of my

Transylvania estates. I determined to know
nothing more of Banfy and immediately took up
my quarters with Kapi in his castle of Aranyos.
Of the splendor displayed by this man I had
never had the least idea before, although all my
life I had been to the courts of Palatines and
Princes in no small number. His wife did not
put her foot to the ground, but was carried to
the very gate in a gilded chair, and she never
wore the same gown twice."

"What have I to do with Madame Kapi's
finery?"

"I am coming to the point. It is just because
of this finery that her husband is compelled to
resort to all kinds of trickery to satisfy the wishes
of his lady. Furthermore your Highness is concerned, for such immoderate luxury only makes
the contrast the more striking between the sim-
plicity of your Excellency's court life and the insolent splendor of these small kings. And it
carries its impression with the strangers who so
frequently visit us; the effect of it is already
felt; for when the Bavarian ambassador came
recently to Aranyos from Ebesfalva I heard him
say in flattering tones to Madame Kapi that she
was the real Princess of Transylvania."

"Did he say that?" said the Prince, beginning
to take great interest in the affair. "Go on with
your story. Did he say that Kapi's wife was
the real Princess?"

"In point of beauty and bearing she is not worthy to tie the shoe of her Highness, the Princess Apafi, if you were to strip her of the costly jewels that she wears in such numbers she can hardly move."

"Go on, go on."

"Now Kapi informed me one fine day that your Excellency had received command from the Palatine to have me arrested and delivered over."

"I— received command— I never heard a word of it!"

"Unfortunately I believed the story, and thinking that I stood between two fires saw no way of escape except to give over to Kapi my Transylvania estates to prevent their falling into the public treasury. In return for this he gave me a written promise that I should have the property back again as soon as I was in a position to receive it. I then determined to flee to Poland during the period of danger. Kapi gave me two guides who were to lead me over the mountains to the frontier, and at the time he sent word secretly to the guard on the frontier that I was a spy sent by the Roman Emperor, who had been finding out the affairs of Transylvania and would now like to get back unseen. These rascals stopped me on the way, robbed me of all my money and papers, and dragged me off to Karlsburg. There, it is true my innocence was proved, but my money and my papers were lost. And

now Kapi asserts that I had actually sold him
all my property and had nothing left but this
leather pouch."

"Be comforted," replied the angered Prince.
"I will give you full satisfaction."

"Your Highness owes it to his own authority,"
replied Balassa, by way of urging on the Prince.
"These nobles act as arbitrarily as if there were
nobody in authority over them."

"Do not be disturbed. I will soon prove to
them that there is a Prince in Transylvania."
Apafi left the audience room very much excited.

Over the heads of two powerful men who stood
in Teleki's way, the storm was already threatening.

CHAPTER X

THE LIEUTENANT OF THE ROUNDS

CLEMENT put his pen behind his ear and read over the beautiful verses he had just written. There were two hundred stanzas all ending in "was," except one that ended in "were."

As Apafi always repented if he had hurt anybody's feelings, so in the case of the traveling student Clement, he did not rest until he had made up to him for the disgrace inflicted. And this he did by making the inoffensive poet Lieutenant of the Rounds.

In those days there were many duties connected with this office, all of which Clement calmly let slip while he wrote chronicles and epics in abundance. Now his glance rested upon an epic in which he had related the victory of Apafi at Neuhäusel. This poetic musing had so engrossed Clement's power of thought that an entire week had passed since his serving-man had run away carrying off his master's spurred boots, and he had not yet pursued the faithless servant in spite of his office as Lieutenant of the Rounds. He kept persistently going around in the same circle; when he looked for his boots, he remembered that his servant had stolen them, and when he started

to go after his servant he became aware that he
had no boots. Under these circumstances where
could he make a beginning ! So he set himself
down and wrote verses without end.

His room had not been swept for a week, so
there was no lack of dust and cobwebs, beside the
ink spots on the floor all around the table. This
table had only two legs, the other two being re-
placed by piles of tiles.

The poet wrote, scratched out, and chewed the
end of his pen. On the window-sill lay a piece
of bread and some cheese and it occurred to the
poet that this food was intended for his consump-
tion. But first he must use the ink in his pen ;
before this was finished, a second, third, and
fourth thought had crowded on the first ; meantime three mice had come out of a chink, sported
about the tempting morsel and then gnawed away
until there was nothing left. After which they
had glided back to their holes.

The poet had worked the Pegasus harnessed
to his plow until his senses were gone. When he
finally roused himself and looked for his bread
and cheese he discovered that only crumbs were
left, concluded that he had already eaten and im-
agined that he was satisfied ; so he set himself
down again and went on with his poetry. While
he was subduing the flesh in this way, there was
a scratching at the door ; somebody rattled the
hinge evidently mistaking it for the latch, and

naturally could not open the door. This noise rudely frightened Clement from his poetic thought. When he had called out several times to no purpose that the door was not locked he found himself obliged to rise and open it to prevent the visitor from breaking the latch or taking off the hinge.

There stood a Wallachian with a sealed letter in his hand. He seemed to be much frightened when the door opened, although that was the fulfilment of his wishes.

"What is it?" said Clement, becoming angry when the peasant did not speak.

The Wallachian raised his round eyebrows, looked at the poet with wide-opened eyes and asked: "Are you the man who lies for money?"

In this choice language the Wallachian described the office of our Clement. His veins swelled with anger. "Whose ox are you?" he thundered at the Wallachian.

"The gracious lord's who sent this letter," answered the peasant, slily.

"What is his name?" asked Clement, furiously, and tore the letter from the Wallachian's hand.

"Gracious lord is what he is called."

Clement opened the letter and read: "Come at once to me where the bearer will lead you."

Clement was already raging, but now the thought that he had been summoned somewhere and had no boots made him beside himself.

"Go," he shouted to the Wallachian. "Tell your lord whoever he is, that it is no farther from him to me, than from me to him. If he wishes to speak with me let him take the trouble to come here."

"I understand, Dumnye Macska." In his terror the peasant had called Clement by the name used by the peasants for the Lieutenant of the Rounds, and at once he hurried out of the room.

Clement drew himself up with a great effort in his high-backed chair, and placed two large books on the floor before him that his visitor should not notice that he was barefooted.

Heavy footsteps were soon heard on the street before the house, and when he looked from the window he saw to his great dismay that his visitor was no other than Count Ladislaus Csaki, attended by two Hungarian foot-soldiers with gold lacings.

"Now, Clement," said the poet to himself, "maintain your dignity. It is true he is a Count and a distinguished man, but one who has fallen into disfavor with the Prince while you are in his favor, and besides that are in an official position." So he hid his feet under the books, placed his pen between his lips and bade Csaki come in. He did not even rise at his entrance. Csaki appeared displeased at this reception.

"You know how to maintain your official dignity," he said to Clement.

"What I am, I am, thanks to the favor of the Prince," he replied, with affectation, and folded his arms proudly.

"I have come to you only at the bidding of the Prince. His Highness has intrusted me with a very delicate affair in which I need your help. The affair must be managed with the utmost secrecy and for that reason I could have wished that you should come to me."

At this explanation Clement suddenly lost his insolent manner.

"I beg your pardon," he stammered confusedly and with head humbly bowed. "I did not know— I pray you be seated."

But as the chair in which he sat was the only specimen of the kind in the room, he jumped up to make room for the Count, and in so doing displayed his feet without their customary covering, at which Csaki burst into a hearty laugh.

"What the devil does this mean, Lieutenant," he exclaimed. "Are you like the Turks who take off their boots in excess of reverence?"

"I beg your pardon. I have not taken them off but they were stolen from me by my servant while I slept. This was my only reason for making your Grace such a rude reply. But I dare hope that your Grace has already pardoned me."

Csaki's good-humor was only increased by this explanation.

"Certainly, if that is all, we will relieve your distress at once," he said. And he ordered the soldier waiting without to bring his own dress boots in the carriage box for the Lieutenant.

Clement was just opening his lips to make some objections—the favor shown him was too great—when he caught sight of the boots; they pleased him greatly, for they were made of royal green morocco, stitched with gold threads, trimmed on each side with broad gold fringe and finished with enameled spurs.

"Put them on quickly," said Csaki to the Lieutenant. "You must be on your way at once without delay."

Clement took one of the boots by the two straps and began to draw it on, first looking in with a satisfied smile, but it was no small task for Csaki wore a very narrow cavalier's boot. Clement, on the other hand, moved on moderately large feet, so that he had to begin from the very beginning as many as three times and give it up from the very beginning as many times, thoroughly tired before he succeeded in getting his foot into the leg of the boot; in these exertions he worked his eyes and mouth so that Ladislaus Csaki had to put his head out of the window, he was so overcome with laughter. Then he came to the heel and there he stuck; he seized the foot gear firmly by both straps and began to stamp himself into it, thumping about the room in this bent position and groaning loudly at every push, till his eyes stood out and the perspiration ran down his face, before he had worked his way into the first boot. The same difficulties attended the second boot; but after he had used six-horse power to get his foot into this insufficient space he looked at his shining tight boots with a glow of satisfaction, though they were not in perfect harmony with the rest of his dusty, greasy, ink-spotted clothing.

"Now listen carefully to what I tell you," said Csaki, seating himself on the only chair with an air of authority, while the student still standing, lifted first one foot and then the other and his face turned green and blue with pain, for the boots began to make havoc with his corns.

"When did you make your last circuit?"

"I don't remember exactly."

"But you ought to know. Why did you not make a note of it? The Prince wishes you to set out at once and make your round without delay, paying special attention to the districts lying between Torocho, Banfy-hunyad, and Bonczida; in addition to the usual questions you are to add this one, Has anybody seen any foreign animals in the surrounding woods?"

"'Foreign animals,'" repeated mechanically the doleful official.

"And if anywhere you receive the reply that such have been seen, you are to go through that locality and examine carefully until you get track of them."

"1 beg your pardon, but what kind of animals will they be?" asked the student, timorously.

"Ch, have no fear, it is neither a seven-headed dragon nor a minotaur. At the worst a young panther."

"Panther"—stammered Clement in terror.

"You are not expected to catch him," said Csaki, consolingly. "You are to hunt out where he stays and then let us know."

"Suppose that beast of prey, whose presence in Transylvania I doubt greatly, should happen to be in the territory of Dionysius Banfy, what shall I do then?"

"Follow him up."

"I beg your pardon, but his territory is baronial, where my authority does not extend."

"Don't be such a simpleton, Clement," said Csaki. "I did not say, did I, that you were to go with an armed guard? The entire expedition must be kept a secret. You and your guide alone are to get track of the beast. We have positive information that he is somewhere in this vicinity. Now a careful investigation is demanded of your skill. The rest will be given over to more fearless workers."

The entire mission seemed to Clement a very strange one, but he did not dare make any objection, and bowed with a deep sigh.

" Above everything else, skill, speed, secrecy. These are the three things that I recommend to your especial consideration."

" I will set out at once, gracious lord, only I must borrow a horse somewhere first, so I shall not ruin these fine boots with walking."

" That would delay matters. You must not exert yourself about a horse; one of my servants shall give up his and you can mount that. Don't forget to think of his fodder, so that you will bring him back something besides skin and bones."

So much kindness fairly bewildered Clement. In all haste he strapped on his traveling bag and his rusty sword; and after he had put in the first a roll of parchment, a pen, and a bottle of ink, declared himself ready.

" That is a light traveling bag of yours," said Csaki.

" 'Integer vitae, scelerisque purus, non eget Mauri jaculis, neque arcu,' " replied the philosopher, with a quotation from Horace, and, the reins being handed him, made ready to mount.

But when the spirited steed noticed that the philosophical student had put one foot in the stirrup he began to kick and circle round, compelling the poet to jump round on one foot until the laughing servant seized the horse by the bridle and helped the inoffensive rider to mount.

But as he had long legs and the soldiers had shortened the stirrups, he had to stoop on his horse as if it were a camel.

Once more Ladislaus Csaki called after him not to forget his injunctions, at which the poet unintentionally struck spurs to his horse and galloped madly away over the stones. Coat, sword and traveling bag flew about the unhappy rider. He held fast to the front and back of the saddle and rode on amid the laughter of the villagers of Torocko, who sat in groups in front of their houses.

First the Lieutenant took the road to Gross-Schlatten. Formerly when he had a servant, the servant constituted his retinue. But now for lack of a servant he was compelled to go from town to town in solitude, following the directions of the village magnate. As he was trotting through a defile he noticed in a thicket a group seated about a fire. At first he thought it was a party of gypsies, until approaching nearer he discovered to his great horror that they were Tartars who were roasting an ox and sat around it in a circle. To turn around was not advisable for the way led straight past the Tartars sunning themselves, so Clement decided it was best to act as if he had no fear, and trotted calmly past the staring group. He pretended to be counting with greatest interest the fruit beside the road, and when he was quite

near took off his hat as if he noticed them for
the first time, murmured hurriedly, "Salem Alei-
kum," and rode on without looking behind. So
far, so good ; but at this moment up jumped two
Tartars and shouted after the rider to stop.
When Clement saw that the two were running
toward him without any weapons, he thought
perhaps they had no intention of murder and
waited for them. But when the two dark-faced
creatures came near, they seized the rider between them, caught hold of his legs and gave
evidence of no less intentions than to strip him
of his fine boots.

"A curse upon your soul !" shouted the furious Clement, laid hold of his rusty sword and
tried to draw it and cut off one of their ears.
But the good blade had not been drawn from its
scabbard for ten years and was so rusted that, in
spite of all his efforts, Clement could not draw it
out. Meantime the two Tartars pulled the
struggling rider this way and that by his legs
and naturally did not succeed in getting off the
tight boots. The Tartars berated Clement, and
Clement berated the Tartars. The uproar
brought the Aga, a man with a figure like an
orang-outang, his brown features framed by a
white beard, who inquired hoarsely what was
the matter.

Clement drew out his warrant of authority
and showed it to the Aga in silence, for rage

stifled his voice, while the two Tartars explained something in a foreign tongue, with angry gestures, and pointed to his green boots.

"Who are you, crooked-nosed unbeliever," inquired the Aga, "that you dare wear light-green, the sacred color of the prophets, that the faithful use only for the dances of their temples and the turban of the Padisha, and that too on your boots that go through the mud? May you be burned alive, you godless giaour!"

"I am the lieutenant reconnoitering in the service of his Excellency, Michael Apafi," declaimed the former student, with pathetic distress. "My person is sacred and inviolable. I am the man who provides the armies of the Sultan with food and drink. I impose the taxes. Let me go for I am a very important personage."

This manner of defense pleased the Tartars. The Aga gave his subjects a tacit sign that meant this was the very man they wanted, and then began to speak to him in a more friendly tone.

"You said that it was your business to announce the taxes. My lord, Ali Pasha of Nagy Varad, has just sent me here to announce a new tax, so I have met you at the right moment although it is nothing for you to do; it will, however, be a sensible thing for you to give this out at the same time."

"I will do so with pleasure," said Clement, eager to get away.

"Wait a moment," said the Aga, motioning to him. "You do not know yet how high the tax is to be. The whole amount is a mere trifle; it is imposed only so that they may recognize our authority. The tax is only a penny a head. That is not much, is it?"

"No indeed," said Clement, agreeing that he might get away the more quickly.

"Don't hurry off," said the Aga, checking his haste. "I should be sorry to see that you did not carry out this order of mine. But as you would not consider it any perjury not to keep a promise given to us I will send one of my good men with you, who shall accompany you from village to village and see that you make the proclamation about the tax."

"By all means, your Grace," said Clement, hoping to get rid of the man in the next village.

"Mount, Zulfikar," said the Aga, to one of his men.

The man spoken to was a lean fellow with an evil, squinting glance. Although he was as dirty as the rest, his features showed that he did not belong to the same race, and if we paid close attention to so unimportant individuals, we might remember that we had already seen him somewhere.

"One thing more," said the Aga to Clement, eager to get off at any price. "As soon as you get home lay aside those green boots, for if I should see them on your feet again you would get five hundred stripes on the soles of your feet, that you would keep until your wedding day."

Clement agreed to everything in his joy to get away at last, and trotted off toward Gross-Schlatten. His Tartar comrade rode faithfully by his side. From time to time the Lieutenant gave a side glance at his companion and then looked away quickly, for as the Turk was cross-eyed Clement never felt sure which way he was looking. And all the time he was considering how easily he could dupe the Tartar, a thought that made him smile to himself, blink and nod with satisfaction.

"You will not play any tricks on me, Lieutenant," said the Tartar, unexpectedly, and in the best of Hungarian, evidently reading these thoughts on his face.

Clement almost fell off his horse with fear, unable to comprehend what fiend he could be to read a man's thoughts on his face, and speak Hungarian in spite of being a Tartar.

"You need not rack your brains any more about me," said the Turk, calmly. "I am a Hungarian deserter once in the service of Emerich Balassa. I helped seize and imprison Corsar Bey, and when the Hungarians began to pursue me for it I turned Turk. Now with the Prophet's aid I shall yet be Pasha, so don't exert your-

self to get the better of me, for be assured you
are dealing with an old fox."

Clement scratched his head in perplexity, and
attended by the deserter, much against his will
concluded his official questions with the announcement of the penny tax which the people
all received with so much favor that most of
them paid it over to the Tartar at once.

But nobody had seen anything of the panther;
and had it not been for their respect for the
green boots with their trimmings they would
probably have laughed in his face when the Lieutenant put that question.

There was still one small Wallachian village,
Marisel, far away in the mountains. Beyond
that began the territorial jurisdiction of Banfy,
and the Lieutenant's authority was at an end.
There too the deserter followed him.

CHAPTER XI

SANGA—MOARTA

THE Lieutenant and his comrade had already been more than twelve hours in the wilderness of Batrina on their way to Marisel. Clement asked everybody he met if the village were not near, always receiving the same answer that it was still some distance farther. Now and then they met a Wallachian peasant with an ox-team; the man shouting to his lazy beasts, trying to goad them into a quicker gait. Then there was a pool to wade through, where a half-naked, picturesque company of gypsies washing the gold out of the sand, stared at the questioning strangers like wild beasts. Sometimes along the road there would be the picture of a saint in the mossy hollow of a tree, with only the dull gilding left of the weather-beaten paint. In the natural niche there would be the pomana,—a pitcher of spring water which some young Wallachian girl, as an act of piety, had placed there for thirsty travelers.

The way led them through valleys and over heights, and the greater part of their way they had to lead their horses by the bridle instead of riding.   On all sides was the forest, tall, slender beeches mingled with dark green firs.

In one place they came to a fork of the roads; one way led along the valley and the other to the top of a bald, steep mountain with out-jetting cliff.

"Which way now?" said Clement.   "I have never been so far."

"Take the traveled road," replied Zulfikar. "Only a fool would climb this steep height.   It probably leads to some foundry."

Clement looked doubtfully around him.   Suddenly he caught sight of a man seated on the rock overhanging the road.   He was a young Wallachian with white face and long curling hair; his leather coat was open on his breast and his cap lay beside him on the ground.   There he sat, bent over on the edge of the high cliff dangling his feet in the air, with his stony face in his hands gazing out into the distance.

"Ho there!" cried Clement, and in a mixture of Hungarian, Latin, and Wallachian asked, "Which way does this road go?"

The Wallachian did not seem to hear the cry. He remained in the same position, staring fixedly.

"He is either deaf or dead," said Zulfikar, when they had both shouted at him in vain.   "We had better follow the regular road."

And they set off on a trot.   The Wallachian

did not even look after them. Evening was near
and the way to Marisel had no end. It went
from valley to valley, never once passing a
human habitation. The rocks in the way and the
streams crossing at different points made it almost impassable. At last in one part of the
forest a column of fire rose before them and the
sound of singing fell on their ears. As they
came nearer they saw the fire of a pyre built up
of whole tree-trunks, in a spot shaded by trees
the foliage of which was scorched by the flames.
Near this was a crowd of Wallachians leaping
wildly with violent gestures; at the same time
they beat the ground with long clubs and seemed
to be treading letters into the ground, waving
their arms frantically, while they howled out
verses that were formulated imprecations, as if
they were driving out some kind of evil spirit.
A circle of young women danced round the
men. The lovely creatures, with their black hair
interwoven with ribbons and jewels, their flower-
embroidered dresses, pleated neckerchiefs, broad-
striped aprons, gold earrings, necklaces of silver
coins and high-heeled red boots, formed an agreeable contrast to the wild, defiant-looking men,
with their high cocked hats on the heavy shocks
of hair, their sunburned necks, greasy waistcoats
and broad girdles. The dance and the songs
were also strange. The women circled in and
out among their husbands, raising a mournful

wail, while the men stamped on the ground and joined in with yells of triumph. The fire threw a red light and dark shadows over the wild group. On a tree stump beyond sat an old piper, and from a goatskin drew forth monotonous tones that mingled with the song in wild discord. When the fire was burned down to ashes the dancers suddenly separated, dragged out the figure of a woman stuffed with straw and dressed in rags, laid it on two poles and carried it to the fire crying wildly in Hungarian, "Tuesday evening,[1] Tuesday evening!" and repeated three times, "Burn to ashes, you accursed witch of Tuesday evening!" Then they threw it into the glowing coals and the women danced round with cries of joy until the effigy was entirely burned, while the men leaped about with wild shouts.

"Who are you? And what are you doing here?" called out Clement, who had until then escaped their notice.

"We live in Marisel and have burned up Tuesday evening," they answered with one voice and with earnest look as if they had accomplished something very sensible.

"Get through with it quickly and come to your village, for I am here at the command of the Prince to ask some lawful questions."

"And I," said Zulfikar, "at the command of

[1] On this day superstition assigns peculiar power to the witches.

the mighty Pasha of Nagy Varad, to impose a
new tax."

The Wallachians looked after the Lieutenant
in silence until he vanished from their sight, and
then said with clenched fists:

"May Tuesday evening carry him off!"   And
then they moved off with the bagpiper at their
head singing as they went to the village.

*   *   *   *   *   *

It was a small straggling Wallachian village
into which the Lieutenant rode with his comrade.
One house was just like another; mud huts with
high roofs, projecting rafters, and enclosed within
quick set hedges. The doors were so low that one
must stoop to enter. Every house consisted of a
single room in which the entire family lived, together with hens and goats.

At the entrance to the village was a large
triumphal arch of stone, and over the main gate
was the torso of a Minerva. In front were figures
of a battle finely cut, and underneath an inscription in large letters in Latin: "This town the
invincible Trojan had built in memory of his
triumph." Behind this were miserable mud huts.

Before a house of mourning on the capital of
a fallen Corinthian column sat Prefika, the oldest
of the old women of the village, weeping paid
tears over the corpse of the young woman on the
bier within.

In front of a grass-grown hill was a grand stone building. In former times it might have been a temple erected to the memory of some Roman hero, but now the Wallachian villagers had made it their church, covering the temple with a pointed roof and spoiling the interior with dreadful paintings. For lack of any other public place the Lieutenant called the people together in this church. The setting sun through the round panes, lighted up strangely the interior of this old building with its walls covered from top to bottom with hideous pictures of saints, whom the monstrous fancies of peasant artists had clad in red cloaks and spurred boots. Among the many pictures was the well-known allegory which represents Death dragging off a king, a beggar and a priest. And scattered among the pictures of the saints were those representing devils with tongues outstretched, holding sinners by the hair of the head. Behind the altar stood the village priest and the Lieutenant.

When Clement had read aloud to the people his warrant of authority he called up the village magnate and asked him these questions:

"Are there any wizards or sorcerers among you who can call on the devil for help?"

At this question there was a timid whispering throughout the company, and after a long pause the priest answered:

"In former years, great and good lord, there was a godless reprobate in our midst who had liver spots on his neck and body; since these are sent by the devil, they did not pain him, even if they were burned with hot coals. We sent him before the Council at Weissenburg, and as he could not stand the test of water he was burned to death."

"Are there any among you who are witches, vampires, people who can harm the children of others, go through the air, turn milk red, hatch out serpents' eggs or find grasses that open locks; or, in short, know how to do anything supernatural?"

To this question there were a hundred answers at once. Everybody strove to tell the questioner his experiences. The young married women in particular crowded about the Lieutenant.

"One at a time," said the Lieutenant, authoritatively. "The judge shall tell what he knows."

"Yes, there was an old witch in the village," said the judge, slily, "we called her Dainitza. For a long time she practiced her evil among us, for her eyes were red. When she chose she could bring on a storm, so that the wind would take the roofs off. Once when she went out to get a hail storm the lightning struck the village in three places. At that the women grew furious, caught her and threw her in the pool. But even there the witch still cried out, 'Take care, you will yet ask me for the water, that you are now giving me to drink.' Then the women fished the body out of the water, where it had caught on a stone, thrust an arrow through her heart, buried her in the valley and rolled a great stone over her grave. But the witch's curse against us still held, all summer long not a drop of rain fell in our boundaries. Everything dried up and pestilence carried off our cattle. Dainitza had drunk up all the rain and all the dew. So we went to her grave, saying, 'Drink, drink your fill, cursed vampire; don't lap up all the water and dew away from us;' and at last the drought ended."

The priest testified that this was true and Clement wrote it down carefully on his parchment.

Now came the third question:

"Is there anybody among you who dares smoke tobacco; either cutting up the leaves and putting them in his pipe, or laying them on the fire and breathing the smoke that rises?"

"There is not anybody, my lord; we do not know this food."

"See to it, that no one tries to learn it; for if anybody is caught doing it, by decision of the states the pipe will be thrust through his nose and the guilty man led through the entire market place."

The fourth question was:

"Is there any one among the peasants here who wears cloth dress, marten cap, or morocco boots?"

"Why not," replied the judge, "if our poverty would permit? not that we long for dyed cloth and morocco."

"It is not allowed; the states of the country have forbidden the peasants to wear clothes fitting their masters."

Now came the fifth question:

"Who were the people who acted contrary to the decision of the states that the peasants should exterminate the sparrows, and mocked those who were appointed to collect the sparrows' heads?"

The judge advanced humbly toward the Lieutenant:

"Believe me, my great and good lord, on account of the drought the sparrows have all left the country. Say to the Prince that we have not been able to find one single one all summer long."

"That is a lie," said Clement.

"It is just as I say," persisted the judge, seizing Clement by the hand and skilfully pressing into it two silver groschen.

"It is not impossible," said the Lieutenant, appeased. "Finally, answer this question: Has any one of you seen wandering about in this region, foreign animals, beasts of prey from other countries?"

"Yes, indeed, my lord, we have seen them in great numbers."

"And what kind of animals were they?" asked Clement, in joyful curiosity.

"Why, dog-headed Tartars"—

"You fool! I am not asking for them. I wish to know whether in your wanderings through the forest you have not seen a foreign four-footed beast of prey with striped skin."

The judge shook his head incredulously, looked at his people and answered with a shrug of his shoulders:

"We have seen no such strange animal. It may be that Sanga-moarta has seen it, for he is forever wandering through the woods and ravines in his foolish way."

"Who is this Sanga-moarta? Summon him."

"Ah, my lord, he is hard to find; he rarely comes into the village. His mother may be here."

"Here she is! Here she is," cried several peasants, and pushed forward an old woman with sunken features, whose head was wound round several times with a white cloth.

"What kind of a foolish name [1] have you given your son?" asked the Lieutenant of her. "Whoever heard of giving a human being the name dead-man's-blood?"

"I did not give him this name, my lord," said

[1] That name is the Hungarian for dead man's blood.

the old woman, with quavering voice. "The
people of the village call him that because no one
has ever seen him laugh. He never talks to anybody, and if you speak to him he does not answer. He did not weep when his father died
and he never cared for any girl. He is always
wandering about in the woods."

"All right, old woman, that does not concern
me."

"I know, my lord, it does not concern you;
but you must hear that the handsomest girl in
the village, the beautiful Floriza, fell in love with
my son. There is not a more beautiful girl in all
the country round! Such black eyes, such long
black braids, such rosy cheeks, such a slender
figure! There was not the like far and wide.
Then too, she was so industrious and loved my
son so. She had sixteen shifts in her outfit, that
she herself had spun and woven, and she wore a
necklace of two hundred silver pieces and twenty
gold guldens— Sanga-moarta never looked at
the girl. When Floriza made him wreaths he
would not put them around his hat. When she
gave him kerchiefs he would not fasten them to
his buttonhole. No matter what beautiful songs
the girl sang as he passed her door, Sanga-
moarta never stopped. Yet she loved him.
Often she would say to him when they met on
the street;—'You never come to see me. I suppose you would not look at me if I should die,'

and Sanga-moarta would say:—'Yes, I should.'
'Then I will die soon,' the maiden would say,
sorrowfully. 'I will come to see you then,'
Sanga-moarta would answer, and pass on. Are
you tired of the story, my good lord? it is almost
done. The beautiful Floriza is dead. Her heart
was broken. There she lies on her bier. Before
the house are the branches of mourning. When
Sanga-moarta sees this and learns that Floriza is
dead he will come out of the woods to look at
his dead love as he promised, for he always
keeps his word. Then you can talk with him."

"Very well," said Clement, who had grown
serious and was almost annoyed that peasants
who had certainly not read Horace's Ars Poetica
should have their own poetry.

"You must watch for your son's coming and
let me know."

"It will be better for you to go yourself," said
the old woman; "for I hardly think that he will
answer anybody else."

"Then take me there," said the Lieutenant.

The entire company set out in the direction of
the house of mourning, at the extreme edge of
the village. This end of Marisel is so far from
the church that it was night before they reached
the house.

The moon had come up behind the mountains:
in front of the houses were fir trees and through
their dark needles gleamed its rays. In the dis-

tance was heard the melancholy sound of a shepherd's pipe. The paid mourner sobbed outside
the door. The wreaths swayed in the breeze.
Within lay the beautiful girl, dead, waiting for
her restless, wandering lover. The moonlight
fell on her white face.

*   *   *   *   *   *

The people surrounded the house. They crept
stealthily through the courtyard and looked
through the window and whispered, "There he
is, there he is!"

The Lieutenant, the priest, the judge and Sanga-
moarta's mother entered the room. Stretched
across the threshold lay the girl's father, dead
drunk. In his great sorrow he had drunk so
much the day before that he would hardly sleep
it off before another day. In the middle of the
room stood the coffin made of pine, painted with
bright roses by the brush of the village artist;
within lay the girl of barely sixteen years. Her
beautiful brow was encircled with a wreath;
in one hand had been placed a wax candle and
in the other a small coin: at the head of the coffin were two wax candles stuck in a jar covered
with gingerbread; at the foot of the coffin on a
painted chair with high back, sat Sanga-moarta,
bent over with his eyes fixed on the girl's face.
The priest and the judge remained standing at the
door in superstitious piety. Clement walked up
to the youth and at a glance recognized him as

the one who had not been willing to direct him on his way.

"Hello, young man, so you are the one who does not answer people's questions?"

The youth verified his words by making no reply.

"Now listen to me and answer what I ask you; I am the Lieutenant of the district. Do you hear?"

Sanga-moarta gazed in silence at Floriza, lost in melancholy and as immovable as the dead. His mother, the worthy woman, took him fondly by the hand and spoke to him by his true name.

"Jova, my son, answer this gentleman. Look at me, I am your dear mother."

"In the name of my master, the Prince, I command you to answer," shouted the Lieutenant, his voice growing more and more angry. The Wallachian was still silent.

"I ask you whether in your wanderings through the forest you have noticed anywhere a foreign beast. I mean a beast of prey, called panther by the learned."

Sanga-moarta seemed to start with terror as if he had been wakened from a sleep. Suddenly he turned his usually fixed eyes to the questioner. Over his face came a feverish color, and fairly trembling, he stammered out,

"I have seen it—I have seen it—I have seen it."

And with that he covered his eyes so that he should not look at the dead.

"Where have you seen it?" asked the Lieutenant.

"Far—far from here," whispered the Wallachian. Then he became silent again and buried his face in his hands.

"Name the place,—where?"

The Wallachian looked timidly about him, shivered as if a chill had gone over him and whispered to the Lieutenant, with timidly rolling eyes,

"In the neighborhood of Gregyina-Drakuluj."[1]

The priest and the judge crossed themselves three times, and the latter raised his eyes most devoutly to a picture of Peter, hanging on the wall, as if he would call on him for help.

"You seem to me a courageous youth since you dare go near the Devil's garden," said the Lieutenant. "Will you show me the way?"

The Wallachian expressed by the pleasure in his face that he would gladly show him the way.

"In the name of Saint Nicholas and all the archangels, do not go there, my lord!" cried the priest. "Nobody who has ever wandered there has returned. The godly do not turn their steps that way. This youth has been led thither by his sins."

"I do not go there of my own accord," said

[1] Devil's Garden.

Clement, scratching his head. "Not that I am afraid of the name of the country, but I do not like to climb around over mountains. However my office requires it and I must fulfil my duty."

"Then at least fasten a consecrated boat on your cap," urged the anxious shepherd of souls. "Or else take a picture of Saint Michael with you so that the devils cannot come near you."

"Thank you, my good people. But you would do better if you would get me a pair of sandals; I cannot go through the mountains in these spurred boots. Your safeguards I can make no use of, for I am a Unitarian."

At this reply the priest crossed himself and said with a sigh:

"I thought you were a true believer, you inquired so zealously about the witches."

"This is only my official duty, not my belief. Send me the Turk."

As he went out, the Pope murmured half aloud,

"You go well together,—two pagans."

"Comrade Zulfikar," called out Clement to the Turk as he entered, fastening on the sandals that had been brought, "you can look out for your own route now, for I must take a little side-dodge into the mountains."

"If you dodge, I will dodge too," replied the distrustful deserter. "Wherever you go, I will go."

"Where I am going, my dear friend, there is nothing to put in your pocket; it must be you wish to bag the devil, for no human being has ever set foot there."

"How do I know where the people live in this confounded country of yours! My orders were to go with you until I reached the starting-point again."

"All the better, for there will be more of us. Help me draw my sword out of the scabbard, so I can defend myself if necessary."

"So you carry a sword that it takes two men to draw. Let me get hold of it."

The two men planted their feet, grasped the sword with both hands and tugged at it for some time. At last it came out of its scabbard, almost throwing Clement over backward. Then Clement took a pitcher of honey, rubbed the rusty sword with the sticky stuff and put it back into its scabbard.

"Now we must be on our way, young man," he said to the Wallachian.

The latter at once took up his hat and his axe from the ground and went ahead without as much as one glance back at the dead. His mother seized him by the hand.

"Will you not kiss your dead love?"

Sanga-moarta did not so much as look—pulled his hand away from his mother's, and went with the two strangers out into the deep darkness of the forest.

* * * * * *

All night long these adventurers wandered through a deep valley from which they could just catch sight of the giant summits rising on all sides; directly overhead glimmered a strip of starry sky. Toward morning they reached the midst of the mountains. What a sight that was! Along the shining crystal peaks stretched dark green forest—on one side rose a crag of basalt, with columns like organ pipes in rows, topped by trees. In front of this crag of basalt a white cloud moved, but the summit and base of the rock were to be seen; from time to time the lightning flashed through the cloud but it was some time before the roll of the thunder rang through the organ pipes. At a little distance is a cleft in the rocks, and the two parts look as if their jagged edges would fit together. Through the ravine several fathoms wide, a branch of the cold Szomas forces its way and is lost again among the thick oaks along the shore. In another place the rocks are piled up in stairs not intended however for human foot, for each step is as high as a house. Again the rocks are tumbled together in such a way that the entire mountain mass would fall into other forms if the rock beneath were moved from its position.

Everything indicates that here the rule of man
has found its limit. From the dizzying height not
a single hut is seen; on all sides are bold crags
and yawning chasms through which the mountain streams roll tumultuously. Only the ibex
wanders from crag to crag.

"Which way are we going?" Clement asked
his guide, looking anxiously about, where there
was every possibility of losing oneself irrecover-
ably.

"Trust yourself to me," replied Sanga-moarta,
and he led them with confident knowledge of
the place through this unfrequented region.

In places where a path seemed hardly possible,
he knew where to find the way over the cleft
rocks. He had noticed every root that could
help one in climbing; every tree-trunk bridging
a chasm; every narrow ledge of rock where one
could step by clinging to its projections; in
short, he moved through this labyrinth with the
utmost confidence.

"We are near the end," he said, suddenly,
after he had climbed a steep wall of rock and
looked over the country, and he stretched his
hand down and drew the others up after him.
The scene was now changed. The declivity of
the rock that they had mounted was under them;
a smooth surface in semi-circular shape formed
a basin hundreds of fathoms deep, where the
dark green water of a mountain lake gleamed.

There was no breeze but the lake was broken with foam. The opposite side of the basin was formed by a group of mountains with fir trees at the base, and where the two mountain masses came together a small stream flowed into this lake, over which the ice that tumbled into the valley made a crystal arch.

"Where will that bring us?" Clement asked, with horror.

"To the head of the stream," replied Sanga-moarta. "It has made its way through the ice and if we follow its track we shall reach the place we seek."

"But how shall we get there? This wall of rock is as smooth as glass, one slip and there is nothing between us and the bottom of the lake."

"You must take care, that is all. You will have to lie down on your back and slip down sidewise. Now and then you will find a bush of Alpine roses that you can cling to; but there is no danger of slipping if you are barefoot,—follow my example."

A blood-curdling pleasure awaited them. The men took off their shoes and clung firmly with hands and feet to the smooth wall of stone. They had gone barely half way when there was a mysterious sound from the opposite mountains; it seemed as if the rocks beneath them trembled.

"Stay where you are," shouted Sanga-moarta to the others. "There is a snow-slide."

And the next moment could be seen the white ball set in motion in the remote mountains, rolling down the steep heights, tearing along with it rocks and uprooted trees, growing every instant more terrible; and as it made great bounds to the valley it shook the mountain to its very foundations.

"Oh my God!" cried Clement, trying to reach the guide with one hand while he clung to the rock with the other. "It will come and kill us all."

"Stay where you are," Sanga-moarta called out to them, when he saw that they were trying to climb up and would so expose themselves to the danger of slipping back. "This slide is going toward that rock and there it will be either broken or held fast."

It was true that the snow-slide, now grown to mammoth size, was rolling toward a jutting cliff that seemed dwarf-like in comparison. The roll of the avalanche had grown so loud that every other sound was lost in its thundering roar. Now the snow plunged against the rock in its path, struck its peak with a fearful bound and gave the whole mountain such a shock that it quivered to its foundations. For a moment the entire vicinity was covered with a cloud of snow flying with the velocity of steam. After the last clap, the thunder ceased. Then followed a frightful cracking. The avalanche had torn the opposing rock from its base and the two plunged down into the lake below them. This, lashed to foam, engulfed the mass and its waves, mounting fearfully, rose to the height of fifty fathoms, where the bold climbers were clinging to the face of the rock. Then the waves settled back, for a few moments took the form of a towering green column which finally subsided, and after some time quiet again ruled over the waters.

Clement lay there more dead than alive, while Sanga-moarta's first look was to see if the bed of the stream had been overflowed by the war of the waters. But the mass of snow had plunged into the lake without raising it a foot; all had disappeared in the bottomless depths; a mountain lake neither rises nor falls.

"Let us go on our way," said Sanga-moarta. "It will be all the easier now that the rock is wet, to climb down."

In the course of half an hour they had reached the mouth of the stream. A wonderful passage opened before them. The stream had its source in a warm spring, which following the course of the valley, was buried under mountains and ava-lanches. The warm water had hollowed out a covered passage, so melting the ice that only its outer surface remained frozen, and this was con-stantly added to by the influence of the atmos-phere, while within it was as constantly melted by the warmth of the spring; the result was that

the stream flowed under a crystal archway with
glittering icicles. Into this passage Sanga-moarta
led his companions. Clement could only think
of the magic palaces in fairy tales, where the enchanted mortal got the sunlight through transparent water. As they were wading along the
stream at one point the underground passage
suddenly grew dark. Heavy masses took the
place of the transparent vaulting. The crusting
of ice was thicker; it changed to dark blue, and
to black; the noise of the waters was the only
guide. The men, up to their knees in the water,
found it growing warmer and warmer until finally they heard a hissing, and through a cleft
in the rock caught sight of the sunlight once
more. At the source of the spring, as they clung
to some bushes to resist the force of the boiling
waters, they found themselves in a deep, well-like
valley.

"We are in the Gregyina-Drakuluj."

It is a round valley with mountains rising
about it several hundred feet high. If you would
look down from their summits you must crawl
on your stomach to the edge of the cliff, and then
unless you have strong nerves you will fall from
the dizzying height. In this valley-bed below
the flowers are always in bloom ; in the sternest
winter season here you can find those dark green
plants with broad indented leaves; those small
round-leaved trees that are nowhere else in the

country. The yellow cups of the leather-leaved water-lilies open just at this time. The place is covered, summer and winter, with freshest green; the wild laurel climbs high in the crevices of the rocks and throws its red berries down into the valley, while all around is cold and dead.

The whole winter through the valley is covered with the rarest flowers. That is why the Walla- chian calls it the Devil's garden, and is afraid to go near it. Yet the miracle has a purely natural cause. In a hole in the depth of the valley is a hot mineral spring that never comes to light, but warms through the earth above; and, as warm waters have their own peculiar flora, these strange plants flourish there beside their quickening ele- ment. The whole place is like a greenhouse in the open air amid storms and ice mountains.

Sanga-moarta beckoned silently to his com- rades to follow him. A feverish unrest was noticeable throughout his whole being. After a few steps he pointed with trembling hand to a dark hollow where there was an iron door.

" What is that ? " cried Clement, reaching for his sword. " Is this hollow inhabited ? "

" Yes," replied Sange-moarta, with blood evi- dently on fire and his temples swollen to burst- ing. " There in that pool she bathes ; here I have listened day after day, but have not had the courage to go near." He stammered in scarcely audible words though they were passionate.

"Who?" asked the Lieutenant, perplexed.

"The fairy," stammered the Wallachian, with quivering lips, and buried his burning lips in his hands.

"What kind of a fairy?" said Clement, turning to Zulfikar. "I am looking for a panther."

"Hush, there is the sound of a key in the door," said Zulfikar, "step back."

The two men had to pull Sanga-moarta from the door. This opened noiselessly and a woman stepped forth leading a panther by a spiked collar of gold. Sanga-moarta had good cause to call her a fairy. A magnificent woman stood there in delicate Oriental garb. The long gold tassel of her red fez fell down over her white turban; above her ermine-embroidered caftan gleamed her ivory white shoulders; her movements were sinuous and bewitching. The three men held their breath while the woman passed by without noticing them.

"Ha, there she is!" whispered Zulfikar, when she had passed.

"Who is she? So you know her," said Clement.

"Azraele, once the favorite of Corsar Bey."

"Where are we then?"

"Be still, or she will hear us."

Meantime the woman had reached the pool, seated herself on a stone bench and loosed her turban. The dark curls fell down over her shoulders.

Sanga-moarta's hot panting was heard in the darkness. The panther lay quietly at the feet of his mistress, his wise head resting on his forepaws. Azraele now took her gay Persian shawl from her waist and made ready to lay aside her caftan. But first she made a few steps toward the cliff, which shut her off from the sight of the men. Sanga-moarta was ready to plunge after her.

"You are crazy," said Zulfikar in his ear. "Are you going to betray us by your curiosity?"

"The boy is in love with the woman," whispered Clement.

At this instant a splash was heard in the water as if some one had jumped in and was playing in the waves. Sanga-moarta tore himself madly from the grasp of his comrades and ran with a wild cry down to the pool At this cry Azraele, in all her enchanting beauty, sprang out of the water, looked with flashing eyes at the bold man, and said to her panther,

"Oglan, seize him!"

Until then the panther had lain motionless, but the instant his mistress called him to a struggle he jumped up with a snarl, caught hold of the Wallachian, and with one movement drew him to the ground.

Sanga-moarta did not defend himself against

the beast, but stretched out his hands entreatingly to the charming woman, appeared to be
drawing in her beauty with his thirsty glance,
while he dragged himself with a groan to her
feet; Azraele gazed at him wildly, and, wrapped
in her cloak, watched her pet panther tear the
youth; for the beast was never drawn to any one
except for his death.

"I'll go to his help," said Clement, mad with
terror,—and drew his sword.

"Stop. Don't be foolish," said Zulfikar.
"There is something more sensible for us to do.
The iron door has been left open; let us slip in
while the lady is occupied and find out what
there is of interest here for our masters. If not
of interest to yours it certainly will be to mine."

With that the two men stole through the door-
way, groped their way along the narrow passage
that seemed to be hewn into the rock and at its
end discovered, by the light of a lamp hanging
from the ceiling, that there were several small
doors on both sides. They opened one door after
another and came to a room with no other door-
way. The light of the outer world came through
the window. Through this they hurried on and
coming to a second iron door, passed through and
found themselves in a large court surrounded by
high walls. By climbing the wall they saw from
its summit the vale of Szamos stretched below
them; and then they discovered a footpath lead-

ing from the wall into the forest below. Down
they ran breathlessly. There first the two men
dared look at each other. Clement thought he
still heard the wild, clear voice of the demon-
woman, the growl of the panther and death-cry
of the Wallachian.

"We have done well to take this path," said
Zulfikar. "For we never could have found our
way back without a guide over the way we
came. From here we shall easily make our
way."

They now found two woodcutters who were
fastening their rafts to the bank.

"What is this castle?" asked Clement.

"Where? What castle?"

Clement looked behind him to point out the
castle, and lo, there was nothing that could be
seen to resemble a castle even from afar. One
rock was like another. The peasants laughed
aloud.

"It is better not to say anything," said Zulfikar; "evidently they do not know what is in
this vicinity. From the outside there is nothing
to be seen but unhewn stone; the bushes cover
the very opening that we came through."

Then they asked their way; and turned back
to Marisel, where they did not stay to be questioned about Sanga-moarta's absence but mounted
their horses and rode off.

Zulfikar would have been glad if Clement

would have gone with him to Banfy-hunyad,
but when he learned that this place was under
the direction of Dionysius Banfy he started off
alone to collect the tax, although the Lieutenant
gave him the comforting assurance that he could
count on blows there more surely than on tribute.

*   *   *   *   *   *

Clement gave Ladislaus Csaki exact information of what he had seen and received as a reward for his discovery a hundred gold pieces,
with the green boots thrown in.

Zulfikar had a more unusual experience.
When he reached Nagy-Varad he gave Ali
Pasha the tax collected and told him what he
had learned of Azraele. Corsar Bey had stolen
her from Ali Pasha when she was thirteen years
old. Ali had offered two hundred gold pieces as
reward to the man who should bring him information of the abode of his favorite, so Zulfikar
came away with the purse of two hundred gold
pieces when he left the Pasha. The Aga over
Zulfikar learning of this, found a pretext to bind
the deserter and sentenced him to a hundred
blows on the soles of his feet unless he bought off
every blow with a ducat.

"That I will not do," replied Zulfikar, "but I
will put in your hands the present that Dionysius
Banfy sent Ali Pasha when I tried to impose a
tax in his name. You give this little box to the

Pasha and I wager that he will reward you with enough for your lifetime."

The Aga caught at the offer greedily, received the carefully sealed box which Zulfikar should have given over to the Pasha, and presented it with the following words:

"See, most gracious Pasha. Here I bring you that princely present which Dionysius Banfy sent you instead of the tax."

Ali Pasha took the box and when he had cut the string, broken the seal and raised the cover, there fell out on his caftan a dried-up grey pig's tail, the most fearful insult, the most horrible disgrace, a man can offer a Turk.

Ali Pasha jumped almost to the ceiling in his anger, threw his turban on the ground, and gave orders to have the Aga, who stood petrified, impaled that instant outside the gate.

Zulfikar walked off, his two hundred gold pieces intact.

CHAPTER XII

THERE was racing and running in the castle of Bonczida. Dionysius Banfy was expected back from Ebesfalva. The castle gate, which displayed a huge crest between the claws of a gilded lion, was overshadowed with green boughs and gay flags. On the street in a long line stood the school children, dressed in their Sunday clothes, with the teacher at their head. Farther back, with Sunday mien, stood the dependents, and in front of a hill were drawn up in orderly ranks the mounted nobility of the county of Klausenburg, about eight hundred men, noble, warlike figures, armed with broad swords and clubs. They had come to greet their superior officer, the general of the nobility. On the walls were Banfy's own warriors; about six hundred, in full armor, with long Turkish guns and with Scythian helmets. On the bastion toward Szamos were eight mortars, and several feet away burned a fire in which the cannoneers heated the ends of their long iron rods to use as a slow match. At every gate, at every door, stood two pages in scarlet cloaks and blue stockings, their entire costume adorned with silver lacings. At the window of the high tower was stationed a lookout to announce with the trumpet the arrival of the lord. The wind struggled above his head with a great purple banner, only swaying the heavy gold tassels that hung from it. From every window eager servants looked out. Lords and ladies appeared expectant. Only three windows were without gay groups. In their place were fragrant jasmine and quivering mimosa in beautiful porcelain jars, behind which one could just discern a pale, gentle woman, leaning on an embroidered cushion, in sentimental melancholy. This was Banfy's wife.

It might have been ten o'clock in the morning when the watcher on the tower inferred the arrival of the first carriages from the clouds of dust along the road and blew his trumpet mightily. The priests and teachers hurried to their pupils; the lieutenants brought their ranks into order and the trumpeters began to play their latest march. Soon came the carriages, attended by troops from the rest of the counties. Before and behind rode an armed throng in whose costume and equipment the greatest splendor of color was shown. The horses were of all kinds and colors: Arabian stallions, Transylvanian thoroughbreds, small Wallachian ponies, slender English racers and lightfooted horses from Barbary. There were horses with flesh-colored manes, with jeweled bridles, and with housings embroidered with butterflies, and in every color. There was, too, all the war equipment of days gone by: the slender Damascene, the spiked mace and those long, three-bladed daggers the points of which dragged on the ground. Each division carried the crest of its county on its gay standards. In front of the band rode the captain of the nobility, George Veer, a stout, muscular man of forty years.

The chief sat in a carriage drawn by five black horses; on both carriage doors was Banfy's crest in gilding. Behind were two hussars. Dionysius Banfy in proud dignity sat in splendor on the velvet cushions of his coach. All the magnificence displayed about him harmonized with his appearance.

The troops drawn up in line lowered their swords before him, the school children greeted him with songs, his vassals waved their hats, music sounded out along the walls, the priests made speeches and the guests in the windows waved their handkerchiefs and caps.

Banfy received all these marks of honor with accustomed dignity and noble nonchalance, like a man who feels that it is all his due. His eyes wandered to the three windows of jasmine and mimosa and his expression grew serious as he saw no one there.

From another window looked down an old man in a long soutane-like coat; but his bearing did not indicate that he took part in the general homage. At his side was a lady in mourning, on whose countenance were unmistakable signs of anger and contempt; and at a window below them stood Stephen Nalaczy with crossed arms, watching the whole procession with a scornful smile.

"Was there ever a Prince with so much splendor as this single baron?" said the lady in mourning to the old man. "I have been present at a coronation, an installation, an inauguration and a triumphal procession, but never before have I seen such a stir made over a single man. If it were a Prince it might pass, but what is this Banfy?—a nobleman like ourselves, with this difference only that he advances arrogantly and knows how to make pretensions; yet this princely splendor is not appropriate for him. I know the proper thing, for I have carried on lawsuits with greater lords than my Lord Banfy."

"Just see how my colleagues crowd forward to kiss his hand," muttered Koncz, to himself. "My learned companion, Csefalusi, takes pleasure in being allowed to assist his Grace from the carriage; well may he, for Dionysius Banfy is a great patron of the Calvinists; for a poor Unitarian clergyman like me a place behind the door is quite good enough."

"Just see—do see—how they carry him on their shoulders to the gate! It is a good thing they do not carry him in a chair the way they do princes;—as if he were their lord because he is serving them to-day!"

"Let the people do him homage," said Nalaczy; "my men will provide salt for the entertainment. He will get his comb cut!"

Meanwhile Banfy had mounted the stairs, the people crowding in at the same time to deposit their load at the end of the hall. In the surging throng the clergy succeeded in maintaining their places only with great difficulty, being knocked about by the godless crowd without mercy, while George Veer forced his way to the overlord with many a thrust of his elbow. As many of the nobility crowded into the hall as it could contain; the rest filled the corridors. The dependents remained in the courtyard and, although they caught only the noise, took great satisfaction in that.

"My noble friends," said Banfy, after it had become somewhat quiet and he had allowed his glance to run over the throng;—"it is not without cause that I wish to see you before me in arms. The history of our poor fatherland is familiar to you, how much our nation has suffered because our princes, either dissatisfied with what they already possessed or else incapable of maintaining it, have persistently called foreign troops into the country. Of these days of contest the historians have described only what was to the credit of the princes, the victories, the battles; they have forgotten to mention that in the year 1617 as a result of the misery caused by the war throughout all Transylvania not a single child was born, but we know it, for we felt it with the people. Now, thanks to Heaven, we are masters in our native land. By the peace of Saint Gotthard both the Roman Emperor and the Turkish have alike agreed not to send any more of their troops into Transylvania, and have put such a restraint upon each other that they have assured us some respite, so that we are not compelled either to take up arms against the one or for the other, but can give our energies to healing the wounds of our fatherland that have bled for a century. For a Golden Age is dawning. The entire land struggles and bleeds; we alone enjoy peace; in our country only is the Hungarian master independent. It is true the country is not large, but it belongs to us, and even if we are a small people we recognize no greater ones over us. But now there are people who would shorten the Golden Age: there are people who do not concern themselves with the cost to the country of a war unwisely begun, if only their ambition, if only their greed, be fattened. And if by chance their opponent conquers they will not be ruined with their fatherland, but will simply turn their coat, join the conqueror and share with him the booty."

"That's a slander!" was hissed from the rear, in a voice that Banfy recognized as Nalaczy's.

The crowd turned threateningly toward the corner from which the voice had come.

"Let him alone, my friends," said Banfy. "Very likely it is some satellite of Michael Teleki's. He too shall have the advantage of freedom of speech. But I, who know the swift mode of thought of the states throughout the country, I can tell you quietly that this rash step will never be taken in lawful fashion. But should secret stratagems, or unforeseen violence attempt to accomplish what would not succeed in open attack, they will find me on the spot. If necessary I will defend the country even against the Prince. Hear now what the intriguers have planned in order to entangle us against our will in snares out of which we have escaped. In spite of the peace, Turks and Tartars at times fall upon our borders, plunder the people, set the towns on fire,—in short, in every possible way obtrude upon us their friendship. A week ago they laid waste Schassburg and before that they made raids in the vicinity of Csik. But that is not my affair. That concerns the Saxon magistrate and the general of the Szeklers. The mouth of his majesty, Ali Pasha, has for a long time been watering for my province but he is not yet quite sure of the way to catch me. Lately he had the circuit Lieutenant of the Prince caught by Tartars and forced him to declare throughout the entire neighborhood that the people were to pay a new tax, a penny a head. The poor peasantry were delighted to get off so cheaply and made haste to pay the tax, without asking me first whether this could be justly levied. In this way the sly Turk accomplished a twofold purpose; in the first place he had compelled the people to recognize the tax, and in the second place he had found out how many taxpayers there were; then he at once imposed the frightful tax of two Hungarian florins a head."

The crowd expressed their indignation.

"At once I forbade all further payments. It is true this tax was not a burden to us, for we are of the nobility, but for that very reason are we the lords of the peasantry that we may not allow them to be robbed of their last farthing. Instead of any reply I sent his Turkish majesty a pig's tail in a box, and if he comes himself to collect the tax I swear by the God in heaven to receive him in such a way that he will remember it all his life."

"We will cut him to pieces," threatened the crowd, clashing their swords and swinging their clubs in the air.

"Now, my faithful followers, go to your tents," said Banfy. "The master of the kitchen will look out for your entertainment. I will decide whether there shall be war."

The excited nobility withdrew amid lively expressions of approval and the clinking of swords.
Only a few with requests to make, remained behind. The Professors from Klausenburg invited
their patron to the public examinations. Banfy
promised to come, and offered prizes for the best
pupils. When they had withdrawn he indicated
those whom he would see in turn. In the first
place he motioned to him Martin Koncz, leader
of the Unitarians in Klausenburg.

"How can I serve you, worthy sir?"

"I have a complaint to bring before you, gracious lord," replied Koncz, bowing and scraping.
"The city council of Klausenburg has taken by violence the market booths belonging to the Unitarian church. I beg you to assist in their recovery."

"I regret, worthy sir, that I cannot help you
in this case," replied Banfy, as he fastened up his
coat. "That is a privilege by establishment
and concerns the Prince. It is true the territory
is mine but the affairs must come up before him
for judgment."

"This is the reply that the Prince made me,
only reversed: 'It is true the decision in the
matter is mine, but the territory is Banfy's, and
you must go to him.'"

Banfy smiled good-naturedly, but Koncz did
not find the affair so entertaining.

"Listen, there is no way for me to turn, even
though justice is most clearly on my side."

Banfy shrugged his shoulders.

"You would like to have justice, worthy sir, but that can hardly be attained."

"Then he is as badly off as I am," cried a voice, and as Banfy looked, he saw Madame Szent-Pali coming toward him. The great lord acted as if he had not noticed the widow and fingered indifferently the diamond clasp of his cloak; but the widow placed herself directly in front of him and began to speak:

"Your Grace has been pleased to look beyond me, but it is in vain. I am here, even though unbidden."

Banfy looked at her without a word, half smiling and half amused.

"Or has your Grace perhaps forgotten my name?" asked the woman, sharply, and smiting her breast. "I am the noble, well-born"—

"And knightly," said Banfy, completing her words with a laugh.

"I am the widow of George Szent-Pali," continued the lady, without allowing herself to be disconcerted,—"whose family in all its branches is quite as noble as is the Prince himself, and that too since the beginning of the world. I have never forgotten my name when asked, and have already stood in the presence of princes and generals greater even than your Grace."

"Well, well, gracious lady, I know that already, I have heard it so often. Tell me quickly now anything good that you may have to say."

"Quickly! I suppose your Grace thinks that a few words will set forth what has been a law-suit between us now for four years, and between the town and my family for sixty-three."

"To cut it short I will tell you the story," interrupted Banfy. "The gracious lady may then make her additions. The gracious lady owns a dilapidated little house in the centre of the Klausenburg market place"—

"The idea! A manor house just as good as your Grace's castle!"

"These barracks have for a long time disfigured the market place. It was in vain the city council entered into negotiations with your family —went before the courts to buy the house and move it off."

"We did not yield. You are quite right. A true nobleman does not sell his property gained by heritage. It belongs to me and within my four walls neither country nor Prince has any authority over me—not even you, General!"

"I certainly did not demand this noble ruin of you for nothing. I offered you ten thousand florins for it. For that sum of money I could have bought the entire gypsy quarter, and yet there is not a single house in it so dilapidated as yours."

"Let my lord keep his money. I do not give

up my house. Two hundred years ago an an-
cestor of mine built it. Cease, I beg, your
scornful words. I was born there; my father
and my mother were buried from there. If it
offends your Grace's sense of beauty to look
down from your magnificent palace upon the
roof of my poor house, yet it does me good to
be able to live out my days in the room in which
my poor husband breathed away his life, and I
would not accept any palace in exchange."

At the mention of her dear departed husband
the lady began to sob; this gave Banfy an opportunity to speak, and he took advantage to reply vehemently:

"As I have said, so shall it be. The masons
are already on the way to tear down your house.
You will receive your ten thousand florins at the
public treasury."

"I do not wish them. Throw them to your
dogs!" screamed the lady, in a passion. "I am
no peasant woman to be hunted from my property. I advise nobody to enter my courtyard
unless he wishes to be driven out with a broom
like a dog. I have been to the Prince, I have
been to the Diet, and here you have an official
document in which the Diet forbids anybody to
trespass on my land. I will nail it to the gate,
it is good legible handwriting, then I will see
who dares force his way into my possessions."

"And I tell you that to-morrow your house

shall be moved off, even if it is surrounded by armed troops. If the Diet pleases it may have the place rebuilt."

With that Banfy was going away full of anger, when Nalaczy met him. The two men greeted each other with forced friendliness, and while Madame Szent-Pali moved away uttering imprecations, Nalaczy began in sweet tones, after a little preparation,

"His Highness, the Prince, wishes to inform your Grace of a very unpleasant incident."

"I will hear."

"During this year the Turk has already forced from us, under one pretext or another, presents on three different occasions."

"He ought not to be allowed to force them."

"If we refuse him he threatens to force on us as Prince the fugitive, Nicholas Zolyomi, living at Constantinople."

"He has only to bring him here and we will drive him out at once, together with his protector."

"Quite true. But the Prince is so wearied of this bitter hatred that he has decided, partly out of fright too, to pardon Zolyomi and permit him to return."

"Let him do so, in God's name."

"Right, quite right. But your Grace certainly knows that the estates of Zolyomi are at present in the possession of your Grace. The Prince, therefore, finds himself compelled to demand of your Grace that you should with all good feeling give over these estates to Zolyomi on his return."

"What!" cried Banfy, stepping back. "And you think that I will give up these estates! The Diet gave them over to me with the burdensome condition that I should equip two regiments for the defence of the country. This burdensome condition I have complied with, and do you think that now I will give up these estates that you may have one more fool in the country?"

"But if it is the Prince's wish?"

"It matters not who wishes it, I will not give them back."

"And shall I carry back this answer?"

"This unmistakable answer," replied Banfy, accenting every syllable. "I do not give them up."

"Your most humble servant," said Nalaczy, bowed mockingly, and withdrew.

"Slave!" Banfy threw after him contemptuously. Then he looked out into the corridor and seeing some of his dependents waiting there hat in hand, he shouted: "Come in, what do you want?"

When the simple folk saw that their over-lord was in a bad humor they hesitated to enter until the castle steward pushed them in.

"We ought to have brought the tithe," began the oldest peasant, with eyes downcast and in

tearful voice, "but we really could not. It was
not possible."

"Why could you not?" said Banfy, harshly.

"Because we have nothing, gracious lord,—the
rain has failed, crops have gone to ruin, we have
not harvested enough corn for the sowing; the
people in the village are living on roots and
mushrooms, so long as they last. After that God
knows what will become of them!"

"There it is," said Banfy. "A new blow of
fortune and we are still longing for war. Here,
steward, you must have the storehouses opened
at once and furnish grain for sowing; and the
poor must be provided with sufficient food for
the winter."

The poor peasant wanted to kiss Banfy's hand
but he would not allow it. The tears stood in
his eyes.

"That is what I am your master for—to
lighten your fate if I see you in need. My
agents will carry out my orders; if my own
granaries become empty they must order grain
for you from Moldavia for cash," and with that
he went away.

* * * * * *

Banfy's wife listened with throbbing heart as
the familiar footsteps came nearer. There she
sat among the fragrant jasmine and quivering
mimosa, as tremulous as the mimosa and as pale

as the jasmine. Everything about her shone
with splendor. On the walls hung polished Venetian mirrors in gold frames, portraits of kings
and princes, the most beautiful of which was
John Kemény's, painted when he was still at-
tached to the Turk, with smooth shaven hair
and a long beard, at that time quite fashionable
with Hungarian gentlemen. On one side of the
room was an artistic cabinet with countless
drawers, inlaid with mother-of-pearl, lapis lazuli
and tortoise-shell. In the middle of the room
stood a beautifully painted table with wonderfully wrought silver candelabra; in glass cases
the family jewels were displayed to view, beak-
ers covered with precious stones; stags enameled
in gold, their heads made to unscrew; several
large silver baskets of flowers, marvels of filagree
work, hardly worth a dollar in weight; the bou-
quets in these baskets were of various-colored
jewels; a gold butterfly alighted on an emerald
leaf, so cunningly made that everything gleamed
through its wings as it swayed gracefully. From
the high windows heavy red silk curtains hung
down to the ground and the sills were covered
with the most beautiful flowers of those times.
Amid all these flowers only the quivering mimosa and the pale jasmine seemed suited to the
lady, so melancholy a contrast did her face make
to the splendor of her house.

The delicate little figure was almost lost in the

high-vaulted room, in which she could with difficulty move one of the heavy armchairs or lift one of the huge candelabra or push aside a hanging. Every noise, every footstep set her nerves quivering. When the familiar step touched her threshold all the blood streamed into her face. She wanted to jump up to meet him but after the door opened she turned pale again and was unable to rise from her seat. Banfy hurried toward his trembling wife whose voice was too stifled for words, clasped both her hands, delicate as dewdrops, and looked kindly into the dreamy eyes.

"How beautiful you are, and yet how sad!"

The lady tried to smile.

"This smile even is melancholy," said Banfy, gently, and put his arm around his fairy wife.

Madame Banfy drew close to her husband, put her arms around his neck, drew his face down to hers and kissed it.

"This very kiss is sorrowful!"

She turned away to hide her tears.

"What is the matter with you?" Banfy asked, and smoothed her brow. "What has happened to you? why are you so pale? what is the matter?"

"What is the matter with me?" replied Madame Banfy, raising her eyes full of tears and sighing deeply; then she dried her eyes, put her arm in her husband's and led him to her flowers as if to turn the conversation. "Just see this poor passionflower, how faded it is; yet it is planted in a porcelain vase and I water it daily with distilled water. Once I forgot to raise the curtains, and just see how the poor thing is faded. It lacks nothing except sunlight."

"Ah," whispered Banfy in subdued voice. "It seems we speak with each other in the language of the flowers."

"What is the matter with me?" said Madame Banfy with a sob, as she clung to her husband's neck;—"my sunlight is wanting—your love!"

Banfy felt himself unpleasantly affected. He sat down beside his wife, drew her gently toward him and asked in the most friendly, though excited voice,

"Do I not know how to express this to you as well as formerly?"

"Oh yes, but I see you so rarely. You have been away now nearly six weeks, and I could not be with you."

"Wife, are you ambitious? would you shine at the Prince's court? Believe me your court is more splendid than his and not nearly so dangerous."

"Oh, you know that I do not seek splendor nor fear danger. When you were banished, when a little hut sheltered us and often only a tent covered us in the snow, then you would lay my head on your breast, cover me with your cloak

—and I was so happy! Often noise of battle and thunder of cannon would frighten sleep from our eyes and yet I was so happy! You would mount your horse while I sank down in prayer, and when you came back covered with blood and dust, how happy I was!"

"Heaven grant that you may be so again. But there is a fortune that stands higher than that of family life. There are times when your mere glance would hinder me—would stand in my way"—

"Yes, I know them. Gay adventures, beautiful women—am I not right?" said Madame Banfy in a jesting tone, but perhaps not without significance in the background.

"Certainly!" said Banfy, springing hastily from his chair. "I was thinking of the fatherland." With that he paced angrily the length of the room.

When a husband falls into a rage over such a jest it is a sign that he feels himself hit. With smoothed brow Banfy stood before his trembling wife, who in the few moments since her husband had entered the room had been a prey to the most varied feelings; joy and sorrow, fear and anger, love and jealousy struggled in her excited bosom.

"Margaret," he began, in a dull voice, "you are jealous, and jealousy is the first step toward hatred."

234 The Golden Age in Transylvania

"Then hate me, rather than forget me!" said his wife, bursting out vehemently, and then regretting it at once.

"What then do you wish of me? have you any ground for your suspicions? You certainly do not wish me to give you an account of the roads I have taken and the people I have spoken with, like the simpleton Giola Bertai, who when he goes away from home takes a diary with him and makes out a report of every hour for his other half. Neither do I keep you under lock and key the way Abraham Thoroczkai does his wife. He has a lock put on his wife's room during his entire absence and when he returns requires the whole village to give an oath that his wife has not spoken with any one in the interval."

Madame Banfy laughed, but the laugh ended in a sigh.

"You evade the question with a jest. I do not accuse you, I do not keep watch of you, and if you should deceive me I should never find it out. But listen; there is in the heart of woman a something, a certain distressing feeling which causes pain without one's knowing why, which knows how to give information whether the love of one who is our all is coming or going, without being able to support itself by reasons. I do not know, and I will not learn where you spend your time, but this I do know, that you stay away a long while at a time and do not make haste to

come home. Banfy, I suffer—suffer more than
you can imagine."

" Madame," said Banfy, looking at her coldly as
he stood before her ; " in this country a suit for
divorce does not require much time."

Madame Banfy fell back in her chair, clasped
her hands over her heart in terror and struggled
for breath. A trembling cry broke from her
lips and they did not close again. It was as if
some one had cut the strings of her heart with a
sword. Half-fainting she stared at her husband
as if doubting whether his words could have been
in earnest or whether she ought not to take
them for a horrible jest.

" You are unhappy," Banfy went on, " and I
cannot help you. You love to dream and I do
not understand you in the least. Possibly my
soul does hurt yours, but it is unintentional. It
is a fact that your feelings hurt mine and that I
will not endure. I recognize no tyrant over me,
not even in love. I will not be importuned even
with tears. Let us tear our hearts apart. Better
for us to do it now while they would still bleed,
than to wait until they fall apart naturally.
Better for us to separate now while we love each
other, than to wait until we come to hatred."

During this terrible speech the lady struggled,
gasping for breath, as if some dread phantom
oppressed her heart and robbed her of speech,

until at last her passion made its way by force
and she uttered the piercing cry :

" Banfy, you have killed me ! "

Her voice, the expression of her face, seemed
to make Banfy tremble ; and though he was
already on the point of leaving the room in
haste, he stopped half-way and looked once more
at his wife. He did not notice at this moment
that the door had opened and that some one had
entered. He saw only that in the face of his
wife, so ravaged with despair, there came suddenly an indescribably distressed smile ; this
forced smile on her agonized features was something terrible. Banfy thought his wife was
losing her mind. But Madame Banfy rose, bustling from her seat and cried out,

" Anna, my dear sister," and rushed to the
door.

Then for the first time Banfy turned toward
the door and saw Anna Bornemissa, wife of
Michael Apafi.

This keen-eyed woman had not failed to take
in the situation in which she had surprised these
married people, although they knew well how to
assume a calm air in an instant ; but she acted
as if she had noticed nothing. She drew Margaret to her breast and extended her hand to
Banfy in the most friendly fashion. Her sister
had not yet fully recovered.

" I heard your voices outside," said Madame

Apafi, "and that is why I came here without being announced."

"Oh yes, we were laughing," said Madame Banfy, and made haste to dry her tears with her handkerchief.

"To what circumstances are we indebted for this extraordinary good fortune?" asked Banfy, hiding his confusion behind rare courtesy.

"As you did not bring my sister to me," began Madame Apafi with smiling reproach, "I came on a visit to my poor relative exiled to Hungary."

Banfy felt the sting under these last words and said as he stroked his beard:

"Here my lovely sister-in-law can do with me what she pleases. She can use me as the target of her wit and overthrow me with her jests. Before the Prince's throne, in the national hall, we face each other as foes. Here on the contrary you are my ruler. Here I am nothing except your most loyal subject, who does homage to your grace and is beside himself with joy that he may have you as a guest."

While he was saying this Banfy threw his arms around the dignified Madame Apafi with familiarity. Not without significance he added turning to his wife, "It is to be hoped that you will not be jealous of Anna."

Madame Apafi took it upon herself to answer in Margaret's place.

"I am more inclined to think that you cannot trust yourself to me"

"If you were my wife that might be so. And that came very near being the state of affairs; there was a time when I wanted to marry you."

"But it did not advance beyond the beginning," replied the Princess with a laugh.

"We recognized each other soon," continued Banfy. "Two such heads as ours would have been too much for one house; there is not even room for them both in one country. We both like to rule and we should have been well sold if we had been obliged to obey each other. It is better as it is; we have both found our corresponding halves; you, Apafi; and I, Margaret; and we are both happy."

With these words Banfy kissed his wife's hand tenderly, which she acknowledged with equal tenderness, and then he left the two sisters alone. Anna with sweet seriousness laid her hand on her sister's, who looked up to her with a smile, like an innocent child to her good genius.

"You have been crying," began Madame Apafi. "It is of no use for you to assume the appearance of good spirits."

"I have not been crying," replied Margaret, asserting her assumed calm with astonishing strength of mind.

"Very well, I am glad that you hide it. It shows that you love him; and if ever you needed to love your husband, to watch over and protect him, it is now."

"Your words bewilder me. You seem to have something extraordinary to say."

"You must have wondered already at my coming here. You can well understand that I have not come without a reason. We have both of us one person to fear, in like degree, and of whom we must be jealous; and if we do not understand each other one of us may lose an individual dear to her."

"Speak, oh speak!" replied Madame Banfy, and drew her sister down to her on a sofa in a corner of the room.

"Our husbands have hated each other from the first. They were always of opposite opinions, in different parties, and had become accustomed to consider each other as foes. Woe to us if this hatred should come to open battle and we should see our dear ones fall at each other's hands."

"I can assure you positively that Banfy cherishes no unfriendly intentions toward your husband."

"I am not afraid of Apafi's overthrow, but of your husband's. The throne to which he was called by force has worked a great change in Apafi. I notice with astonishment that he is beginning to be jealous of his power. Already at Neuhäusel he expressed himself in the presence of the Grand Vizier as disturbed because Gabriel

Haller had aspirations toward the Prince's crown; in consequence of which the Vizier had poor Haller beheaded at once without my husband's knowledge. Even now Apafi recalls the message which your husband once had sent to him, that in a short time he would tear his green velvet cloak from off his shoulders."

"Oh my God, what must I fear!"

"Nothing so long as I have not lost my husband's favor. While others sleep I am awake at my husband's side and keep watch for the manifestations of his feelings; and God has given me the strength to be able to struggle against monsters who would drown in blood the memory of his rule. In spite of all this, now and then there appears in my husband a condition of mind when my influence loses all its magic, when he steps out of his own nature and his gentleness turns to a brutality demanding action. Then his eyes, which at other times overflow with tears at the death of a servant, become bloodshot and seem eager for murder; he who at other times is so cautious, then becomes hasty. And this condition, I blush to acknowledge to you, is drunkenness. I do not bring it up against him as a complaint, the man we love has no faults for us, we forgive him everything"—

"With one exception—his infidelity."

"That too—that too," the Princess made haste

to add. "When his life is at stake we must for-give that too."

"Oh, Anna," said Margaret, in distress, "you leave me to suspect mysteries that you do not re-veal."

"What you must learn, you shall. A little time since, your husband with proud recklessness set himself against a mighty party which joined with kings against kings. It may be said that your husband intends to thwart fate. He is proud enough not to take into consideration the peril which he has raised up against himself in this way. Or perhaps he thinks that those who are whetting their weapons against a ruling king would defer an instant if one of your people should show his face against them. Banfy has insulted, mocked and threatened the men, and tangled the threads in their fine-spun plans; in fact he has insulted both them and the Prince face to face, and that too in the presence of each other."

Madame Banfy folded her hands timidly.

"I see the storm that is gathering over Banfy's head."

"In his drunkenness Apafi has let fall allusions in my presence that have filled my soul with ter-ror, and for the sake of others I am not willing that Apafi's hand should be the one to strike him. On all sides they are going to seek occa-sions of quarrel with him. I will exert myself to keep off the blow, but if it must fall you shall ward it from him. We two must keep the love of our husbands to the uttermost that we may be able in this spiritual power to throw ourselves between them if they should attack each other. Think how terrible it would be if one should fall by the hand of the other, and one of us should have caused the other's mourning!"

"What shall I do? Oh my God, what can I do, where does my strength lie?"

"Your strength? In love, watchfulness and self-sacrifice," replied Madame Apafi, striving by her own strong soul to fill her weak sister's with courage.

The fate of two men was in that moment given over into the hands of two angels: and the fate of these two men was one with the destiny of Transylvania.

CHAPTER XIII

THE NIGHT

WHEN Dionysius Banfy left his wife's room and went down the back stairway to the hall of the ground floor, he saw a young rider bound into the courtyard. The rider was covered with dust and foam; when he sprang from his horse, the tired beast lay down. The rider asked hastily for Banfy, who recognized in him Gabriel Burkö, and went to him with the question:

"What's the matter?"

"My lord," began the exhausted rider, recovering his breath, "Ali Pasha has attacked Banfy-Hunyad."

"Very good," said Banfy, who appeared to take pleasure in the fact that fate offered his agitated soul something to crush. "Call George Veer," he shouted to his men. "And do you tell me, as soon as you have your breath, just what has happened."

"I must be quick, my lord, I have come out of the midst of the fight. A troop of Kurdish raiders came to Banfy-Hunyad yesterday. Your Grace's captain, Gregory Sötar, suspecting that they had come to plunder, marched against them with the hussars of the castle, engaged in conflict with them and after a short struggle drove them from the walls. Not content with that, however, he gave the signal for an attack and pursued the retreating troops in the direction of Zeutelke. While the Kurds were fleeing before us we saw ourselves suddenly attacked on the flank. In a trice the entire open space was covered with Turkish riders, who crowded upon us like a heap of ants. I cannot give their number definitely but this much I know;—three horse tails were visible in their midst, and that means that there is a Pasha in the army. Sötar could no longer make his retreat to Hunyad."

"The Devil!" interrupted Banfy.

"Every one of us had to encounter two or three. Sötar himself took his spiked club in one hand and his sword in the other and shouted to me as I came near: 'My son, leave the battle-field, force your way through, hurry to Bonczida and tell the news.' What more he said I did not hear, for the struggling masses separated us. With that I threw my shield over my back, laid my head on my horse's neck, used my spurs and galloped off the battlefield. A hundred horse-men hurried after to catch me; the arrows fell like hailstones on my shield; but my clever horse took in the danger, doubled his speed and so the pursuers lost me."

"You come straight from Bonczida?"

"I could not resist, gracious lord, making a

détour to Banfy-Hunyad to inform the people there of their peril so they might flee to the mountains in time."

"That was wise on your part. So the inhabitants have taken to flight."

"Far from it. Directly in front of Madame Vizaknai's gate I told the people the frightful news. Their faces turned pale, then suddenly the lady of the house came out with drawn sword and stood in the midst of the people with flashing eyes, as if she had the spirit of a hundred men, and she said to them: 'Are you men! If you are, seize your weapons. Go upon the walls and know how to defend the place where your children live and your fathers are buried. But if you are cowards, then take to flight. The women will stay behind with me and show the furious foe that when it is a matter of fighting for hearth and home nobody is too weak.'"

Banfy called out to his squire in a hoarse voice to bring him his shield, lance and helmet, and motioned to the panting messenger to go on with his story.

"At these words, there was a cry of rage among the people. The women ran for arms like so many furies and by the side of their husbands who were changed into heroes by the decision of their wives, they mounted the walls. Everybody took what he could find, scythes, shovels or flails. Madame Vizaknai was everywhere at once; gave orders, encouraged the fighters, had the church barricaded, oil and brimstone boiled and the bridges torn down, so that when I rode out of the town it was already in a state of defence. I swam the Körös, to avoid that long way, and came through the forests and bypaths."

By the end of this story, Banfy seemed to be beside himself. He did not wait for armor or helmet, shouted for a horse and as he mounted, called back to Veer;— "Follow me to Banfy-Hunyad. Let the foot soldiers ascend Mount Gyalu by a détour; the horsemen may follow me to Klausenburg. When you are near, light fires on the mountains that I may make an attack on the enemy at once with the van of the cavalry."

"Would it not be better for your Excellency to stay with the main army?" said Veer, anxiously.

"Do as I bid you," said Banfy, and giving spur to his horse he bounded off. Ten to twenty horsemen joined him.

"What does he mean," said Veer, "that he neither waits for us, nor tells his wife nor the Princess, who is a guest here?"

"When I informed him that Madame Vizaknai was defending Banfy-Hunyad he was dismayed," said Burkö, by way of explanation. "She is a youthful love of his whom he forgot in later life, but now that he hears of her bravery the old love seems to have sprung up again."

George Veer was quite content with this explanation, ordered his troops to mount at once and rode off, first giving orders to inform Madame Banfy of a trifling engagement with the troops at Klausenburg. The command of the infantry he intrusted to Captain Michael Angyal, who did not set out until evening, for the way to the snow mountains was a shorter one.

*   *   *   *   *   *

When George Veer reached Klausenburg he did not find Banfy there; the general had gone on an hour before with two hundred horse. Veer ordered his troops not to halt long and followed after Banfy, but could not overtake him. He kept ahead all the way, sometimes several hours' march. It was already late at night when Banfy with his two hundred riders reached the point where the Körös cuts its way through the wooded valley. At the bridge the Turks had encamped. The Bedouins lay there with their long weapons, on the watch. It was not possible to take them by surprise. In the direction of Banfy-Hunyad there was a glow on the heavens, sometimes sinking, sometimes mounting high again. Banfy left his men in concealment on the further bank, while he himself, attended by only four men went down to the river to find a ford. The Körös is here so furious that it sweeps the horseman from his horse; but fortunately, on ac-

count of the drought of the hot summer, it had
so fallen that Banfy soon found a place where it
flowed quietly, and waded through with his comrades. Then he sent one of them back to bring
the rest, but he himself remained gazing fixedly
in the direction where the fire was in sight.

Meantime, one of the six Bedouin horsemen on
guard noticed the three riders, and the leader
called out to them to stand. Banfy tried to retreat, but three Bedouins sprang on him from
behind and three more rushed toward him, lances
in rest.

"Bend down on your horses' necks and seize
your spear in your left hand," Banfy shouted to
his men, and drew his sword against the assailants; so in the darkness of the night they fell
upon one another silently. Banfy was in the middle. The lances of the three Bedouins whizzed
through the air at the same time. Banfy's
comrades fell on both sides from their horses,
while he with his left hand skilfully wrested the
lance from one of the guards and with the right
hand dealt him a blow that cleft his skull. When
Banfy saw that he was alone he turned at once
on his two foes and struck one down with his lance
and the other with his sword. Three more horsemen came furiously toward him from the bank.
"Come on," growled Banfy, with that grim
humor so characteristic of certain warriors in the
moment of danger. " I'll teach you how to

handle the spear," he added, with a smile;
shielded on the rear by a group of trees, he
thrust his sword into its sheath, grasped his spear
with both hands and within two minutes all three
lay stretched on the ground. Then he looked
round and saw with joy that the enemy at the
bridge were too far away to notice the fight, and
his two hundred horsemen were already at the
bank, and now crossed noiselessly. Some of the
Bedouins on the ground still groaned and
sighed.

"Knock their skulls in, so they will not betray
us by their noise."

"Shall we not wait for Veer's troops?" asked
the standard-bearer.

"We cannot, we have no time," said Banfy,
directing his glance toward the reddened horizon,
and the little band moved quietly across fields
and thickets. Soon there was the sound of a
distant roar and when they had reached the top
of a height before them Banfy-Hunyad came in
sight. The leader breathed more easily. It was
not the town that was on fire but only some hay-
ricks. The roofs of the houses had been taken
off by the inhabitants in advance, so that the
enemy could not set fire to them. Church and
bell-tower too were stripped of their roofs, and
one could see by the glare of the fire that they
were surrounded by the Turkish army, while
from the top of the tower brimstone and pitch

with heavy beams fell like a rain of fire on the
assailants and crowded them from the walls.

Ali Pasha had not waited for his artillery
which had been detained by the bad roads, because he thought he could take by storm in a
single attack a place defended only by peasants
and women; but it is well known that despair
makes soldiers of everybody and axes and
scythes are good weapons in the hands of the
resolute.

At this spectacle Banfy's face suddenly glowed;
he thought he saw a woman's figure on the bat-
tlement of the tower.   At once he put spurs to
his horse and rushed forward like a whirlwind,
calling back to his men:

"Do not count the foe now; time enough for
that when he is down."

And within a quarter of an hour the small
band reached the camp before the town.   There
everybody was asleep.   While one part of the
army made the attack there was time for the
other to rest.   Even the guards had let their
heads droop in sleep; there they lay by their
staked horses, and were only roused from their
dreams when Banfy had already ridden wildly
through their ranks in every direction.   The
Baron, who intended to hasten on alone to the
relief of the besieged, in a trice ran down the
confused troops who, startled from their sleep,
seized horse and lance and mistaking one another

for the enemy crowded together and cut down
their own troops. In vain did the Turkish
leaders strive to control the frantic men.

Meanwhile, Banfy appeared boldly and unexpectedly in the midst of the Turkish army storming the church. The front ranks gave way in
terror at his unexpected onset but at once an
advancing brigade made up of Ali Pasha's chosen
Mamelukes, brought the fugitives to a stand. A
giant Moor stood at the head of the troops. His
horse too was an unusually tall one, sixteen
hands high. He himself was seven feet tall;
his great swollen muscles shone like steel in the
fiendish light of the burning hay-ricks; his broad
mouth bled from the blow of a stone and the
whites of his eyes shone in a ghastly fashion from
his black face.

"Halt, Giaour!" roared the Moor, with a voice
that sounded above the thunder of battle, and
made his way toward Banfy. In his clenched
fist shone a broad scimitar that seemed too heavy
even for him.

Two hussars riding before Banfy fell at one
blow from the monster; one to the right, the
other to the left of his horse. As he raised his
arm for the third blow the Moor rose in his
saddle and shouted: "I am Kariassar, the Invincible! Thank God that you fall by my hand."
And with that he threw his sword backward and
dealt a frightful blow in the direction of Banfy's

head.   The Baron drew his sword coolly in front
of his face and when Kariassar struck, made a
very skilful movement at the hand of the Moor
and struck off four fingers at once from Kariassar's hand, so that they fell noiselessly to the
ground.   An expression of terror and rage over-
spread the dark features.   He threw himself
quickly with a frightful roar at Banfy, and paying no heed to the wounds received on face and
shoulders, with his left hand grasped the Hungarian's right and gave him such a push that, had
not Banfy been firm in his saddle, he must have
fallen from his horse.   It seemed as if the Moor
were still able with one hand to crush him.   As
Banfy was a good rider he used his spurs, and
while the giant struggled with the master, pull-
ing at his lacerated arm with lion strength, the
battle-horse turned himself suddenly against the
Moor, dealt him a blow in the thigh with his
hoof, bit his breast with his foaming mouth and
pushed against him with his teeth.   Kariassar
cried out with the maddening pain and letting go
the Baron suddenly, reached for his dagger with
his left hand and drew it from its sheath.   Just
at this moment Banfy struck at the giant's neck
and the monstrous head rolled to the ground.
While the blood gushed out in a threefold stream,
the headless figure remained seated upon his un-
guided horse,—a terrible spectacle !   At sight of
him the frightened Mamelukes scattered, dashing

over hedges and fences on their horses, riding one another down.

At the same time the people who were defending the church broke down the barricades and made a sally on the assailants. At their head was Madame Vizaknai with drawn sword—behind, the clergy as standard-bearers, with the church banners.

The great army of besiegers, now fallen between two fires, parted and opened a free course for the scythes of the peasants, and for the tschakany. This last is a mighty weapon; in the hands of the expert its blow is almost unfailing. The long pointed blade strikes with such weight as it falls that there is neither helmet nor shield it cannot go through, and the sword offers no defence against its crooked steel.

Soon the two armies met. The janissaries who, though half dead still struck with their hangers at the feet of the horses riding over them, scattered like chaff.

Madame Vizaknai sprang toward Dionysius Banfy and seized his horse by the bridle.

"The danger is great, gracious lord. The Turks are twenty times our number. Come behind the church wall."

"I'll not go a step further," replied Banfy, coldly. "Save yourself behind the barricades."

"Neither will I," replied Madame Vizaknai.

"I can defend myself," said Banfy, fiercely.

"So can I," replied the woman, proudly.

New forces streamed out from every direction as if they had come down from the clouds or up from the ground. Foot soldiers and horse, with long weapons, bows and lances arose from every side with a shout that reached the heavens:— "Ali, Ali, Allah Akbar!"

The Hungarian force, with backs to the church drew themselves up in line of battle and waited the attack. From the end of the street a gleaming troop of horsemen appeared to be advancing. It was a picked company of spahis on stately Arab horses; the housings gleaming with emeralds in the firelight. In the middle rode Ali on a slender snow-white barb; in his hand a crooked sword with diamond-set hilt and on his head a turbaned helmet. His long beard fell over his silver armor. When he was within range of Banfy he called a halt and drew up his men. Until then Banfy had not touched his pistols, the wonderfully carved ivory handles of which were just in sight above the saddlebags. Now he drew them and handed them both to Madame Vizaknai.

"Take them," he said, "you ought to have something for self-defence."

Just then Ali Pasha sent a herald who brought this message to the Hungarians:

"My lord, Ali Pasha, commands you unbelieving giaours to surrender. Every way of escape is closed; spare yourself further useless efforts, lay down your weapons at his feet and surrender yourselves to his mercy."

The herald had hardly uttered the last words when two shots were heard and he fell dead from his horse. Madame Vizaknai, instead of any reply had fired off both pistols at him.

Ali Pasha, infuriated, gave a signal to the troops around him and there was a shower of darts and balls from every side upon the little Hungarian band

Madame Vizaknai stepped up to Banfy's stirrups and resting against him one hand and swinging her sword with the other, said :

"Fear nothing, my friend."

Her words were followed by a sound as of thunder and a whizzing of darts. Madame Vizaknai's body came between Banfy and danger. When the noise of the firing passed over he felt her hold on his arm grow weaker;—an arrow had struck the lady just above the heart.

"The arrow was meant for you," said Madame Vizaknai, with feeble voice, and sank down dead on the ground.

"Poor soul !" said Banfy, looking down at her. "She always loved me and never showed it."

And then blood flowed instead of tears.

The Hungarians were surrounded by the Turks and could not force their way through at any point. Already Banfy was fighting with the eighth spahi who, like all the rest, gave way before his extraordinary dexterity. Ali Pasha was beside himself with rage.

"So then, you cannot kill this detestable dog," he roared, in his anger, and striking the people before him with the flat of his sword, he galloped toward Banfy.

"I stand before you, you miserable hog, son of a dog," he said, gnashing his teeth.

"Keep your names for yourself," said Banfy; rode up to the Pasha, and let fall on his helmet so mighty a blow that it was shivered, and Banfy's sword too, and both men drew back stunned. Ali took a round shield from one of his armor-bearers and a steel tschakany was handed Banfy. The tschakany fell with frightful force on the shield, making a hole. Ali Pasha drew his sword and this time Banfy saved his life only by a skilful spring to one side.

"I'll play ball with your head," said Ali, scornfully.

"And I will make a broom out of your beard," replied Banfy.

"I will have your coat of arms nailed up in my stable."

"And I will have your hide stuffed with sawdust and use it for a scarecrow."

"You rebel of a slave!"

"You barber's apprentice made into a general!"

Every taunt was accompanied with a fresh thrust.

"You shameless kidnapper!" shouted the Pasha. "You carry off Turkish girls, do you? I will carry off your wife and make her the lowest slave of my harem."

Everything swam before Banfy's eyes; he had received three wounds that took from him all humanity.

"Cursed devil!" he roared, and gnashing his teeth, grasped his tschakany in the middle, bounded nearer to Ali and whirled his weapon with lightning swiftness about his head so that it flew about in his hand like the arms of a windmill, now driving at the opposing shield with the handle and now with the ball-like end of the weapon, serving alike for attack and defence. Ali Pasha, overwhelmed by this unwonted mode of attack tried to withdraw, but the two warhorses shared their masters' struggle by biting each other in the neck and chest and could not be separated. The spahis, who saw their master reel, threw themselves between the two and drove off the hussars surrounding Banfy. When he saw that all his men were fleeing toward the church he quickly let fall one last blow on Ali's shield, which struck through, and as he surmised from Ali's roar, just at the point where the shield fits on the arm. Banfy had no time for a second blow for he was surrounded on all sides. Just

then there was heard in the rear of the com-
batants a familiar braying of trumpets, and a
fresh war cry sounding from all sides mingled
with the confusion.

"God! Michael Angyal!" George Veer had
arrived with his troops.

"God! Michael Angyal!" shouted the leader,
towering above the rest in his coat of mail with
a bearskin thrown over one shoulder; with a
notched club he forced his way through the midst
of the surprised Turks.

The attack was skilfully made. The knights
crowded forward from all sides and threw the
army of the Turks into confusion at every point
at once so that no division could bring help to
another, and the outer ranks were constantly
trampled down by this superior foe.

Ali Pasha had received a bad wound on his
arm from Banfy's last thrust, that took away his
courage; he put spurs to his horse and gave the
signal for retreat. The army of the Turks was
driven headlong out of the town. The leaders
strove to bring the troops to the mountains of
Gyerto, where they thought they could gather
their forces again in the passes.

Outside the town the battle went on in spite of
the order to retreat. The Hungarians scattered
the burning hay and in the darkness of the night
became so mixed with their foes that they could
only be distinguished by the war cry. The re-

treating army of the Turks in the darkness and
confusion now fled toward the enemy, now cut
down their own comrades, and in their effort to
imitate the war cry of the Hungarians met with
still greater misfortune, for since they could not
pronounce Michael Angyal but shouted Michael
Andschal instead, they were the more easily
recognized by the Hungarians. The Turkish
army was utterly defeated. They left more than
a thousand dead in the streets and vicinity of
the church; and had it not been for the mountain ravines where it was not advisable for the
Hungarians to follow, they would have been completely annihilated.

George Veer ordered the trumpet to sound for
the rally of the scattered troops, while Banfy in
his restless rage sought to pursue the fleeing foe.
In vain! Every way was closed by the hastily
felled trees.

"We are forced to let them escape," said Veer,
sheathing his sword.

"Maybe not," said Banfy, excited, and rode up
a hill where he appeared to see something. Suddenly he shouted joyfully :—"Look there! The
signal fires are just being lighted." And it was
a fact! The signal bonfires were seen blazing in
a long line along the Gyalu mountains.

"There are our men!" shouted Banfy, with
fresh enthusiasm. "The Turk is in a snare!"

And he collected his forces again and galloped

toward the barricaded streets, giving no heed to the warning of the more cautious Veer.

*   *   *   *   *   *

Ali Pasha had meantime sent ahead his tents, camels and the booty-laden wagons, with Dschem-Haman to open up the road over the mountain. While Dschem-Haman went forward in the darkness, leveling a road, he suddenly heard a conversation on the steep rocks towering above his head and saw a troop of armed men come in sight. Both troops spoke at once,—" Who are you? What are you doing?"

" We are carrying stones," replied Dschem-Haman. " We too are carrying stones," shouted those above.

" We are Dschem-Haman's men, who are clearing the stones out of the way for Ali Pasha,— and you, are you not Csaki's men?"

" We are gathering stones to throw at the head of Ali Pasha, and are Michael Angyal's men," was the reply from above; and at the same moment there fell on the head of the Turk a rain of stones, as if by way of confirmation.

" Is Angyal here too?" growled the Turks, starting back in terror and alarming those in the rear, who feared they were about to be surrounded. At this information the army of the Turks formed in a solid mass, rear and van alike harassed by the fear that the Hungarian forces in possession of the mountain-heights would begin at daybreak to roll down huge rocks.

Ali Pasha tried to force his way through, now in one place and now in another, but was beaten back every time with frightful loss, by masses of rock and trunks of trees rolled down from above. The boldest rangers, who had fought hand to hand in hundreds of battles, fled terror-stricken before these thundering rocks which so crushed everything in their path that horse and rider could not be distinguished from each other. Ali, seeing that he and his entire host were all but caught, tore his beard with rage that he must lay down his arms before an army to which his own was even now superior in numbers.

"There is nowhere either help or defence except with Almighty God!" he cried, broke his sword in two in his despair, drew his pistol and aimed it at his own breast. At that instant a hand tore his weapon from him and Ali Pasha saw Zulfikar before him.

"What do you want, you madman?" he shouted at him. "You surely would not have me fall into the hands of these unbelievers alive!"

"I will set you and your army free," said Zulfikar.

"By the soul of Allah, you make great promises, and if you should be able to fulfil them I would make you second in command."

"That is not necessary. Promise me a thousand ducats and send me to Banfy as messenger."

"So you can betray my position to him, you dog!"

"I do not need to do that, he can see for himself from the mountain height, and in any case you are as well done for as if you were dead already, so you have no choice whether you will believe me or not. Within ten days you and I and your noblest knights will die of hunger; in this one respect all are alike and have no advantage over one another."

"And what will you attempt, miserable slave?"

"Influence Banfy to withdraw his troops from the road leading toward Kalota and so leave us a way of escape."

"And you think that is possible?"

"Either it is possible, or it is not possible. Where death is certain, a man is not risking his life. If I can speak with Banfy this evening, you can think of escape by night. If it succeeds, good; if it does not, you can come back here again."

"The boy speaks boldly. Well, act according to your judgment. I trust it to you. God sees all. Go."

Zulfikar laid down his arms and followed the defile leading toward Kalota. As he came to the Hungarian outpost he saw the length of the street, long rows of trees with Turks hung to the branches; but this sight did not disturb the composure of the deserter. He walked boldly into the midst of the enemy and when they stopped him, said quietly in Hungarian, " Take me to Dionysius Banfy, I am his spy!"

" You lie!" they shouted. " Hang him to a tree!"

" I can prove it," continued Zulfikar, firmly, took a folded letter out of his turban and gave it to the captain.

In the letter were these words. " I, Gregory Sötar, inform the captains that the bearer of this letter, Zulfikar, is my faithful war spy. He is to be allowed free pass everywhere." The captain gave back the letter sullenly and motioned to two soldiers to lead him to Banfy, and in case the latter did not recognize him, strike him down at once. Banfy recognized him at the first glance as Pongracz, once servant of Balassa, and motioned to his servant to leave him alone with him.

" So you have turned Turk?" Banfy asked.

" Do not ask, my lord, I have a great deal to say beside that. Let me tell my story quietly to the end and I will be brief. Emerich Balassa turned me out of his house when he learned that I had assisted you in carrying off Azraele."

" Good," said Banfy, contracting his eyebrows.

"The girl has fled from me too and I do not know where she has gone."

"I do, my lord. But the worst of it is that there are others who know too. Near Gregyina-Drakuluj there is a hidden dwelling among the rocks that is her property."

"Still," cried Banfy, frightened. "How do you know that?"

"Balassa entered a complaint to the Prince that his wife had been stolen. The affair is not so trifling as you think. Azraele is the Sultan's daughter, who was betrothed to Ali and carried off by Corsar. Balassa's poison alone saved Corsar from a silken rope, while Balassa has given up his native land for the sake of the girl. This woman has brought misfortune to everybody who has rejoiced in the possession of her. Now it is your turn. After the Prince had promised the disgraced Ladislaus Csaki everything in his power if he would discover the place where you had concealed the girl, Csaki craftily commissioned the Lieutenant of the circuit to make inquiries among the people whether a panther had not been seen in the forest, for he felt quite sure that this tamed beast would wander widely. In this way they got trace of the hiding place among the rocks, saw the girl,—and all is betrayed."

"Hell and the devil!" said Banfy, turning white.

"Hear the rest. Csaki communicated his plan to Ali Pasha, who was the one concerned; according to this plan, when Ali fell upon Banfy-Hunyad, Csaki with his thousand Wallachians was to go up into the mountain under pretext of a hunt and storm Gregyina-Drakuluj."

"Unheard-of knavery!" cried Banfy, with his hand on his sword.

"It is possible, my lord, that you may yet get there in time," added the deserter, cunningly,— "if you do not delay too long."

"Let us start at once," said Banfy, pale with rage. "I'll teach these sycophants to touch the possession of a free nobleman while he himself is fighting against the foe of his fatherland. A few hundred men will be enough to hold Ali Pasha in check here; with the rest I'll wager that I can make it uncomfortable for Ladislaus Csaki if he crosses my borders."

And at once Banfy sent orders to his men to start for Marisel in perfect silence; he ordered the few troops remaining to light a great many fires in the forest to make the enemy believe that the entire force was still there, and he himself hurried on to Azraele's hiding place. For Zulfikar he counted out five hundred gold pieces for his information.

Ali Pasha, according to agreement, had attacked by night with his entire force the line of military posts left by Banfy and held by a few hundred men; had driven them back after a short resistance and leaving behind two thousand dead and all his baggage, and swallowing down his vexation at a great defeat, had hurried away toward Gross Nagy Varad. From him too Zulfikar received the thousand gold pieces stipulated; he had done a service alike to the Hungarian and to the Turk, and had allowed himself to receive pay from both parties.

CHAPTER XIV

THE COURT OF JUSTICE IN THE BANQUET HALL

A BLAST of hunting horns echoed from the mountains of Batrina and the din of the chase drew nearer. A group of distinguished-looking riders was seen in the cavalcade and at their head rode Ladislaus Csaki.

"After him! After him!" rang out from all sides. Evidently the beast had been started when the group of riders, coming out of a thicket into a clearing, met a group from the other direction in which all recognized Dionysius Banfy as leader, and astounded they cut short their chase.

Banfy rode toward the group with a scornful smile. "Welcome, my lords, to my estate! I am very glad that this good fortune is mine. Probably you have lost your way, otherwise you are my guests and so welcome. But why do you stare at me so wildly? you call to mind the Hindoo proverb; 'He who hunts a deer in the forest often comes upon lions.'"

"We consider you neither deer nor lion," replied Csaki, blushing in his confusion to his very ears;—"but we expected to find ourselves on lawful ground."

"Quite right," replied Banfy, with an offended

laugh. "You are on my territory and that is comparatively lawful. I really do not know how I can express my pleasure at this honor. Doubtless you are weary; I invite you to my house at Bonczida to a friendly meal."

"Thank you," replied Csaki, angrily, "but at present we cannot accept."

"That is my affair. I am not accustomed to allow those to go away hungry and thirsty who have come to me as guests. I cannot treat you as poachers so I must look upon you as my guests, I suppose."

"There is still a third condition possible."

"I recognize none."

"Your Excellency shall learn it at once from me."

"Very good, but there will be time for that over the midday meal. Let us turn our horses toward Bonczida, my lords."

"I have already said that we would not accept the invitation."

"What do you say? have you then so poor an opinion of my hospitality as to think that I will not myself drag you away by force? You must not overlook Bonczida: since you already know my game, you must now make acquaintance with my domestic animals. At all events, I shall take you with me, even by force."

"Have done with jesting, Banfy; it is not in place here."

"I think that it is you who are jesting, for I am perfectly serious when I say that I intend to take you with me even against your will."

"We will see."

"You may be assured that you will," said Banfy; he blew his horn and from all sides appeared armed men out of the forest. Csaki's men were surrounded.

"This is certainly treason!" cried Csaki, infuriated.

"Oh no, only a little Carnival fun," replied Banfy, laughing. "This once the game catches the hunter. Forward, my men, take the horses of these gentlemen by the bridle and follow me with them to Bonczida. If any one of them does not go willingly, fasten his legs firmly to the stirrups."

"I protest against this violence," said Csaki, raging. "I call upon you to bear witness that I have entered a protest against this law of violence."

"And I, on my part, call on everybody to witness," said Banfy, laughing as he imitated him; "that I have invited these gentlemen in the most friendly fashion to a banquet."

"I protest it is violence!"

"It is diversion—Hungarian hospitality."

Some of the gentlemen laughed and the rest cursed. Finally, since Banfy had the power, Csaki's men sullenly yielded to the act of violence and allowed themselves to be led away to Bonczida.

Along the road Csaki called out to all who met them. He called on them to bear witness that Banfy was doing them an act of violence, while Banfy in turn laughingly strove to make it clear to them that the noble gentleman was a little befogged and that they were playing him a joke befitting nobility.

"You will be sorry for this yet," snarled Csaki, beside himself with rage.

As they were passing through a village one of Csaki's suite, a young nobleman called Szantho by his comrades, made his way out of the throng and before they could pursue him, was out of sight.

"The Devil take him!" said Banfy. "However we can sport merrily without him can we not, my Lord Ladislaus Csaki?"

Gradually Csaki regained his composure and laid aside his anger. As they came to Bonczida he wore a smiling countenance for he saw that it would be unbecoming and ridiculous in the presence of ladies to wear an angry expression, so without annoyance he allowed himself to be presented to Madame Banfy and Madame Apafi as a guest picked up by the way.

Banfy crowned his insult by pointing Csaki to the seat of honor at the upper end of the table near his wife, placed himself opposite and be-

stowed on him constantly the highest expressions
of honor, at the same time allowing the most biting scorn to show through. Csaki did not dare
have it seen to what extent he felt this. The
merrier their spirits grew toward the close of the
meal, the more exasperated Csaki became. He
sat on burning coals and had to smile. At last
Banfy thought of one more vexation for him.
Taking up his glass he drank to his health.
Csaki had to accept the civility and empty his
glass and so face Banfy's laugh. Every drop of
the liquor turned to poison under this scornful
laughter; and the torture was so subtly veiled
that the two ladies did not notice any of it. As
the guests were at their merriest, the middle door
flew open and without any announcement there
entered Michael Apafi, the Prince, to whom the
escaped Szantho had carried the news of Csaki's
capture.

The two ladies hurried toward the unexpected
guest with cries of joy and surprise, while the
gentlemen at once discerned the threatening
storm on the countenance of the Prince and became serious. Banfy alone knew how to maintain his customary distinguished serenity, which
was wont to express even anger with smiles. He
sprang hastily from his seat and met the Prince
with a joyful face.

"Your Highness has come in the very moment
that we had emptied our glasses to your health.

I call that an unexpected but most opportune appearance."

Apafi received his greeting with a slight nod and leading the ladies back to their places took Banfy's chair at the table.

Several of the guests hastened to offer their seats to Banfy, but the Prince motioned to him :

" You may remain standing, Banfy. We wish to make a friendly trial of your case."

"If we may be permitted to be the judges, your Excellency,"—interrupted the learned Csehfalusi, " the necessary inquiries have already been made."

"I alone will pass judgment," said Apafi, "although I do not know whether the master in Bonczida is Dionysius Banfy or I."

"The law of the land is master of us both, your Highness," replied Banfy.

"Well answered. Then you certainly mean to remind us that a Hungarian nobleman in his own house does not allow any one to sit in judgment on him. It is only a little 'Carnival fun' that is under discussion. You began it, you gave it this name, and we continue it."

Tense expectancy was on the faces of those present for they did not know whether all this was to end as a joke or as something serious.

"You seized by violence our messenger Ladislaus Csaki and brought him to your house."

"Indeed!" said Banfy, with feigned astonish-

ment. " Is that his office ? why did not the
Count say at once that your Highness had sent
him to hunt on my estate ? And then when
your Highness has a desire to hunt within my
preserves, why do you not inform me instead ?
I could have far better deer shot for your Highness than Ladislaus Csaki can."

" This is not a question of deer, my lord baron.
You know perfectly well what the affair turns
on. Do not oblige me to speak more plainly in
the presence of the ladies."

At these words Madame Banfy would have
risen but the Princess held her back.

" You must stay," she whispered in her ear.

" Thus far I do not understand a word of all
that has been said," Banfy remarked in an ag-
grieved tone.

" You do not ? then we will recall to your memory a few circumstances. In your forests a panther has been seen by the peasants."

" That is possible," replied Banfy, with a laugh.
(For a Hungarian noble may be permitted to jest
with his guests but never to be rude, no matter
how much he may be annoyed.) " It is quite possible that the panther is a descendant of the one
which came into the country with Arpad, and so
might be called an ancestral panther."

" It is no joke, my lord. That beast of prey
has torn to pieces in the sight of several persons
a Wallachian, on whose account I sent out the

lord, Ladislaus Csaki, to hunt down the beast and
kill him.　And Csaki had seen the creature and
given chase when you met him in the forest."

"My lord, Ladislaus Csaki has merely mistaken
his own tiger skin for a panther."

"Do not sneer.　The lair of that monster has
been discovered.　Do you understand now?"

"I understand, your Highness.　For that reason it was a pity to put my lord Csaki to so much
trouble.　So it was he who discovered the building which I had hewn in the rocks in my love
for a hot spring.　This will hardly earn him the
title of a Christopher Columbus."

"We still mock, do we?　So you do not wish
to bend your proud head to the dust?　What if
I knew the secret which caused you to have that
lair made so quietly?"

Balfy began to change color.　He answered in
a low tone of voice like a man who found it hard
not to speak the truth.

"The cause of this, my lord, is quite simple.
Borvölgy too I had discovered, and hardly had
the news of it spread abroad when the public
took possession of this spring: again near Gregyina-Drakuluj I found a spring of mineral waters, and to prevent everybody from going there
I had a little pleasure house made in secret among
the rocks."　By these last words, Banfy intended
to signify to the Prince that he would like to

spare his wife, but he accomplished quite the opposite effect.

"Ah, my lord, that is base hypocrisy!" cried
out the Prince, passionately, and struck his
clenched fist on the table. "You wish to use
your wife as a cloak and yet you are keeping in
that place a Turkish girl, on whose account the
Sultan is now preparing war against our country."

Madame Banfy uttered a piercing cry. Her
sister whispered in her ear, "Be strong. Show
your resolution now."

Banfy bit his lips in anger but he knew how to
control his feelings and answered quietly:

"That is not true. I dispute it."

"What! Is it not true? there are people who
have seen her."

"Who has seen her?"

"Clement, the Lieutenant of the Circuit."

"Clement, the poet? lying is the poet's trade."

"Good, my lord baron! Since you deny everything I shall convince myself personally of all
these matters. I shall myself go to the place in
question and if I find proof of the accusation
brought against you, be assured that a threefold
punishment awaits you; for the abduction of the
Turkish girl, for the violence done a messenger
of the Prince and for your infidelity. But one
of these charges is alone sufficient to bring you
down from your fancied height. Csaki, conduct

us to the place mentioned. My lord, Dionysius Banfy, will remain here in the meantime."

Banfy stood colorless and as if rooted to the ground. His wife had risen, and summoning all her strength with a mighty effort, advanced to the Prince and said:

"My lord,—pardon my husband,—he knows of nothing—the guilt is mine; that woman whom you are looking for found herself pursued and turned to me for protection and I hid her in that place without the knowledge of my husband."

Each word that she spoke seemed to cost the pale, weak woman more than human strength.

Banfy blushed and dropped his eyes before her. Madame Apafi looked at her sister triumphantly and pressed her hand.

"Good! that is noble. You were strong."

Apafi saw through the generous deceit and turned angrily toward Banfy, determined that he should not escape him in this way.

"And you permit your wife to take risks which might easily plunge your family—yes, your country—into peril! for this you deserve punishment. It is my wish that here in the presence of your guests, to my satisfaction, you set her right." Madame Banfy sank down on her knees before the guests, with an air of resignation, and dropped her head like a criminal who awaits her punishment.

"That is not my custom," replied Banfy, hoarsely.

"Then I will do it," said Apafi, and stepped up to the lady.

"This deed of yours deserves to be punished by imprisonment."

"That I will not permit, my lord," muttered Banfy, between his teeth.

He was already white as a corpse. All the blood seemed to have settled in his eyes as at a focal point. All his muscles quivered with rage and shame.

"My lords,"—rang out a bell-like voice, the sound of which was grateful in this rude contest of men. It was Madame Apafi who had stepped between the prostrate lady and the men.—"Formerly noble men were wont to honor noble women."

"You are on hand again, to defend those whom I bring to justice," said the Prince, with annoyance.

"I am on hand to save your Highness from an injustice; to defend my sister is always my right; when everybody fails her then it certainly is my duty."

With these words the Princess put her arms around Margaret who, feeling herself supported by the stronger nature suddenly sank down in a faint in her sister's arms, her overtaxed physical and mental strength failing her. Banfy would have hastened to his wife's aid but Madame Apafi held him back.

"Go," she said, "I will assume the care of her."

"So you intend to remain here?" said the Prince to his wife, in a tone wavering between anger and sympathy.

"My sister needs me—and you, I see, do not."

Since Apafi had heard his wife speak his voice had become noticeably dejected, and fearing that she would utterly rout him he left the battlefield in great haste with only half a triumph.

The Prince was naturally very much dissatisfied with this result. He felt that Banfy had been struck in a weak spot and at the same time that the blow was not deadly. The great lord had been affronted but not humbled. So much the worse for him!

What will not bend must break!

CHAPTER XV

THE DIET OF KARLSBURG

THE states of the country were already assembled in Karlsburg, in the stately palace of John Sigmund. Only the Prince's place was still vacant. There sat in a row the Transylvanian patricians, the leaders of the Hungarian nobility, the most influential by intelligence, wealth, and bravery; the Bethlens, Kornis, Csakis, Lazars, Keménys, Mikes and Banfys. The will of these mediæval clans represented the nation, their deeds shaped its history, their ancestors, grandfathers and fathers, had fallen on the battlefield in defence of their princes or, in case they had risen against them, on the scaffold; and yet their descendants did not fail to follow the example of their forefathers. A new prince came to the helm and they took up the sword fallen from the hand of their fathers to wield it for or against him, as fate willed.

In picturesque contrast to the splendor of the Hungarian nobles were the deputies and nobility of the Szeklers in their simpler costume and with their serious inflexible features; and the Saxon states with their simple faces and their ancestral German costume.

The crowd gathered in the galleries and behind the balustrades formed a gay picture. Here and there one or another familiar figure was pointed out and sometimes a threatening fist was shaken at some offender. Finally a blare of trumpets announced that the Prince had come. The seneschals threw wide the doors: the crowd cried huzza! and the Prince entered attended by his courtiers. At their head marched Dionysius Banfy as first marshal, with the national standard in his right hand. By his side Paul Beldi of Uzoni with the princely mace, as general of the Szeklers. Behind them came solemnly the prime minister, Michael Teleki, carrying wrapped in silk the official seal.

All these lords were in splendid court costume. In the middle came the Prince himself in long, princely caftan with ermine bordered cap,—the sceptre in his hand. Around and behind him crowded the ambassadors from foreign courts. In the first row was the Sultan's representative, in jeweled costume; then followed the ambassadors of Louis XIV., Forval, a courtly, good-looking man in a silk-trimmed dolman, with gold lace on his hat and an embroidered sword-knot, and an abbé with smiling face, wearing a lilac robe and purple girdle. Then came Sobieski's representative in cloak with slashed sleeves, so like the Hungarian dress. All these lords took their places on the right and left. The ambassa-

dors of the foreign courts remained behind the
Prince's seat and several of them carried on a
lively conversation with the Hungarian nobles
while the tedious protocol of the last Diet was
being read.

Among the last was Nicholas Bethlen, whose
features became familiar to us in Zrinyi's hunt-
ing-party. He was a lively, sensible man who in
his youth had traveled through all the civilized
countries of Europe and had made the acquaintance of the most important men, even of princes;
yet his national character had not been impaired
although he had adopted the most advanced ideas
of his time. The French say that it was he who
first acquainted them with the hussar costume,
and by the pattern of the cloak which excited
admiration on his figure, Louis XIV. had several
regiments equipped.

When Bethlen caught sight of Forval, whom
he had known in France, he hastened to him and
greeted him cordially. Forval, hearing that something was being read aloud, said to the young
nobleman :

" Will you not lose the thread of the delibera-
tion ? "

" The present business can go on without me;
the measures which are now being carried turn
on the question how many dishes a man should
set before his servant; or at the most how the
poor can be made to grow rich so they can pay

their taxes. As soon as they come to important matters I will be in my place."

"Come then and tell me meantime, which are worthy men here and which are not. In Transylvania everybody is known, of course."

"This classification is not at all easy. Before I had ever been out of Transylvania, and while I belonged either to one party or the other, I was convinced that all the adherents of my party were worthy men but those on the opposite side were worth nothing. But since I have lived in foreign lands and been somewhat withdrawn from the sight of political machinery I begin to see that one may really be as good a patriot, as brave a fighter and as honest a man in one party as in the other. It all depends on which is managing affairs more intelligently. However, if you wish I will share with you my party views; you can then form your own opinions. This man of proud bearing at the Prince's right is Dionysius Banfy, the one at his left is Paul Beldi; both are among the most distinguished lords of the country and both are decidedly opposed to the impending war. At the same time they are opposed to each other. On one point only do they stand together. Banfy is evidently in league with the Roman Emperor and the other with the Turk. According to their opinion Transylvania is quite strong enough to drive out any foe which forces its way into the territory, and sensible enough not to strive after the possessions of others. Now turn your eyes toward that man with thin hair at the Prince's left. It is this man's clearness that holds the two in check. He is a near kinsman of the Prince's, and when the Hungarian National party has been overthrown he will again take up the unsuccessful campaign. The contest between the strength and cunning of these three men is going to offer an interesting spectacle."

"What if the peace party should prevail?"

"Then the nation will have closed its career."

"And the king cannot oppose this?"

"Here, my friend, we are not at the court of Versailles where the king may be allowed to say 'L'État c'est moi.' These men here are, each one of them, as mighty as the Prince himself. There strength acts in union with the Prince; but let him try to act in opposition to the will of the nation and he will soon discover that he stands alone. In the same way these lords would be isolated if they should undertake anything against the decision of the nation."

"Tell the truth. Do you hope the war-party will carry off the victory?"

"Hardly, this time. I do not yet see the man who could accomplish it. In the entire Hungarian nation there is no man who could serve as ideal to this war-loving people. The leaders have gone to ruin. Rakoczy has changed parties. Teleki knows how to overthrow parties but not how to create any. Besides he is no soldier and in such a position a warrior is needed; he represents cold reason and here a soul of fire is needed. He does not feel a mission within him, he has only an interest in having Hungary go to war. One of the great Hungarian lords, that smooth-faced youth there, has sued for the hand of his daughter in order to interest him in his party. You can be assured he will not end where he has begun. One idea leads him on,—power. Fate is changeful and he avails himself of every means."

This cold consolation was not agreeable to Forval; meanwhile the tedious reading had come to an end and Bethlen returned to his seat.

The Prince explained to the lords, with great depression of spirits, that the affair which had occasioned their coming together would be explained by Teleki; he then wrapped himself more closely in his caftan and settled down into a corner of the throne.

Teleki rose, waited until the murmur of the people had gradually subsided, then cast a tranquil glance at Banfy and began as follows:

"Noble Knights and States, you are acquainted with the events which have recently taken place in Hungary; even if you were not acquainted with them, you would need only to cast a glance about you and you would see the sad faces worn

with despair which swell our assembly; these are
our Hungarian brothers, once the flower of our
nation, now withered leaves which the storm has
driven. You have not refused to share with your
brothers in their misfortunes your hearth and
your bread, and you have mingled your tears
with theirs; but they have turned to us, not for
the bread of charity, nor for woman's tears—you,
Bocskai, and you, Bethlen, whose portraits look
down upon us in silent reproach, whose victorious
banners covered with dust wave above the
princely throne, why could you not rise in hero
form to seize these banners and to thunder out to
this irresolute modern generation: 'The exiles
demand of you their home, you must win back
for the homeless their fatherland by war!'"

. . . .

Here Teleki paused, as if he awaited objections.
Everybody was wrapped in silence, feeling that
thus far it was only a matter of rhetorical figures.
This silence constrained Teleki to avoid the bom-
bastic in his speech.

"You meet my speech with silence. This is
the same as, 'Qui tacet, negat.' I will not believe
that your heart is cold and that it is for that reason you do not become excited. You waver because you are taking counsel with your strength,
but you must know that not alone shall we move
to the field of battle; the confiscated churches,
the fate of the clergy dragged away to the gal-

leys, has forced weapons into the hands of all the
Protestant princes of Europe. Even the King of
Belgium, who has least concern for our fate, has
by force rescued the clergy of our faith from
Neapolitan galleys. The sword of Gustavus
Adolphus too has not yet rusted in its scabbard.
Yes, even the Catholic princes and those who
acknowledge Mohammed are ready to grant their
assistance in our affairs. See, the King of France,
at present the mightiest ruler of Europe, not only
in his own land but also in Poland recruits armies
for us. If it should be necessary the Sultan will
not hesitate to break the enforced peace; or if
he should not do this, still it will be an easy matter to assure ourselves of his border troops for
pay. And now when the noise of battle roars
about us on all sides, when everybody has seized
his sword, ought we alone to leave ours in the
sheath ? We, who have the most duties to fulfil
toward our brothers and even toward ourselves ?
What happened to them yesterday, may happen
to us to-day. What country shall then give us
refuge ? therefore, sons of my fatherland, listen
to the entreaties of the exiled as if you were in
the same position; for I tell you the time may
come when you will be in the position of your
brothers, and as you treat them Fate will treat
you."

With these words Teleki came to an end; he
fixed his eyes on Dionysius Banfy as if he knew

in advance that he would be the first to oppose him. Banfy arose; it was evident from his countenance that he had done violence to his feelings in order to keep cool.

"Noble comrades,"—he began in an unusually calm voice,—"sympathy for the unfortunate and hatred for old enemies are both passions befitting men. The life of states however offers no room for passions. Here we are not kinsmen nor friends, nor even enemies. Here we are only patriots who reckon coolly; for the decision will determine the fate of the whole country, quite apart from the question of how many will weep or lament in consequence of the decision. This is the real question,—'Shall we stake the existence of Transylvania for Hungary, that it may arise again by our blood?' Let us not follow the voice of our hearts; this would lead us to feel only, the head must think. At present, Transylvania lives in peace. The people begin to feel prosperous. The towns are building up. The garb of mourning is gradually disappearing and on the bloody battlefields the blade shoots into the ear. Now the Hungarian within Transylvania is his own master; no stranger forces tribute from him; he has neither foe nor patron; nobody dares mix in his councils: the neighboring powers are under obligation to protect him, and he has no homage to pay them. Consider this well before you hazard everything for one chance. Do you wish to see Transylvania once more turned into a great battlefield and your subjects into armies? and there is still the question whether these armies would be victorious. Even if our fighting force were sufficient another important question arises:—Who is to be our leader? Not one of us has inherited the spirit of Bethlen or Bocskai. Neither I, nor my lord Teleki. On whom can we count outside ourselves? on the mood of Louis XIV.? his policy is easily made to waver by a pair of beautiful eyes; and when we should be in the deepest distress it is possible that a little intrigue at Versailles might be the cause of our being left alone on the battlefield."

A slight cough of vexation was heard from Forval.

"However," went on Banfy, "Sobieski will not pick a quarrel with the Emperor his present ally, for our beautiful eyes, unless there is every other cause. Nor will the Sultan so easily break his oath as my lord, Michael Bethlen, imagines. What course is there left us? To call into Hungary the Tartar Nomads? The poor Hungarian people would certainly return most hearty thanks for such assistance! The brave Nicholas Zrinyi, who stands as the ideal to every Hungarian, once related a fable bearing on this which deserves to be handed down. The devil was dragging a Szekler along on his back. A

neighbor of his met him and said: 'Which way
are you going, my good friend?' 'I am being
dragged to hell,' replied the other. 'Indeed,
that is truly unfortunate,' said the other. 'It
would be still more unfortunate,' replied the
rogue, 'if the Devil should seat himself on my
back, drive his spurs into me and make me carry
him.' I leave you to make the application. For
my part I should not know how to decide aright
which I ought to fear more, the enmity of the
one, or the friendship of the other. And what
is to be the result of this war? If we conquer
with the aid of the Sultan Transylvania becomes
a Turkish pashalic. If we are conquered we
sink into the condition of an Austrian province,
while now we are, by God's grace, an independent country. Hungary's fate anticipates
improvement in every case, and it lies just as
heavily on my heart as on the hearts of those
who think that the sick man can be healed by
the sword. But nothing is to be attained in this
way. How much blood has already flowed without the slightest result! Let us try at once another way. Ought not the Hungarian to possess
so much strength of soul that he can overthrow,
by intellectual superiority, the foe whom he cannot conquer by force of arms? Subdue your
conqueror. You who in understanding, activity,
wealth and manly beauty are the first of the
kingdom, why do you not take the high position

which is becoming you? Were you there where the Pazmans and Esterhazys spread themselves no empty place would then remain for a Lobkowitz. If, instead of fighting these small battles without result, you would fight it out with your intelligences and your influence you might make your land prosperous and that without the cost of a drop of blood. It rests with you to conjure up again the period of Louis the Great. At that time when the foreign prince was so enamored of his chosen people he understood how to become a Hungarian and so, with the help of the nations, became strong and powerful. If in your eyes the prosperity of the nations is of the first importance, change your rôle : let the states of Transylvania undertake to promote peace between the Emperor and the nation, to get back for you your property and your rank and I will be the first to offer a helping hand for that purpose, and Michael Teleki surely will be the second. If you do not accept this proposition then consider what you can do. So far as that prophecy goes of first one and then another, you need not be concerned about Transylvania. I will wager that everybody who crosses Transylvania by force of arms, let him be who he may, will find a force to match him. I also wager that this Transylvanian fighting force will never for the love of anybody rashly cross the borders of a foreign country."

"So then you think Hungary is a foreign country!" rang out a mocking voice from the crowd.

This interruption disturbed Banfy's composure. He turned angrily toward the corner from which the remark had come, and when he met the cold, disdainful glances of the Hungarians grouped together, he forgot himself; everything swam before him, and throwing his kalpac on the ground he cried out:

"As you say, quite right. You have always been strangers to us; nay more, stepchildren! You have always done wrong and we have always suffered for it. We have fought and you have trifled away the results of our conquests. Three times have your dissensions plunged your country into the grave, and three times has Transylvania brought it to resurrection. We have furnished you heroes and you have furnished us traitors." These last words Banfy had fairly to shout to make himself heard above the increasing din. Soon all were shouting confusedly. The Hungarian lords sprang up from their places and broke out in anathemas against Banfy. The more serious of the peace-party shook their heads thoughtfully when they saw that this inconsiderate expression of Banfy's was the occasion of stirring up so much violence of feeling.

Beldi rose; and the rest who would gladly see peace restored, shouted: "Let us listen to Beldi."

At this moment a young man suddenly made his way forward and stood in front of Banfy with glowing face and his hand resting on Teleki's seat. It was Emerich Tököli.

"I too ask for a word," he shouted, with a voice that drowned all else. "By law and justice, speech is mine at this bar. If you in Hungary deny your mother and would make boundaries between her and you, then I too will speak. I am just as strong a landed nobleman in Transylvania as you, proud little god, whose father was one of those heroes in whose name you are heaping up insults on the mother-country."

Beldi tried to get to Tököli to restrain him from speaking, but just then he was seized from behind by the hand, and when he looked around he saw to his surprise his son-in-law, Paul Wesselenyi, who called him out into the entrance hall "just for a word." Beldi went into the hall while Tököli's thundering words sounded through the entire room, drowning out the ceaseless noise. In this entrance hall a veiled lady waited for Beldi. When she uncovered her face it was only with the greatest difficulty that he recognized his own daughter Sophie, the wife of Paul Wesselenyi, so much had sorrow changed and broken her. She had wept her beautiful eyes out.

"We are fugitives from our country," sobbed Sophie, falling on her father's breast. "Our estates in Hungary have been taken from us. My husband has been driven from his castle and is fleeing for his life."

Beldi grew serious. This unexpected Job's messenger brought war to his soul. Within thundered Tököli's voice summoning them to an uprising and Beldi no longer was in a hurry to check it.

"Stay with me," he said, sorrowfully. "Here you can live in peace until the fate of the country meets with a change."

"Too late," replied Wesselenyi. "I have already enlisted as common soldier under the standard of the French general, Count Bohan."

"You, a common soldier! You, a descendant of the Palatine Wesselenyi! And what is to become of my daughter meantime?"

"She is to remain with you and to be widowed until the struggle for Hungary is over."

When he had finished speaking he placed his young wife Sophie in Beldi's arms, kissed her brow and went away with dry eyes.

Within the people were clamoring. Beldi saw his daughter sob and a bitter feeling began to blaze in his breast, not unlike revenge. He began to feel almost content that within there was a cry for war and he stood ready to draw his sword—he, the leader of the peace party!—to rush into the hall of the Diet and cry aloud, "War and retaliation!"

At this moment the pages conducted to the door of the entrance hall an old man, pale as death who, recognizing Beldi, hastened to him and addressed him with trembling voice:

"My lord, surely you are the general of the Szeklers, Paul Beldi, of Uzoni?"

"Yes, what do you wish of me?"

"I am," stammered, in dying voice, the sick old man, "Benfalva's last inhabitant. The rest have all been carried off by war—famine—pestilence. I alone am left; after I came away the place was entirely deserted; I too feel my release near and so I have brought with me to give over to you, the public seal, and the—village bell— give them over to the nation—let them be kept in the archives—and let it be written above: 'This was the bell and the seal of Benfalva, in which village everybody to the last man is dead'!" At this Beldi let his hand fall from his sword hilt in dismay and freed himself from the embrace of his daughter who was still clinging to him.

"Go home to your mother at Bodola, and learn to bear your fate nobly."

He then took the seal out of the hand of the death-stricken old man and hurried back into the hall just as Tököli had finished his speech, caus- ing a terrible effect on the entire assembly. The French ambassador pressed his hand. Beldi took his place at the Szeklers' table and laid down the

seal. He was universally respected and when
they saw that he was ready to speak there was
perfect silence.

"See," he said in excited tones; "a desolated
village sends here to the country its official seal
by its last inhabitant, and he too is at the point
of death. . . . Of such villages there are already enough in Transylvania and in time there
may be still more. Famine and war have laid
waste the most beautiful portions of our country.
. . . This seal, my lords, you must not forget
to place among the symbols of your victories."

These last words Beldi uttered hardly above a
whisper yet they were heard in every corner of
the hall, so deep a silence reigned. A tremor
passed over the faces of the men.

"Outside the door I hear some one weeping,"
Beldi went on with quivering lips. "It is my
own daughter, the wife of Paul Wesselenyi, who
has been driven from her country and who has
thrown herself sobbing at my feet that I in revenge for her wrongs may allow retaliation to
prevail. . . . And I say to you, let my child
weep, let her perish, let me—and if necessary my
entire family, be set apart for destruction, but
let nobody in Transylvania suffer on account of
my sorrow—even if every one of you has agreed
to the war—I am against it— My lords—do not
forget, I pray you, to lay among your trophies
this seal. and soon the rest too."

When he had spoken, Beldi took his place
again. Long after his words were ended the
silence of the grave reigned throughout the hall.
Tekeli, ascribing this silence to disapproval rose,
sure of his position, and made the states give
their votes. But this one time he had not taken
the public pulse correctly, for the majority of the
states, affected by the previous scene voted for
peace, so great was the influence of Beldi and
Banfy still over the country.

Teleki looked in confusion toward his son-in-
law. The latter muttered bitterly with clenched
fists and tears in his eyes:

"Flectere si nequeo superos, Acheronta mo-
vebo."

When the assembly had broken up Forval and
Nicholas Bethlen met.

"So then there is no future hope of seeing
Transylvania take up arms," said the Frenchman,
somewhat dejectedly.

"On the contrary we just begin to hope with
good reason," replied Bethlen, laying his hand
on his friend's shoulder.

"Did you listen when the young man spoke?"

"He spoke beautifully."

"It is not a question of beautiful speaking. I
think that is the man you are looking for."

"A King of Hungary?"

"Or a fugitive fleeing from country to country,
just as the dice fall."

CHAPTER XVI

THE LEAGUE

IN accordance with a good old custom every festivity must close with a banquet, so this noisy Diet was closed with a still noisier revel at which Michael Apafi again presided, and this time with justice, for according to the old chronicles a skin of wine was not enough for him at a sitting.

Wine gives a peculiar fire not only to love but also to hatred. If ladies are at table we must look out for our hearts; but when men are together then our heads are in danger.

After the feasting, in true Transylvanian fashion the drinking was continued standing. The entertainment took on a livelier cast and the Prince turned to each one of the lords as they stood, holding out a full beaker to them and challenging them to drink.

"Drink! to my health! to the welfare of the country—or to whatever else you please!" The men were all in good spirits, quarreling with each other good-naturedly and becoming reconciled again. One man only who never drank, Michael Teleki, remained sober.

Beware of those who remain sober when everybody gets drunk! Teleki went round among the lords who were drinking together on a wager and joking, and had for some time been moving stealthily about Banfy, when Banfy noticed him and turned toward him jestingly.

"How sad you are!" he said, with a pitying laugh; "just like a man who has lost a palatinate."

This remark came very aptly for Teleki. With a smile out of which gleamed a deadly dagger, he replied:

"No thanks to you! If Paul Beldi had not been present you would have been alone with your vote. But it has happened once more, in the presence of so influential a man as Paul Beldi we must all bow. His words are for all the country like the amen in the prayer."

Teleki bowed with a show of deep respect as he thrust this poisoned steel into the great lord's heart, for there was nothing could so touch him as to have somebody considered greater than himself, especially when it was a man who deserved it. Teleki now turned to Beldi, drew him into the recess of a window and gently demanded speech with him.

"I have always regarded you as a very noble-hearted man; to-day I learned, although to my own disadvantage, to recognize you as doubly so. The Diet knows only that you sacrificed your love for your daughter when you voted for peace. I know besides that you sacrificed at the same time your hatred for Banfy."

"I—I never hated Banfy!"

"I know why you have concealed this hatred. You think that your reasons for it are not known to anybody. Oh my friend, we who are men know well that one may pardon a dagger thrust but never a kiss!"

Beldi drew himself up and knew not how to answer this man who had thrust the most painful sting of jealousy into his heart, broken off the point and now left him with a smile.

At this moment Banfy came up behind him. In Banfy burned the desire to make Beldi feel his arrogance and he sought an opportunity of coming to blows with him. Beldi did not notice him at first and when the Prince, by chance, reached that part of the hall at that moment and with friendly words offered him the jewel-studded beaker in his hand, Beldi thought that the invitation was to him alone and never once suspecting that anybody else was reaching for the beaker, he took it from the hand of the Prince and drained it off to his health at the very moment that Banfy reached out his hand for it. Banfy grew purple with rage and turning haughtily to Beldi, he said in an insulting tone:

"Not so fast, Szekler, you might at least, since I am the general of the country, show me sufficient respect not to take the glass from my very lips. I would have you understand that if you continue in such insolence we may easily come to blows."

Had Beldi been in any other state of mind he would have excused himself for his mistake with his wonted moderation, but now the desire had been roused within him to measure his strength. He looked at Banfy calmly from head to foot and said with suppressed anger:

"I would have you understand, Dionysius, that I am a heavy Szekler. If by chance I should happen to fall on you I should crush you so that you would not again on this earth sound your horn."

"What foolishness is this?" said the Prince, coming between them. "I am surprised at my lords. Drink now! Inter pocula non sunt seria tractanda!"

And the Prince compelled the two great lords to approach each other and placed the hand of the one in that of the other. Then he let the matter rest and went on, thinking that it was only a quarrel over the cups.

But Teleki observed that after this scene both lords left the hall, and soon learned that they had gone away from Karlsburg suddenly, so giving free play to the further plans of the minister. Teleki and his faithful men remained alone with the intoxicated Prince.

"Drink, my lords, be merry!" said Apafi

"Let not a man of you leave me! Who has gone already?"

"Beldi!" shouted several.

"Very well, the poor fellow has not seen his wife for a long time; let him go to her. And who else?"

"Banfy!"

"Hm! He too! Why did he go?"

"He went home to reign," said Ladislaus Szekeli, scornfully; he was one of Teleki's creatures.

"He cannot stay in a place where he feels that any one is his superior," Nalaczy added.

"Just to please his Excellency I am sure I shall not lay down the Prince's crown."

"That he does not need at all," Teleki rejoined. "He knows how to rule in Transylvania without a crown. What he commands the country must comply with, and what the country commands he pushes aside with disdain."

"I should like to see him!" muttered Apafi, angrily.

"And yet 'tis so. We wish war, he does not, and we must yield. We wish peace and it occurs to him to carry on war at his own expense with our ally. The throne is ours, the country his."

"Do not say that, my lord Michael Teleki."

"Do you too speak for me, Nalaczy. What answer did he make in the affair of Zolyomi?"

"He sent word," Nalaczy made haste to take up the conversation,—"that if the country de-

manded back from him the Gyalu property for
Zolyomi he would like in exchange the Szamos-
ujvar estate."

"What!" cried the Prince. "The estate which
the country set apart for my revenue? my own
princely income?"

"So he said; and otherwise he will not consent
even if Zolyomi should set the Turk against us
this very day."

"I will soon settle that with him. Not another
word, my lords."

"The affront to the Prince," Teleki joined in,
"your Highness may overlook as long as it
pleases you, but Banfy's conduct toward the people, toward the nobility,—that we cannot let pass
in any such way. He has recently taken a violent course against the noble lady Szent-Pali;—
the ancestral house of the poor widow offended
the house of my great lord because it interfered
with the view from his palace; at once he ordered
the poor woman's house to be appraised and
pulled down. The authorities gave her a letter
of protection but my lord tore this in two and
ordered the work of destruction to go on and the
home of the poor widow's ancestors to be razed
to the ground. The country might build it up
again if it chose, he said. Such a deed in ordinary times my lord, costs the doer his head."

Apafi was silent. The flame of anger leaped
into his eyes.

"But that was not all," continued Teleki; "the insult of the individual vanishes when the fate of the country is at stake. This great lord who knows so well how to talk about the blessings of peace—let us see how he exerts himself for its maintenance. He takes the sword out of our hand, closes our lips that we may not raise any protestations because Kecskemet has been burned to ashes and its inhabitants massacred; and then he himself assembles an army and incites the Turks to war against the country while we are unable to make such royal gifts as might have some effect against his schemes. Three letters have come to us, one from the Pasha of Nagy Varad, another from the General of the forces at Ofen and the third from the Sultan himself, in all of which satisfaction is demanded of us for the defeat which the Pasha of Nagy Varad suffered at the hands of Banfy, or else an indemnity of a hundred and fifty thousand piastres. Since it is useless to talk of satisfaction with Banfy will it please your Highness to consider where we can raise the money demanded?"

"Nowhere!" said Apafi, furiously, breaking his glass against the table. "I will show that I am in a position to gain satisfaction from any man even one so mighty as Banfy."

"Then I could wish that your Highness would acquaint us with the manner of this satisfaction, for we know that Banfy will not appear if sum-

moned. If we should compel him by force he
has shown that he alone is stronger than the
whole country. He orders the countries to assemble, the frontier troops to march, and we
might have the same experience that my lord
Ladislaus Csaki had when Banfy seized the official
sent for his arrest and held us up to ridicule."

"What would you counsel, since you know
how to give counsel in such affairs?" Apafi
asked, with annoyance.

"I know of only one remedy that will heal the
evil thoroughly."

"Prescribe it. What are the means?"

"The jus ligatum."

In spite of his drunkenness Apafi shrank from
this suggestion; he threw himself into an armchair and gazed fixedly at Teleki.

"Are you not ashamed?" he mumbled in the
broken sentences of the drunken—"to propose a
secret league against a free nobleman?—in viola-
tion of the fundamental law of our country to
bind yourself in secret against him?"

"The shame does not fall on me," replied
Teleki, quietly and steadily, "it rests rather in
the fact that the country has not sufficient power
to bring a rebel to justice; that in our fatherland
there is a man who can openly defy the law and
deride the decisions of the Prince. When in such
a case there is no alternative except the jus liga-

tum, the shame for such a state of affairs does not fall upon me but on the Prince!"

Apafi sprang from his seat in anger and paced the room with long strides. The lords watched him in deep silence. At length he stopped beside Teleki and leaning on the back of his chair asked:

"How do you think the league can be brought about?" Nalaczy and Szekeli smiled at each other; evidently the idea had impressed the Prince. Teleki motioned to Szekeli to bring writing materials and a roll of parchment and arranging these before him replied:

"We will draw up at once the counts of the indictment that can be brought against Banfy; your Highness shall sign them and in secret we will win over the nobles of the country to agree to Banfy's arrest and to stand by the league before any legal steps are taken."

At this many of the lords present began to chew their beards thoughtfully. Teleki noticed the movement and said pertinently:

"As I observe that nobody here has the courage to give his signature first, I have a man all ready who alone is in a position so far as power is concerned to oppose Banfy and when once this man has signed all the rest will follow."

"Who is that?" asked Apafi.

"Paul Beldi," was the answer.

The Prince shook his head.

"He will not do it.   He is far too honorable a
man."   These words spoken in the bravery of
his intoxication threw Teleki completely out of
his composure.

"Are we then planning a dishonorable action?" he demanded of the Prince, vehemently.

"What I meant to say was that he would not
voluntarily begin action against anybody, for he
is a peace-loving man."

"But I know his weak spot which you have
only to touch with your little finger to rouse him
to blows and make a lion out of a lamb.   I will
bring him to the point."

At this moment the door opened and to the
astonishment of all the Princess entered.   This
time her appearance was no chance.   It was easy
to see by the excitement in her face that she
knew well what had happened.   The lords grew
confused and Apafi himself was so dismayed, in
spite of the irascibility incident to his drunkenness, that he whispered to Teleki,

"Put that paper aside."

Teleki alone remained composed and instead
of putting it aside spread it out the more.

"What are my lords doing?" asked Madame
Apafi; she was pale and her bosom heaved.

"We are taking counsel," answered Teleki,
firmly.

"You are taking counsel?" asked Anna, approaching nearer to the table.

"At the same time we would put to your Grace the question, who gave you the right to disturb us when we are making decisions about the most important affairs of the country?" continued Teleki, in a hard tone of voice.

"You are making decisions about the most important affairs of the country," replied Madame Apafi, slowly repeating Teleki's words, while she looked at him sharply; then suddenly she broke out in a resonant voice,—"and that over your wine cups! You consult about the fate of the country while the man at its head is intoxicated, so that you may bring all to confusion."

Teleki sprang from his seat and turned to the Prince.

"May it please your Majesty to dismiss us? Evidently a domestic scene is in progress."

"Anna," cried Apafi, red with shame and the glow of the wine, "leave this hall this instant. It is our order and from this day on for a week do not appear again before our eyes."

"Very well, Apafi. I have nothing more to say to you for you are not in your senses. But to you, my Lord High Counsellor, who are always sober, I have a word to say:—I raised you from the dust; I helped you to your present position; in gratitude for this you have forced yourself between my heart and the Prince's so that whenever I would approach my husband I find you in my path. You have taken the sceptre out of the

Prince's hand and in its stead you have forced into his hand the headsman's sword, so that he begins to rule by that. Now let me tell you that if I am not allowed to get to the Prince's heart yet I will stand in the way of the headsman's sword. Whenever it is to fall I shall be found between the blow and the victim; and you two choice menials,—barons—you Szekeli and you Nalaczy who cannot yourselves tell now how you so suddenly became great lords, remember that the wheel goes down as often as up and that the judgment which to-day you pass against others by to-morrow may be carried out against yourselves. And the rest of you intriguing lords, who get courage for your timid hearts out of the wine cups, remember, and shudder at the thought, that in the bumpers in your hands not wine, but the blood of the innocent, foams. Shame on you all, that you give your Prince wine that you may demand of him blood! And now, your Highness, add two weeks more to my term of exile."

With these words the Princess quickly left the hall. The lords were silent and dared not look at each other. Teleki rose, closed the door, dipped his quill and said:

"Let us continue from where we left off."

CHAPTER XVII

DEATH FOR A KISS

PAUL BELDI took the direct route from Karlsburg to Bodola. All the way he was tormented by the thought which Teleki's words had called up again. In itself a kiss is a very innocent matter but if another knows of it, has noticed it ?—if this should be only one pole of the world of distrust about which the soul revolves bringing up now this, now that, which might have happened before and after,—and then too another knows of it ?— The husband thought that a kiss nobody knew about caused no defect in his wife's virtue—but now it lived on the lips of others; perhaps still more; perhaps the world was dragging his honor in the dust while he supposed it well guarded, and the first sound of the derision to him so deadly had just reached his ear, and that too from his most hated foe. .   .   .

Night interrupted his thoughts. The horses were tired out, Beldi had given them no rest, had had no fresh relays,—only on and on. He wished to get home as quickly as possible—to have under his eyes that wife who had cost him such disgrace —who knows how much !— But is it sufficient satisfaction to see a woman weep or die when a

man still lives on whom he might take revenge?
—a man too who had been his enemy from the
time when they had both served as pages of
Gabriel Bethlen and who now sought out the
most sensitive spot in his heart to tear it with his
ruthless hand.

"Turn about!" he shouted to the driver.
"Take the road to Klausenburg."

The old servant shook his head, turned into a
side road and soon lost the road so completely in
this wandering by night that he was at last
obliged to confess to his master that he did not
know himself where they were. Beldi trembled
with inward emotion. Looking about him he
saw not far off a light, and quite out of temper
he bade the coachman drive toward it. They
drove into the courtyard of a lonely country
house. The barking of the great house-dog
brought out the master, in whom Beldi recognized
old Adam Gyergyai one of his dearest friends
who, as he recognized Beldi, hurried forward to
embrace him, beside himself with joy.

"Good-evening, my dear friend," said the
good old man, covering his guest with kisses:—
"I do not ask what good fortune has brought
you to me."

"To tell the truth, I have lost my way. I was
on my way to Klausenburg. I shall go on this
very night, and with your permission leave my
horses here to rest."

"What have you to do there that is so pressing?"

"I must carry some news," said Beldi, evasively.

"If that is all, why need you hasten so? You can certainly trust it to a letter and one of my servants on horse shall carry it at once to the place while you stay here."

"You are right," said Beldi, after some consideration;—"it will be better for me to manage the matter by letter." So he asked for writing materials, sat down and wrote Banfy. Writing usually brings a certain soberness to one's thoughts, so this letter was in quite a moderate tone. He informed Banfy that he summoned him to Szamos-Ujvar to adjust an affair of honor. With that Beldi sealed the letter and intrusted it to Gyergyai with the request that he be so kind as to send it.

"So you are writing to Banfy, my good friend," said the old man, looking at the address of the letter. "You could have talked with him a little while ago. What have you two to arrange with each other that is so urgent?"

"You remember, my friend," replied Beldi, "that you saw me once in the lists with Banfy, at the time of the tournament when George Rakoczy was the master?"

"Oh yes, you had overcome all other contestants but could do nothing against each other."

"On that occasion you said that you would like to see which one of us would carry off the victory in a real engagement."

"Yes, I remember that too."

"Now you shall see."

Gyergyai looked Beldi in the eye.

"My friend, I do not know what this letter contains but from your expression I infer your thought. I have heard my father say that a man should not send off the same day a letter written under excitement, but should lay it under his pillow and sleep on it. The advice is not bad. Do not send your letter off before morning; in fact I will not send it to-night."

Beldi complied with the old man's advice. He put the letter under his pillow, lay down, fell asleep and dreamed. In his dream he was happy with his wife and children. The noise of a wagon passing by in the morning awakened him. The first thing that his hand touched was his letter to Banfy. He broke it open, read it through again, and—was very much ashamed that he had written anything of the kind.

"Where was your understanding, Beldi?" he asked himself with a smile, tore the letter in two and threw it into the fire. "How they would have laughed at you!" he thought. "They would have said you were an old fool to whom it had occurred late in life to be jealous of the mother of his children on account of a kiss given by a man in his cups and received against the lady's will." What a weapon he would have given Banfy if he had announced that he was not sure of his wife on Banfy's account. "We will go straight to Bodola," he said gently to his servant when he entered, and then he took leave of his host.

"And what about the letter you were going to send?" asked Gyergyai with concern.

"I have already conveyed it—to the flames!" replied Beldi, smiling, and went on his way with his feelings quite changed. As he approached Bodola he noticed from a distance the members of his family who had been watching for him from the castle balcony; as soon as they recognized his carriage they hurried down to meet him. When he reached the foot of the castle hill there they all were,—his wife and children; they threw themselves on his neck with cries of joy and he kissed each one several times over, but especially his dear devoted wife on whom he feasted his eyes. It seemed to him that her eyes were brighter, her face more charming, her lips sweeter than ever. "What fools men are!" thought Beldi. "When they do not see their wives they are ready to believe everything bad of them, and when they do see them they forget it all."

He was so abandoned to his joy that he did not observe that there was a stranger in the family circle, but the stranger made haste to attract his attention. He was Feriz Bey, a handsome, well-built young Turk, with frank, noble features resembling a Hungarian's.

"You do not notice me, or perhaps you do not remember me," said the youth, stepping up to Beldi.

Beldi glanced at him and thought he recognized him, but did not venture to call him by name until his younger daughter Aranka hanging on her father's arm said with a childlike laugh:

"Have you forgotten Feriz Bey? I knew him at once."

Beldi extended his hand to the youth with a cordial greeting.

"My father sends me to you with an urgent message and had you not come I should have ridden after you. When your family rejoicing is over call me, for my mission admits of no delay."

Beldi was surprised at the serious tone of the youth, and as soon as he reached the castle called him aside to a private room. Then the young Bey gave him a roll fastened with a yellow seal and tied with cords. Beldi broke it open and read as follows:

"May heaven protect and defend you and your family. Transylvania is in peril; the Grand Seignior is aroused by the conflict between

Dionysius Banfy and the Pasha of Nagy Varad.
It is reported that this nobleman is in corre-
spondence with the Roman emperor. See to it
that the country bridles Banfy; you have still
force sufficient. The Sultan has sworn that if
the Prince should not prove a match for him
and know how to command he will drive them
both out of the country and intrust the control
of Transylvania to a pasha. The pashas of Nagy
Varad and Temesvar, the princes on the frontier
and Tartar Khan have received orders to hold
themselves in readiness to make their way into
Transylvania from all sides at the first signal.
Keep that noble lord under check for death
hangs over your heads by a mere thread.

"Your good friend,
"KUTSCHUK PASHA."

Beldi's face grew dark as he read these lines.
So then it was in vain for him to put Banfy's
name out of his mind; this letter called it up
again and in an aspect still more hateful. He
folded the letter, and in a few words gave the
serious youth a reply for his father.

"Inform your father that our action shall an-
ticipate the threatened evil. I send my thanks
for the warning."

With this reply Feriz Bey left the castle.
Beldi remained alone in his room; deep in
thought he paced back and forth, and racked his
brain to find out some way to meet the peril, but
he saw none. It was not to be expected that a
man of Banfy's pride would make any conces-

sions to the Pasha, especially after his victory
and in a just cause. And yet the justice of the
cause must give way to the welfare of the country. Deep in these and similar thoughts he did
not notice that some one was knocking at his
door. When no answer was made to the thrice-
repeated knock the door opened and Beldi, rousing himself from his meditation, saw Michael
Teleki. Beldi was at first so bewildered that his
speech forsook him. "You seem surprised at my
coming," said Teleki, noticing Beldi's astonishment. "You are amazed that I should have
followed you such a distance after an absence of
barely twenty-four hours. Great changes have
taken place. Transylvania is threatened by a
peril which must be prevented at once."

"I know it," replied Beldi, and let Teleki read
Kutschuk Pasha's letter with the exception of the
signature.

"You know more than I," said the minister;
"what I wished to say of this affair is a secret
which not even walls may hear."

"I understand," said Beldi, and at once gave
orders that no one should come into the entrance
hall, stationed guards under the windows and
had the curtains drawn. Only one way was left
unguarded, and that was a door in the arras at
the back of the room, which led by a narrow
hallway to his wife's sleeping room, an arrange-
ment often found in the houses of the Hungarian

nobility. By way of precaution Beldi closed even that door.

"Do you feel safe enough?" he asked Teleki.

"One thing more. Give me your word of honor that in case the information communicated to you does not meet your approval you will at least guard it as a secret."

"I promise solemnly," replied Beldi, tense for the development. With that Teleki drew out a sheet of parchment folded several times, spread it out and held it under Beldi's eyes without letting it go out of his hands. It was the League formed against Banfy signed and sealed by the Prince. The farther Beldi read in the document the gloomier he grew. Finally he turned to Teleki and thrust the paper from him with loathing.

"My lord, that is a dirty piece of work!"

Teleki was prepared for such a reception and summoned his usual sophistry to his aid.

"Beldi," he said, "this is no time for strait-laced notions. It is the end and not the means in this case. This is the worst only because it is the last. It is the last because there is no other way left. If anybody in the country has attained to such despotism that the arm of the law is no longer strong enough to bring him into the courts, then he has only himself to thank if the state is compelled to conspire against him. The man who cannot be reached by the executioner's axe is struck by the dagger of the assassin. When Dionysius Banfy set at naught the commands of the Prince and began war on his own account he put himself outside the law. In such a case when the justice of the state has lost its authority it is natural to take refuge in secret justice. If anybody has wronged me and the law cannot procure me satisfaction I make use of my own weapons and shoot him down wherever I find him. If the country is wronged by anybody who escapes punishment, it must make use of the jus ligatum and have the man seized. The general welfare demands this and the general peril drives us to it."

"God's hand controls us," said Beldi. "If he will destroy our fatherland let us bow our heads and die with a quiet conscience—die in the defence of liberty; but let us never raise our arms to the destruction of our own hereditary justice. Rather let us endure the evils that have their origin in this freedom, than lay the axe to its very root. Let war and conflict over freedom enter our land rather than any conspiracy contrary to its laws. The one sheds the blood of the nation but the other kills her soul. I disapprove of this League and will fight against it."

At this Michael Teleki rose, fell on his knees before Beldi and said with his hands raised to heaven:

"I swear by the Almighty Living God: so

may he grant me salvation, protect my life, pros-
per my wife, my children, as I am your true
friend; and because I know that Banfy's every
effort is directed to destroy you and your home
therefore do I announce to you that if you love
your life, that of your wife, your children, you
must meet this impending danger by signing the
League. Now I have said all that I could to
save you and the fatherland and that too at my
own peril. I wash my hands in innocence."

Beldi turned in calm dignity toward the
Prince's minister and said in a tone of firm conviction:

"Fiat justitia, pereat mundus."

*   *   *   *   *   *

A few minutes after Teleki's arrival at Bodola
a rider came bounding into the castle yard. It
was Andrew the faithful old servant of Madame
Apafi, who inquired for Madame Beldi, handed
her a letter from the Princess and added that
this was the more urgent as he had recognized
Teleki's carriage in the courtyard, which he
should have preceded.

Madame Beldi broke open the letter, and
read:

"MY DEAR FRIEND: Michael Teleki has gone
to your husband. His purpose is to ruin Banfy
secretly by Beldi's hand. The nobles have taken
an oath to break the law. Fortunately every

one of them has a wife in those heart the better feelings are not yet dead. I have called on each one separately to guard her husband against Teleki's malice. I hope to attain the greatest result through you. Beldi is the most distinguished among them; if he agrees to the League the rest will follow his example; but he is also the most honorable man and the best husband. I count on your firmness; use every means.

"Your friend,
"ANNA BORNEMISSA."

Madame Beldi almost gave way when she read this letter. Teleki had been talking for half-an-hour with her husband and the servants had brought word that every one had been ordered away from the lords' vicinity, even from the entrance hall. The entire situation became clear to the lady's mind at once. She was terrified! perhaps it was already too late and she could not get to her husband. What should she do? Then she remembered the secret way from her room to her husband's and she hurried along, reached the arras door, stood there and listened. She heard only the voice of Teleki, who spoke with growing passion amounting to vehemence. She looked through the key hole and saw how Teleki knelt before her husband and with upraised hands and oaths sought to persuade him. At this sight Madame Beldi was terror-stricken. Why did the proud, powerful man kneel before Beldi? What was he swearing so passionately?

Suddenly Banfy's name rang·on her ear. Horror seized her, and at the moment when Beldi answered : " Let justice prevail though the world fall," she thought in her ignorance of Latin that her husband had consented, and in her despair she pressed the latch of the door. When this did not open she pulled at it with frenzied strength and shouted passionately ; " My husband, my beloved master! Lord of my heart! Do not believe one word Teleki says, for he will ruin you ! "

At this passionate outcry the man started up in affright and Beldi arose with annoyance, went to the door and said to his wife angrily : "Stay in your own province, my wife."

Madame Beldi lost her presence of mind entirely. The thought that her husband might assent to Teleki's plan made it impossible for her to comprehend the situation. She forgot that even the best man is ashamed to have it publicly known that he is under the control of his wife, and merely to prove the contrary would be inclined to be untrue to the very convictions he would have followed without compulsion. Consequently Madame Beldi rushed into the room, sank down at her husband's feet, clung to his knees and called out in an impassioned voice :

"Sweet lord of my heart! By the Almighty God, I implore you, do not believe this man. Do not be influenced by him to bring innocent blood

on your head. You have always been just. You
cannot turn hangman!"

"Wife, you are mad!"

"I know what I am saying. I saw him on
his knees before you. He who believes in God
does not kneel before any man. He means
through you to ruin Dionysius Banfy. Woe to
us if you do that, for if he is the first you will be
the second."

When Teleki saw his secret disclosed in this
way he was furious.

"If my wife did that to me," he said, violently,
"I would tear her eyes out of her head. If anybody wished to help me for my own safety I
should thank him for it rather than leave him to
be met by my wife in an insulting way."

Beldi called out angrily to his wife to leave at
once.

"I shall stay even if you kill me: for this is a
case of life and death. Here the peace of your
family is at stake and in that I have a right. I
too may speak. I beg, I entreat you, undertake
nothing against Banfy."

Beldi was ashamed of this attack upon his
manly supremacy and could hardly control himself. When his wife mentioned Banfy he started
as if a viper had stung him. The effect of this
name did not escape Teleki and he said ironically
and with meaning:

"It seems women pardon certain things more

readily than their husbands." The sharp allusion
went through Beldi's soul like lightning. The
kiss came into his mind. The kiss! Pale and
speechless he seized his wife by the arm and her
sob only serving to fan his jealousy, he dragged
her through the arras door and locked it behind
her. There she lay sobbing violently, cursing
the princely counsellor loudly and beating against
the closed door with her hand. Beldi sat down
white as death and with teeth set, called out to
Teleki:

"Where is the document?"

Teleki spread it out before him on the table.
Without a word Beldi took his pen and with
steady hand wrote his name under that of Michael
Apafi's. A smile of triumph played about Teleki's
lips. When that had been accomplished there
was once more a threatening, an accusing knock
at Beldi's heart. He laid his hand on the paper
and turned with serious glance toward Teleki.

"I make one condition," he said, hoarsely. "If
Banfy does not oppose his arrest with weapons
right and justice must be granted him according
to legal forms."

"It shall be so—just so," replied the Prince's
counsellor, and reached for the paper.

And still Beldi did not give it up. Still he did
not let it go out of his hand.

"My lord," he said, "promise me also, that
you will not put Banfy to death secretly, but

when he is arrested you will bring suit against him according to the usual mode of procedure, in a regular court of justice. If you do not assure me of this, then I will tear this paper in two and throw it into the fire with the Prince's signature and mine."

"I assure you, on my word!" promised the Princely counsellor, at the same time inwardly smiling at the man who while he was still upright showed himself weak, and when he had already fallen strove to show himself firm.

With the League signed Teleki went the same day to Ladislaus Csaki, from him to Haller and then to Bethlen. As soon as they saw Beldi's name they signed, for all hated Banfy. In every house the husbands fell out with their wives. Nowhere did Teleki escape calumny. Nevertheless the League was established.

So Transylvania made her own grave.

CHAPTER XVIII

WIFE AND ODALISQUE

SINCE that painful interview Madame Banfy had not seen her husband. Fate had willed that Banfy should remain away continually; he was hardly back from the assembly at Karlsburg when he was called to Somlyo where his troops had taken a stand against the Turks. During the few hours he had spent in his house in the intervals, his wife had secluded herself from him and had not admitted any of the retinue to her presence. She did not leave her room, and received nobody.

One day both husband and wife were invited to be god-parents at Roppand, in the house of Gabriel Vitez to whom a son had been born, and who knew nothing of the existing variance. It was impossible to refuse the invitation. On the appointed day Madame Banfy from Bonczida, and her husband from Somlyo, to their mutual surprise met at the house of rejoicing. At first they shrank from meeting each other; their inclination had long sought such a meeting but pride had restrained them. So they were both glad and indignant at this accident but could not express both feelings. In a circle of friends their conduct must be such that no one should know that this meeting was not of daily occurrence with them.

Toward the close of the festivity and banquet, which lasted until late at night, Vitez took care that all his guests should be lodged with due comfort. The wives were with their husbands, the young girls had an apartment to themselves and the young men the rooms assigned to the hunters.

For Banfy and his wife a pavilion in the garden had been fitted up, which promised to be the quietest spot as it was quite separated from the noisy court. As an especial mark of attention the master himself conducted them there. It had been some time since they had slept under the same roof but in the presence of so many acquaintances they could not show their feelings and were compelled to accept the provision made for them. It was not enough to accompany them there himself but the host indulged in many jests and finally left them alone after many times wishing them good-night.

The pavilion consisted of two adjoining rooms. They looked very pleasant; in one of them a merry fire blazed high in the chimney and the tall clock in the corner ticked familiarly. Behind the parted brocade curtains of the high bed were seen the snow-white feather-beds inviting to rest, and two small red-bordered pillows on them. In the other room partly lighted by the firelight was a sofa covered with a bear's skin and with one cushion of deerskin. Evidently it had not been expected that anybody would sleep here.

Banfy looked at his wife sadly. Now for the first time, since he could no longer come near her he saw what a treasure he had had in this beautiful and noble woman. Gentle, sorrowful, with eyes downcast, his wife stood before him. In her heart too many traitorous feelings were pleading for her husband. Pride and injured wifely dignity, that inflexible judge, began almost to waver. In a noble heart love does not give way to hatred but to pain.

Banfy stepped nearer to his wife, took her hand in his and pressed it. He felt the hand tremble, but there was no return of his pressure. He kissed her gently on the forehead, cheeks and lips: the lady permitted this but without return, and yet—had she looked up at her husband she would have seen in his eyes two tears of most sincere penitence. Banfy sat down speechless with a sigh, still holding Margaret's hand in his. It needed only a friendly word from his wife and he would have thrown himself at her feet and wept like a repentant child. Instead of that Madame Banfy with a self-denying affectation said:

"Do you wish to stay in this room and shall I go into the other?" Her frosty tone touched

Banfy. He sighed deeply and his eyes looked sorrowfully at the Paradise closed against him by his wife's joyless countenance. Sadly he rose from the chair, drew his wife's hand to his lips, whispered a barely audible "Good-night" and with unsteady steps entered the next room and closed the door.

Madame Banfy made ready to undress, but sorrow filled her heart and she threw herself on the bed, buried her face in her hands and remained lost in grief.

Can there be a greater pain than when the heart struggles with its own feelings, than when a wife attains to the conviction that the ideal of her love whom she adored next to God, is only an ordinary man, and that the man whom she had loved so devotedly is deserving only of her contempt? yet she is not able to stop loving him. She feels that she must hate him and separate herself from him; she knows that she cannot live without him; she would gladly die for him and yet no opportunity for death offers. Only an unlocked door separated them,—they were only a few steps apart. How small the distance and yet how great!

She sank into a deep revery. The fire had entirely burned down and the room was growing darker and darker. Only the woman's figure with her head buried in her hands was still lighted by the glowing coals. Suddenly it

seemed to her in the stillness of the night and of
her thoughts, as if she heard whispers and
stealthy steps at the door. Madame Banfy
really did hear this but she was in that first
sleep when we hear without noticing what we
hear; when we know what passes without heed.
There was a whispering outside the window too,
and it seemed to her that she heard besides a
slight noise of swords. Half asleep, half awake,
she thought she had risen and bolted the door
but this was only a dream; the door was not
fastened. Then there was the noise of the latch
—she dreamed that her husband came out to her
and entreated her.

"Let us separate, Banfy," she tried to say, but
the words died on her lips. The figure in the
dream whispered to her, "I am not Banfy, but
the headsman," and took her by the hand. At
this cold touch Madame Banfy cried out in terror
and awoke. Two men stood before her with
daggers drawn. The lady looked at them with
a shudder; both were well-known figures; one
was Caspar Kornis, Captain at Maros, and the
other was John Daczo, Captain at Csik, who
stood there threatening her with the points of
their bared daggers at her breast.

"No noise, my gracious lady!" said Daczo,
sternly. "Where is Banfy?"

The lady, wakened from her first sleep, could
scarcely distinguish the objects about her. Ter-

ror robbed her of speech. Suddenly she noticed through the door that the passage-way was filled with armed men and with that sight her presence of mind seemed to return at once. She took in the significance of the moment and when Daczo, gnashing his teeth once more asked where Banfy was she sprang up, ran to the door opening to her husband's room, turned the key quickly and shouted with all her might:

"Banfy, save yourself! They want your life!"

Daczo ran forward to stop the woman's mouth and wrest the key from her. With rare presence of mind Madame Banfy threw the key into the coals and cried:

"Flee, Banfy, your enemies are here!"

Daczo tried to get the key out of the coals and burned his hand badly; still more infuriated he rushed at the lady with his dagger unsheathed intending to thrust her through, but Kornis held him back.

"Stop, my lord, we have no orders to kill the lady nor would it be worthy of us. Let us rather break in the door as quickly as possible."

Both men pushed with their shoulders against the door, Daczo cursing by all the devils, while Madame Banfy on her knees prayed God her husband might escape.

*　　*　　*　　*　　*　　*

Banfy had fallen asleep and he too had a distressing dream. He thought he was in prison, and when Margaret's cry rang out he sprang in terror from his couch, tore open the window of the pavilion without stopping to think and with one bound was in the garden. Here he looked round him quickly. The house was surrounded on all sides by armed Szeklers and the rear of the garden was bordered by a broad ditch filled with stagnant rain-water. Among the foot-soldiers was a group of four or five stable boys standing beside the horses from which the leaders had just dismounted. There was no time to plan. Under cover of the darkness Banfy hurried up to one of the servants, struck him a blow that made the blood flow from nose and mouth, sprang on the horse he was holding and struck the stirrup into its flank. At the outcry of the servant thrown down by the horse but still holding to the halter the Szeklers came running up with wild cries. It suddenly occurred to Banfy to put his hand in the saddlebags where there were always pistols, and seizing one he fired two shots into the crowd pressing about him. In the confusion that resulted he made his horse rear and fled through the garden. The stable boy still clung to the halter and was dragged along until his head struck against the trunk of a tree and he lay there senseless. Banfy galloped to the ditch and crossed it with a bold leap. His pursuers dared not follow him and had to go round by the gate, by which Banfy gained on them several hundred paces, gave rein to the beast, maddened by the noise of pursuit, and chased away over sticks and stones, hills and valleys, without aim or direction.

*   *   *   *   *   *

"A curse on the woman!" growled Daczo, when he learned that Banfy had succeeded in escaping, and he threatened the wife with clenched fist. "You are to blame that Banfy has escaped us!"

"Thanks to Thee, Almighty God!" said Margaret, with hands upraised to heaven.

The Szeklers, exasperated at the husband's escape, rushed at the wife with weapons aimed to kill her.

"Let her die!" "Death on her head!" they roared, with inhuman fury.

"Kill me. I shall be glad to die," said Margaret, kneeling before them. "I had only that one wish left, to be able to die for him. I am in God's hand."

"Get away from here!" cried out Kornis; struck down the Szeklers' weapons with his sword and covered the kneeling woman with his ong cloak.

"Are you not ashamed of yourselves! Would you kill a woman, you mob more pagan than Tartar! Since you have let Banfy escape, go after him!"

"We will kill her!" "We will put an end to her!" roared the Szeklers, and tried to pull Kornis away.

"You cursed beasts! who is in command here? am I not your captain?"

"Not ours," replied a stiff-necked Szekler. "Our captain is Nicholas Bethlen and he is not here!"

"Go find him. But first one word; if a man stays in this room I'll crush him to pulp!"

This did not humble the Szeklers, however, until some one cried: "Let us go to Bonczida!" The others took up the cry "To Bonczida!" and went off with loud curses and in great disorder.

Caspar Kornis took Madame Banfy at once to a carriage and had her driven to Bethlen castle, which was at that time Beldi's property, hoping that if Banfy knew his wife were imprisoned he would be more manageable.

* * * * * *

After Dionysius Banfy had freed himself from the snare set and the sound of the pursuit grew faint, he began to take his bearings in the starry night, and chose his way so successfully through forests and over stubble fields that by daybreak the towers of Klausenburg were in sight. Rage now took the place of fear. At first he thought that the night attack had been only an attempt of his personal enemies, planned without the knowledge of the Prince by those who knew well that it was easier to get approval for a deed done than for one to be done. But the attempt had not succeeded and the lion escaped from the toils of his foes had still strength enough and the will necessary to turn on his pursuers and impress them with respect for the law.

In the open field outside the town Banfy's troops were going through their manœuvres in the early morning, when their leader rode up to them with haggard face, head bare, without his caftan and without his weapons. His chief men hurried to him in terror and met him with a questioning look.

"I have just escaped from a murderous attack," said Banfy, with husky voice and breathing hard. "My enemies fell upon me; I have escaped but my wife is in their hands. By their voices I recognized Kornis and Daczo among my pursuers."

"In fact Daczo's name is worked on the trappings of this horse," said Michael Angyal, who came up just then.

Banfy's face was perturbed as if he could get no clear idea of either past or present.

"I cannot understand the whole affair. If the attack followed a command of the Prince then there must have been a suit, a summons or certainly a sentence. If it was only private revenge then my hand is more than a match for both these good Szeklers. In that case stay here out-

side the city ready for an attack, while I hurry
back to my castle. In a few hours I shall know
what course we must take."

Banfy rode into town accompanied by Michael
Angyal. As he turned the corner of his palace
he had to pass the place where Madame Szent-
Pali's house had stood. Only a corner stone was
left, and as Banfy chanced to look that way he
saw sitting on this one stone the former mistress
of the house, who was waiting there for the lord
with her face lighted with fiendish joy, and as
he turned his head aside greeted him mockingly.

"Good-morning, my gracious lord."

But Banfy galloped on defiantly. At the castle gate his steward from Bonczida was already
waiting for him. After the Szeklers had forced
their way into Bonczida he had escaped; but not
willing to make a sensation with his Job's message had told nobody, and now only whispered
briefly to his lord that everything in the castle
from top to bottom was upturned and that the
Szeklers had entertained themselves after their
own heart. Banfy answered not a word. He
called for his armor and his war-horse and made
his preparations quietly.

"My gracious lord would perhaps do well to
make haste," urged the steward. "The Szeklers
are already in the house."

"It is well," answered Banfy, pacing up and
down with folded arms.

"No, my gracious lord, it is not well. They have destroyed everything in the rooms, cut the carpets, divided up the valuables, let the wine in the cellar run out and finally stolen the horses."

"It is no matter," answered the magnate, gloomily. What did he care at that moment for all the valuables, wine or riding horses?

"They have done even more, my lord. They have forced their way into your wife's sleeping-room, used the portrait of the gracious lady as a target and disfigured it horribly."

"What! the portrait of my wife!" cried Banfy, laying his hand on his sword. "The portrait of my wife did you say?" he repeated, with flashing eyes. "Ah," he cried, tearing his sword from its sheath and turning his face upward with an expression never before seen on it. He was like an exasperated tiger in chains, with bloodshot eyes, thick swollen veins in his brow and bloodthirsty lips.

"May God have mercy on them!" he cried out in a fearful voice, and throwing himself on his horse rode out to his troops.

"My friends," he cried, before he reached the ranks, "a swarm of hornets has fallen on my castle and plundered it. They have destroyed everything in my rooms, cleared my stables, robbed my family treasures; but I care not for that, let them gorge their fill, let them have what they never knew before, let them steal me even,

I should still be master and even after this rob-
bery, with one hand could pay off all these beggarly Szekler princes. But they have abused the
portrait of my wife—of my wife! And I will
have my revenge for it—a frightful revenge!
Follow me. The trees in the garden at Bonczida
have not borne any fruit for some time now but
they shall bear some."

The general battle-cry of the troops showed
that the army was ready to follow Banfy. The
leaders drew up their men in ranks and the trumpet had sounded the second time when a company
of twelve horsemen came in sight of Banfy's
army. In the central figure they recognized the
herald of the Prince, a broad-shouldered man of
giant size who rode up to Banfy and the officers
around him, and said :

"Halt!"

"We are halting. If you have eyes you can
see," said Michael Angyal.

"In the name of his Excellency the Prince I
summon you, Dionysius Banfy, to appear in three
days before the court in Karlsburg to defend
yourself in legal form against the indictment
found against you. Until that time your wife remains in custody, as hostage for your deeds."

"We will come," replied Michael Angyal.
"You can see for yourself that we were on the
point of starting out only we did not know until
now which way to go."

"Still, my lord captain!" said Banfy. "One should not use mockery with a messenger from the Prince." The messenger turned then to the officers:

"This summons does not concern you. For you I have another message to give in the name of the Prince."

"You may keep it to yourself or I will say something to you that will make your ears tingle," sneered the captain, aiming his pistol at the herald.

"Down with your pistol!" Banfy called out to him. "Let him give the Prince's message. Give him opportunity to speak freely."

The herald straightened himself in his saddle and surveying the soldiers said in a loud voice:

"The Prince forbids you to give further obedience to Banfy; any man that takes up weapons for him is a traitor to his country."

"That's what you are yourself," growled Michael Angyal.

The next moment the disorganized troops had turned with rage and threats toward the herald: a hundred swords flashed at the same time above his head.

"Stop!" said Banfy, in a thundering voice and at the same time standing before the herald. "The life of this man is sacred and inviolable. Keep your places. Let no man put his hand to his sword. I order you—I, your leader."

" Three cheers ! " shouted the brigades, and at the word of command formed in ranks and stood like a wall.

" You will not bear me ill-will," said Banfy to the herald who had turned pale, " that these men have this once more obeyed me. Go back to your Prince and tell him that I will appear before him within three days."

" We will be there too," shouted the captain. The herald and his retinue moved away. Banfy dropped his head in deep thought. The trumpet sounded, for the banners were unfurled, but Banfy still stared into space, speechless, heavy-hearted and gloomy.

" Draw your sword, my lord," Angyal said to him. " Put yourself at our head and let us start, first for Bonczida, and then for Karlsburg."

" What is that you say ? " said Banfy. " What do you mean ? "

" Why, that since the law has expressed itself by the sword, the sword shall be our defence."

" Such a case at law would be called civil war."

" We did not start it : neither shall we add fuel to the flame."

" It is no longer a war against my personal enemies but against the Prince, and he is the head of our country."

" And you are his right hand. If they are going to light the torch of war in the country it shall not be extinguished in your blood."

"And why should my blood flow for that? have I committed a capital crime? can anybody accuse me of such?"

"You are powerful and that is reason enough to kill you."

"It is all the same to me. I will go and what is more, alone. My wife is in their hands. They have it in their power to make me suffer their vengeance. If there were no other reason for my appearing, to set her free is my duty as a knight."

"With weapons you can set her free more easily, and also yourself."

"I have nothing to fear. I have never done anything for which I need blush in the sight of the law. Even if they should intrigue against me, still stay here, summon my troops at Somlyo and throw yourself into the breach there when injustice is practiced against me."

"Oh, my lord, the army is worth nothing when its leader has surrendered himself. To-day it would still go through fire for you and be ready to hail you as Prince; but to-morrow if it should learn that you had obeyed the summons it would disband and deny you."

"You must not tell any one of my intention. I will take a carriage at once and drive to Karlsburg; you tell the troops that I have gone to Somlyo to collect the rest of my army; keep them together under good discipline, till news of me comes."

With that Banfy rode off to Klausenburg, while Michael Angyal sullenly sheathed his sword and proclaimed to the troops that they might go to rest in case they were tired.

*   *   *   *   *   *

An hour later we see Banfy in a carriage drawn by five horses, rolling along the way to Torda. A servant on horse led by the bridle a saddle-horse. The farther Banfy separated himself from the seat of his power the greater his anxiety became; his soul was irresolute and he began to see spectres brought nearer by every step forward. Pride alone kept him from changing his purpose. Everything seemed to him different from what it had formerly been. He thought he read the feelings toward him of those whom he met, in their faces and forms of greeting; if anybody smiled he thought it was from pity, if the greeting was sullen he saw hatred. Now he stopped and questioned all those with whom he had even the slightest acquaintance; people whom he formerly deemed unworthy of a glance or else looked down upon. Misfortune recalls to the memory of men the faces of acquaintances, and a man who once would have even repelled the hand-shake of a friend now extends his hand to a foe while yet afar off.

Suddenly he saw that an open carriage was coming toward him from Torda, and that the one seat was occupied by a man wrapped in a grey duster, in whom Banfy as he rode past recognized Martin Koncz, the Bishop of the Unitarians. He called to him to stop a moment. The Bishop on account of the noise of the wheels did not hear him, took off his hat and drove on. Banfy considered this an intentional avoidance and looked upon it as a bad omen. The man who once had borne all perils so lightly now shrank back before every fancy of his brain. He ordered his carriage to stop, mounted his horse and told his coachman to drive on to Torda and wait for him there. Then he galloped after the Bishop's carriage. When the Bishop saw him riding up he had his carriage stopped, while Banfy breathlessly shouted from a distance:

"So then you will not enter into conversation with me?"

"At your good pleasure, my lord; I did not know that you wished to speak with me."

"You know already what has happened to me, I suppose. What do you say to it? what ought I to do?"

"In such a case my lord, it is as difficult to give advice as it is to receive it."

"I have determined to obey the summons."

"As you say, my lord."

"I certainly have nothing to fear. I feel the justice of my cause."

"It is possible that you are in the right my

lord, but you will hardly receive justice for that reason. In the world of to-day everything is possible."

Banfy caught the allusion. He had once used the same words to the bishop and now he had not sufficient strength of soul to withdraw proudly, but allowed himself to continue the discussion.

"It is true the Prince is my enemy, but the Princess has always defended me and I can put confidence in her character."

"The relations between the Prince and his wife are at present strained. It is said that he has even forbidden her to enter his apartment."

This news seemed to stun Banfy, but one consoling thought was left to him.

"I do not suppose they will venture to do me an injustice for they know that I have troops in Somlyo and Klausenburg ready for action, who may call them to account."

"My lord, it is difficult to lead an army when one is in prison; and remember that a live dog is a more powerful beast than a dead lion."

These words caused a change in Banfy's decision. For some time he rode along beside Koncgin's carriage, still considering; after a long time he replied gloomily:—"You are right," gave spurs to his horse and rode back to Klausenburg, resolved not to be enticed away from the centre of his troops.

When he reached the spot where barely six

hours before the troops had shouted their huzzas in his honor, to his great astonishment he came upon a group of gypsies who seemed to be hunting for something on the ground.

"What are you doing here?" he said, when he was in their midst. At this question their chief came forward and recognizing Banfy, took off his cap humbly.

"My gracious lord, the gypsies have come out to gather up the cartridges which my lords the nobles had scattered here."

"Where are the noble lords now?"

"Oh, my gracious lord, some have gone in one way and some in another."

"What do you mean? Where have they gone?"

"When they found that your Grace had left Klausenburg, they scattered to the four winds."

Banfy turned pale.

"And Michael Angyal?"

"He was the first to hurry away."

Banfy felt a dizziness seize him; tears stood in his eyes. Thus to be deserted by all, by man, by fate and even by his own consciousness! What was left to him of all his power! whither should he turn? what should he plan? every way was closed to him. He could neither use the sword nor fight with the arm of the law, nor flee. Mechanically he allowed his horse to carry him on. With gloomy face he sat in his saddle, staring vacantly at the ground and at the clouds. In heaven, on earth even as in his own heart, all was desolate. Nowhere did he find a place of refuge. The one passion of his soul, which had entirely filled it, was pride. Now that this was gone the world was empty. He rode on and on wherever his horse took him. Before him stretched out great forests. He thought: " What lies beyond these forests ? high mountains ; and what beyond those ? still higher peaks ; and what further ? summits of snow—and not a house to offer me refuge." So at the first stroke did everybody turn from him ? was the man who the day before had ruled half Transylvania and had castles at his disposal not to find a hut to shelter him that night ? was he to be an object of ridicule to his foes and not have the satisfaction of being able to laugh in the hour of death ? was he to die ingloriously like a hunted beast ? He considered how he could arrange it so that since he must die at least he should not be derided after death.

Gradually an idea began to develop in his mind. With this thought the color came back to his cheeks, and as if strengthening him to a decision he heard an inner voice saying:

" Yes, thither, thither."

He turned the bridle of his horse toward the

forest before him and disappeared among the trees.

*   *   *   *   *   *

The storm raged, the trees creaked in the wind, the rain fell and the swollen streams roared. The horizon was surrounded by steep rocks and at their feet in a pathless valley a rider stumbled along, who from the heights above looked like a mere ant. May God be gracious to him in this storm, at night, in such a place! It is Gregyina-Drakuluj.

*   *   *   *   *   *

Before our eyes is a splendid Oriental apartment, hundreds of wax candles are lighted, but the ceiling is too high for their gleam to reach; two rows of columns support the heavy architrave, slender columns with the heads of animals for capitals, such as are found in Persian temples. The space between the columns is hung with bright draperies, the walls are covered with arabesques. This was the hidden apartment of the Devil's Garden, and the one who dwelt here, woman, fairy or demon, was Azraele. Here she shaped the future, made endless plans, dreamed of power and battles, and new countries in which she should be queen, of new stars in which she should be the sun.

Suddenly she heard a sound as if some one had

ridden over the vaulted ceiling : steps were heard
in the passage adjoining and there were three
knocks at the door. She sprang hurriedly from
her couch, drew the heavy bolts and pulled open
the door. There stood Dionysius Banfy, sad,
silent and dispirited, with no greeting for this
beautiful woman. A shiver passed over him. It
is true he wore a tiger-skin over his usual clothing, but the heavy rain had penetrated it.

"You are wet through," said Azraele. "Warm
yourself quickly. Come here and rest."

With these words she drew Banfy to a sofa,
took off his cloak and covered him with her own
lined with fur, and placed a cushion under his
feet. But Banfy was cold and silent. His misfortune seemed written on his face even to a less
keen eye and to a mind more free from suspicion
than Azraele's. It could not be concealed that
his proud features no longer bore the stamp of
the lord in power but of a fallen king, whose fall
had been the lower since his height was great ;
who had not come because he wished to leave all
that was dear to him but because he was left by
everybody. Not for all the world would Azraele
have shown that she noticed the change in Banfy's
face. She tripped off like a doe and came back
bearing a great silver tray of gold drinking cups.

"Not the gold ones, they do not break when
you throw them at the wall. Let us have our
wine in Venetian crystal." He seized the first

glass and said in bitter scorn, "This glass to my friends!" He drank it off and hurled it in contempt to the wall where it was shattered to pieces.

At once he seized a second. "This second glass to my enemies!" and emptying the glass he hurled it with mad laughter into the air. It went almost to the ceiling and when it fell dropped on a cushion, and did not break.

"See, it mocks me still and is unbroken!" said Banfy, with blazing eyes.

Azraele sprang up, caught up the glass and crushed it under her feet.

Then Banfy took the third glass.

"This glass for Transylvania!" And he emptied it, but when he had taken it from his lips the smile died from his face and instead of hurling it at the wall he set it on the table. A cold shudder ran through his whole frame at the meaning of his own words, "This glass for Transylvania!" He did not take his hand from the glass but timorously attempted to raise it from the table, when the glass without visible cause cracked and fell into fragments in his hand. The diamond ring on his finger had scratched the glass and like all badly cooled crystal, it went to pieces at the slightest scratch. Banfy sprang back in terror as if he had seen an omen.

The girl took up his glass and with lips quivering with passion cried out, "And this glass for love!"

The words recalled Banfy from his bewilderment to the present surroundings.

"For me there is no love!"

"Your heart has been full of lofty plans. Fate had determined you to be the ruler of a country and perhaps the hero of half a world,—a man who should fill a page of history with his name."

"All that is past," said Banfy, "I am nobody and nothing!"

"Ah!" cried Azraele. "Have your enemies triumphed over you?"

"A curse upon their heads! I had sympathy and I fell."

"Is Csaki among them?"

"Yes, he pursues me most bitterly."

"And have all your faithful friends left you?"

"The fallen has no faithful friends."

"You could hire mercenaries and begin the fight. You certainly are rich enough for that."

"My wealth has gone!"

"You might get help from a foreign country."

"I have fallen, and know what is before me— I must die! Yet my enemies shall not have the triumph of making my death a festival and of laughing when I am pale with death. I will die alone!"

"I will show you something!" and with these

words she drew aside the rug, lifted a trap-door and there was a low room, with thick short columns among which casks were ranged.

"True," said Banfy, "that is the powder I hid there after John Kemény's fall."

"See this long fuse," said Azraele, drawing forth a thick woolen cord connected with the casks; "while all is still here below and above is the roaring of the storm and your enemies, there shall come an earth-shaking thunder which shall send the rocks crashing against one another and carry word to heaven and hell that nobody need seek you here on earth!"

"Azraele, you are a demon!"

An hour later the hall was dark; no light was visible except a glow as of a fiery-eyed monster piercing the smoke, and a slowly creeping snake of fire which ran along the length of the room. Banfy slept for a long time then suddenly awakened. All was dark about him. His bewildered brain required some time to recall who he was and why he was there. He felt a cold breath of wind through the room and presently he discovered that the door was open and the outer air was pouring in. Gradually he recalled it all, and taking some coals from the fire lighted a wax candle. This single light was not sufficient to let him see through the entire room, but the first thing he saw was the fuse cut in two. Pierced through with the cold air he drew his cloak about him. A paper fell at his feet and taking it up he read the following words:

"My lord, you read hearts poorly. You have forfeited your power and when all had forsaken you you thought me alone faithful, who loved in you only your power. The man who rises I adore: I hate the falling. You should have taken Corsar Bey's fate for warning." . . . Banfy could not read it through. His face was darkened with shame to be so degraded.

"It is cowardice and disgrace for a man who has lived as I have to be willing to die this way; for a man who has always faced his enemy to hide himself away now in his last moments— shame on him! That I could forget the wife who freed me from my enemy's hands by the sacrifice of herself! It is not too late. I cannot save my life now but I can my pride. No one hereafter shall boast that he betrayed me. My enemies shall not say that I tried to hide from them and they found me. I will go boldly into their presence as I should have done at first."

With this decision Banfy went out into the hidden court where he had left his horse. To his surprise he found that it was not there; the odalisque had taken it. At that he could but smile.

"I should regret it very much if she had not stolen me too at the same time."

He went back into the hall, lighted again the

fuse, came out again, closed the iron door and made his way along the bank of the Szamos. Toward noon he sat down on the bank to rest and had sat there hardly a quarter of an hour when he heard the sound of horses' hoofs approaching and looked up. The thicket concealed him and at the head of an armed band of men he saw Ladislaus Csaki and Azraele riding on one horse. The girl seemed to be pointing out something to him in the direction of the cliffs, at which the man was evidently delighted. Banfy smiled scornfully:—Poor Tartar! As soon as the band had passed Banfy continued on his way. Soon he met in the forest a poor peasant cutting wood.

"Do you know in which direction those armed men have gone?" he asked him.

"Yes, my lord, they have gone to seize Dionysius Banfy. A great price is set on his head."

"How much?"

"If a nobleman takes him, he is to receive an estate; if a peasant, two hundred ducats."

"That is not much though I suppose it will be enough for you. I am Dionysius Banfy."

The peasant took off his cap.

"Is there any place you wish me to guide you to, my lord?"

"Guide me to the place where they will pay you the two hundred ducats."

*   *   *   *   *   *

In another quarter of an hour a frightful explosion reechoed in the mountains and made the earth quake for half a mile around. The enchanted hollow of Gregyina-Drakuluj was in inaccessible confusion.

Fortunately for Csaki he had delayed a little, otherwise he with his followers would have all been destroyed there. When he came back Banfy had already been arrested and he robbed of the glory of having captured his foe. He hurried at once to meet him and by way of exquisite revenge took with him the odalisque who looked at Banfy as coldly as if she had never seen him before. However, since Banfy had voluntarily surrendered himself, he had quite regained his former strength of spirit and looking down at Csaki, he said,

"So then, your Grace intends to wear my cast-off clothing from now on."

Azraele hissed like a snake whose tail had been stepped on, when she heard these words of biting scorn; while Csaki colored to his ears and forced a smile.

"Does your Excellency wish any favor from me?" asked Csaki, with insulting kindness.

"You have none to give and I have need of none. What I demand is that since I have appeared,—yes, even under arrest without knowing why, you shall now let my wife go free."

"So then at last you will go whimpering back to your wife?"

"That is not what I meant. I do not intend to go back to my wife; on the contrary I wish that as soon as I am led into prison she shall be set free from the same."

"It shall be as you wish, most gracious lord," replied Csaki, with ironical friendliness.

Banfy gave him an unutterably contemptuous glance, turned to one of the jailers present and began a conversation with him without giving any further heed to the grandee.

*   *   *   *   *   *

When Teleki learned of Banfy's arrest he ordered him brought to Bethlen castle at once. In Bethlen castle the provost of Klausenburg, Stephen Pataki, received him, at sight of whom Banfy jestingly asked:

"So you have been appointed my confessor, have you?"

Pataki wept, while Banfy smiled lightly. The Provost conducted Banfy up the steps, showing him the greatest respect. Deeply affected he remained standing at the threshold. In the room was a lady in mourning who at sight of him turned pale as death and leaned against the table unable to move. Banfy felt all the blood rushing to his heart. The next moment he rushed passionately to her and cried,

"My wife! Margaret!"

The lady, speechless, threw herself in her husband's arms and sobbed violently.

"They did not set you free?" asked Banfy, turning pale.

"Of my own accord I did not go," replied Margaret. "I could not leave you in the prison."

Tears gushed from Banfy's eyes. He sank down at her feet and covered her hands with kisses.

"So long as the world believed us happy we could avoid each other," said Margaret, with stifled voice. "Misfortune has brought us together again." . . .

She bent over to kiss her husband's brow; Banfy was completely overpowered; his feelings were all at once so mightily overcome that even his strong heart could bear no more.

CHAPTER XIX

THE JUDGMENT

THE Diet assembled at Karlsburg opposed the secret procedure against Banfy. Paul Beldi himself was the first to say distinctly that even if Banfy's arrest through conspiracy had been permitted his judgment must be given in the presence of the Diet and not before any secret tribunal, and demanded that personal safety should be assured him.

The Prince appeared in the assembly, angry, with heavy head and red eyes; the usual sign with him of perplexity. As Teleki had no authority over the Diet he had the Prince dissolve it, making him believe that Banfy if brought before the national assembly would escape on the way, or would know how to turn his two-edged sword in such a way as to overpower the Prince.

In the presence of the judge the opposition made by Kozma Horvath to the illegal procedure was in vain. The conspiracy brought thirty-seven indictments against Banfy, advanced by Judge Martin Saros-Pataki.

Banfy stood indicted. The greater number of the counts were so unimportant that no answer needed to be brought against them. They did

356

not dare to introduce among them his pretensions to the throne—that remained a secret indictment.

Banfy answered in manly fashion to every
charge. It was in vain. Defend himself as he
would those who had arrested him knew too
well how great a wrong they had done him, now
to let him live. The case came to a verdict and
he was sentenced to death.

On the day that this happened nobody could
gain access to the Prince except the confederates
in this secret league, who with hasty, eager expressions went in and out of the Prince's apartments continually. Toward evening they succeeded in rousing the drunken Apafi to ratify
the decision. This Prince usually so gentle, so
kind-hearted, now poisoned with terror did not
know himself.

Ever since noon saddled horses and carriages
in waiting had been standing before the gate.
Suddenly Ladislaus Csaki came hurrying out of
the hall, concealing a paper in his pocket and
calling for his horse; he mounted, motioned in
silence to the lords following him and galloping
off. The other lords too as if pursued, hurried
into the carriages standing in a row before the
palace, and taking leave of each other with
mysterious whisperings, quickly fled so that the
Prince in a few moments was left alone. Teleki
was the last to leave him. The Prince accom-

panied this lord to the vestibule, his countenance showing deep sorrow; he could hardly let Teleki go. The latter withdrew his hand coldly from the Prince's.

"You need have no fancies about this, my lord. The principles of a country are concerned here, not a human life. If my own head stood in the way I should say cut it off and I say the same about the head of another."

And with that he went away.

Apafi did not stay in his room, he felt the need of fresh air. Within something threatened to choke him so oppressive was the air,—or was it his spirits? He went out into the vestibule. The cool night air soothed his bewildered spirits and the sight of the starry heavens was good to his clouded mind. Leaning against the balustrade he gazed in silence into the still night as if he expected that some star greater than all the rest would fall from Heaven, or that somebody miles away from him would cry out. Suddenly a cry did strike his ear. With a shudder he looked about but remained speechless in terror. His wife stood before him, whom his lord councillors had kept away from him for weeks by causing a division between the stupefied husband and the high-spirited wife. When the last grandee had withdrawn her loyal men had informed her that the Prince had signed the death sentence and the shocked wife, forcing her way through castle guards had rushed to her husband; now meeting him in the vestibule she hurried to him and in her excitement cried out:

"Accursed man, do not shed the blood of that innocent one!"

Apafi drew back timidly before his wife.

"What do you wish of me?" he asked, sullenly. "What are you saying?"

"You have signed Banfy's death sentence."

"I?" asked Apafi dully, and reached for his wife's hand.

"Away with your hand, the blood of my kinsman is on it!"

"You do not approve it? I did not wish it;" stammered Apafi. "The lords compelled me to it."

The Princess clasped her hands together and looked at her husband in despair.

"You have brought blood on our family, a curse on the country, a curse on me that I did not leave you to die in the hands of the Tartars. Even virtue becomes through you a crime!"

Apafi was contrite. In the presence of his wife all his spirit was gone.

"I did not want to kill him"—he stammered. "I do not now either—and if you wish I will grant him amnesty. Take my seal ring; send a rider to Bethlen after Csaki; show favor to your kinsman and leave me in peace."

The Princess called in a piercing voice, "Who

is here?" Among the courtiers who hurried forward, the steward was the first.

"Take four of the Prince's racers," said Anna, meanwhile she wrote the pardon with her own hand, had her husband sign it and stamped it with the seal. "Take this letter and hurry with it to Bethlen castle. If the horse falls under you, take another. Do not delay a minute anywhere; a human life is in your hands."

The grooms led up the racers. The steward mounted one, fastening the rest by the bridle, and chased away.

* * * * * *

At about the same hour, perhaps the same minute, Paul Beldi called out to his groom the order to mount the swiftest horse and ride to Bethlen and say to the castle warder that he would cut his head off if Banfy received the least harm at Bethlen. He too did not wish to meet his wife in this hour.

And perhaps in the same hour, perhaps in the same minute, Teleki pressed the hand of his future son-in-law Emerich Tököli, and whispered in his ear;—"We are one step nearer;" under the pressure of the youth's iron hand the betrothal ring that bound him to Teleki's daughter broke, and Teleki regarded it almost as a prophecy that the hand of the youth should be stronger than his.

All Transylvania was alarmed that night.
Wolfgang Bethlen could not sleep in his bed the
whole night through. Stephen Apor grew so
uneasy that he had to make confession : Kornis
became so confused on the familiar road home
that he was compelled to spend the night under
his carriage. And what took place in the heavens? About midnight a shower came up; such
that the oldest inhabitant could not recall its
like. The lightning set fire to forests and towers, and floods poured from the riven clouds.
The alarm-bell sounded everywhere. God's
judgment held sway that night. Almost the entire nation was sleepless. Only the reconciled
husband and wife slept quietly and sweetly. At
times the lady wept in her dreams; tears fell on
her pillow; she dreamed of her happy bridal
days or of the sweet moment when she laid her
first child in her husband's arms. Her husband
lay with calm countenance, at odds with the
world but reconciled with himself—with the better half of his soul. The happiness which had
fled from him in the palace sought him out in the
prison. The hanging lamp threw its pale light
on their sleeping forms. In this frightful night
four single riders galloped separately toward
Bethlen castle, hardly a thousand paces apart.
By the lightning flashes they saw each other at
times and each one struck spurs the harder to
his horse. The first rider reached the castle gate

and gave the signal with the horn; the draw-
bridge fell threateningly, the rider sprang into
the courtyard and laid a letter in the hand of
the warder who hurried forward. It was Paul
Beldi's message.

The second rider who reached the castle, ordered the gate opened in the name of the Prince.
He gave the castle warder a second paper. It
was Ladislaus Csaki. The warder turned pale
as he read this message.

"My lord," he faltered, "I have just received
an order from Paul Beldi who threatens me with
death if any harm happens to the prisoner."

"You have your choice," replied Csaki. "If
you obey, it is possible that he will have your
head cut off to-morrow. If you do not obey, I
will kill you to-day." The warder trembled as
he bowed.

"Raise the draw," ordered Csaki. "Let no
one enter the castle without permission. Whoever acts contrary to my orders is a dead man."

*   *   *   *   *   *

Husband and wife slept peacefully. A minute
later the door opened with a slight noise and
Stephen Pataki entered, terror-stricken and with
difficulty restraining his tears. He stepped up
to Banfy to awaken him. As he touched his
hand, Banfy, seeing Pataki who in his emotion
could not speak, tried to rise without waking his

wife but she opened her eyes at that very moment and Pataki, who did not wish her to know the terrible message, said in Latin:

"Rise, my lord, the death sentence is here."

Trembling at the speech in a foreign tongue whose meaning Pataki's face so ill concealed, Banfy's wife asked in terror what it meant.

"Nothing, nothing," said Banfy, with a tender smile, embracing his wife. "An urgent message that I must answer at once. I will return soon; lie down and sleep quietly."

With these words he laid his wife back in her pillows and kissed her tenderly several times, after each kiss saying:

"My soul, my love, my blessing, my Heaven."

Madame Banfy did not suspect that this was the parting kiss of a man on his way to death. He looked at her so smilingly, feigning joy in his countenance when he stood on the threshold of death.

At this moment the horn rang out before the castle gate. The messenger of the Princess had arrived and demanded admittance in the name of his Excellency. Csaki mounted the stairs in haste and just as Banfy had calmed his wife about his leaving, he pushed open the door suddenly and cried out,

"Why this long parting! Be ready! The sentence awaits its execution!"

At these words Madame Banfy sprang from

her couch with a convulsive scream, reached both arms to her husband, looked at him for a moment in silence then laid her hands on her heart and sank back dead among the pillows.

Banfy looked at his foe with deadly bitterness; his veiled eyes seemed to Csaki to hurl forth more curses than any lips could have spoken.

"Miserable wretch!" he thundered at him, "who ordered you to kill my wife too?"

Csaki turned his head aside and called out harshly,

"Make haste, the time is short."

"Short for me but it will be long for you, for the time is coming when you will curse life and not die as peacefully as I do. Leave me alone. I wish to pray and I cannot call on God in the same room where you are."

Csaki went away, shocked in spite of himself.

Banfy put his hands to his brow and prayed.

Heavy thunder rolled through the Heavens.

"Oh God, who in thy anger dost thunder above, take my blood for my sins. Let no drop of it fall on the head of those who have shed it. Grant that my country may never expiate my death. Guard this poor land from every misfortune. Keep thy vengeance far from the head of this people and mid all perils be their shield. Forgive my enemies my death as I forgive them."

The thunder rolled terribly. God was angry. He did not wish to hear this prayer.

Banfy went back to his dead wife, kissed her white face for the last time and then went quietly to Csaki.

"I am ready."

*   *   *   *   *   *

After another quarter of an hour Csaki permitted the messenger to enter.

"What do you bring?" he asked the steward.

"The Prince's pardon for the prisoner."

"You have come too late."

The head of the highest noble of Transylvania had already fallen to the ground.

*   *   *   *   *   *

The tragedy comes to an end with the death of the hero. Other forms, other leaders, continue the course of events. The fate, the form, the history of Transylvania is changed. The sword-stroke that killed Banfy marked off an epoch. The ruling figure was buried in the earth of Bethlen chapel and no one inherited that spirit.

Only when misfortune threatens Transylvania, so says the chronicle,—to the terror of the people, to the astonishment of the world, the blood of the fallen patriot is wont to gush forth from this humble grave.

www.ingramcontent.com/pod-product-compliance
Lightning Source LLC
Chambersburg PA
CBHW011652010726
47499CB00010B/3233